STRANGERS *at the* RED DOOR

Also by Dennis Bock

Olympia
The Ash Garden
The Communist's Daughter
Going Home Again
The Good German

STRANGERS *at the* RED DOOR

A Novel

Dennis Bock

HARPER PERENNIAL

Published by Harper Perennial, an imprint of HarperCollins Publishers Ltd

A section of a chapter in this work was published in a different form in *Glimmer Train* (Winter 2012) Issue 81 as "Improvised Explosive Device."

HarperCollins Publishers Ltd
Bay Adelaide Centre, East Tower
22 Adelaide Street West, 41st Floor
Toronto, Ontario, Canada
M5H 4E3

www.harpercollins.ca

HarperCollins Publishers
Macken House, 39/40 Mayor Street Upper
Dublin 1, D01 C9W8, Ireland

https://www.harpercollins.com

Library and Archives Canada Cataloguing in Publication

Title: Strangers at the red door : a novel / Dennis Bock.
Names: Bock, Dennis, 1964- author
Identifiers: Canadiana (print) 2025021315X | Canadiana (ebook) 20250213184 | ISBN 9781443476539 (softcover) | ISBN 9781443476546 (ebook)
Subjects: LCGFT: Novels.
Classification: LCC PS8553.O42 S77 2025 | DDC C813/.54—dc23

Printed and bound in the United States of America

25 26 27 28 29 LBC 5 4 3 2 1

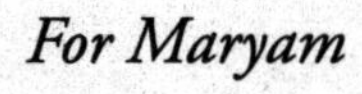

For Maryam

ONE

WHEN MILDRED CHEN ENTERED THE BACK OFFICE OF HER HONG Kong bookshop and began preparing the delivery for the crossing, she knew nothing yet of the troubles that would rise to confront her in the coming days. She was only eager to get the new delivery over the border and return home in time to help her aunt close up the shop for the evening.

She worked quickly, stripping a dozen copies of a popular romance of their dust jackets, then used the covers to disguise an equal number of copies of the book that had changed her life, and would soon change it again in a way she could not begin to imagine on that late-March morning.

She placed the camouflaged copies in the cardboard box marked with the title of the decoy romance, secured its flaps with packing tape, and fed the original covers of the banned novel into a paper shredder. Now, the evidence safely destroyed, she carried the delivery out to the front room, where her old aunt was arranging the display window.

"Don't forget to eat something over there," her aunt said. "It'll be a long day. You're always forgetting to eat something. Promise me."

The bookseller named Mildred Chen was used to this gentle mothering from the woman who'd raised her since the age of five. Her aunt was a kind and solemn woman, given to selfless worry and the long, meditative pauses of an old, tired soul.

"Yes, yes," she said. "I promise."

Mildred had inherited her father's easy smile and bright, inquisitive eyes, and from her mother she'd received the uncompromising idealism that could not be mistaken for naïveté. Both of her parents were graduate students at Peking University when they died many years ago. She was forty years old, spoke and read Cantonese and Mandarin with equal facility, and discussed politics with few people other than her aunt, from whom she'd learned the bookseller's trade and the fine art of book smuggling. With the box of contraband propped heavily against her chest, she exited the bookshop and hailed a cab.

By now Mildred had done enough of these day runs over to the mainland to know much more than simply where to find a decent meal in Shenzhen. She knew the routines and the temperament of many of the customs officials at the checkpoints she passed through. After dozens of crossings, she'd mastered the feigned ignorance and the nimble flirtation required to distract these men from her true purpose. Years ago, on one of her first crossings, she'd encountered a crotchety guard who went as far as to unseal her box of books in order to verify the claims she'd made on her declarations card, which on that distant morning stated she was carrying nothing more dangerous than an authorized biography of a well-loved Beijing pop star. Simple as it was, the strategy of the counterfeit dust jacket had proven remarkably effective over the years; and so, thirty-five years after the death of her parents, Mildred Chen, co-owner with her aunt of Utopia Street Books, maintained the illusion that she was a guileless purveyor of cookbooks, popular romances, fantasy and thrillers, gardening books, and sensational celebrity tell-alls. For good reason she was called "the book lady of Hong Kong" by some of the customs agents who presided over these crossings, and this with no small degree of affection. They found her manner appealing and enjoyed the way this attractive importer of books allowed but politely resisted their fawning attentions. Otherwise stern and unforgiving in their duties, these men usually just smiled and wished her a good day.

AT THE LUOHU crossing, half an hour north of the city centre, she checked the box and continued on to present her documents on the mainland-China side of the border. The official in his booth issued the transit pass with hardly a glance at her paperwork. He gave her a courteous smile and waved the next traveller forward, and Mildred proceeded to the oversized-luggage clearance area. While she waited for the box to appear on the carousel, she opened her phone and read a few messages for the bookstore about coming deliveries and expected returns and queries from book reps and publicists. They were all routine concerns, nothing out of the ordinary.

She switched over to a VPN and pulled up an article on BBC Chinese about an Iranian film director and actor turned dissident who'd been living in the Japanese consulate in Hong Kong for the past three years. Accompanying the story was a photograph of an elegant woman addressing the United Nations General Assembly, taken some years before she was forced to seek asylum at the consulate in Hong Kong. Not twenty-four hours ago, Beijing, overlords of the former colony, had issued an ultimatum in accordance with their close ties with Tehran. The waiting game had gone on long enough, the report said. Unspecified diplomatic measures would follow if the dissident wasn't turned over within the next ten days. Not since the Tiananmen crackdown in 1989 had diplomatic relations between Beijing and Tokyo been so badly strained. The ultimatum was a highly unusual tactic in the diplomatic world. The Japanese government had yet to issue its response.

The poor woman might be barking mad after three years of confinement, Mildred thought. The consulate likely had its comforts—decent food, books, internet—but would be a prison, nonetheless. Standing here, waiting for the box to appear on the baggage carousel, she doubted that she herself would survive such a repressive ordeal without losing her mind.

She closed the page, and when she saw a customs agent walking toward her, she pocketed the phone and prepared a warm smile. Quite used to the sort of friendly intrusions she'd come to expect from various officials here, she was not alarmed when he asked her to follow him. The man was one of the more personable border agents, a certain Inspector Duàn. He was in his mid-forties and wore the black tie and blue dress shirt of his official station. The small jag in her itinerary would cause some minor delay—half an hour, perhaps; but by the time he was finished with his questioning, or more accurately, his flirting, the queue might be shorter and she'd collect her box and be on her way.

He led her through the busy hall and down a narrow corridor to a windowless interrogation room containing a table, two chairs, and a dormant video camera set on a tripod, its lens turned sleepily to the floor. He asked her to be seated, and so she sat. She trusted he'd take the other chair and begin immediately with the interview that would soon settle into the light-hearted banter that characterized these occasions when she was pulled from the queue. Instead, he abruptly left the room, closing the door behind him.

She waited, watching the door, confused and unsettled by this surprising departure from what she'd come to expect, and felt the first spark of anxiety catch within her and begin to smoulder. She took a long, deep breath and tried to calm her nerves. Surely this was nothing more than a scheduling conflict or bureaucratic hiccup. The man's shift had just ended, she imagined, and another official would be along shortly to tell her to be on her way. Or the sudden need for a toilet had embarrassed the poor fellow, something as banal as that. Think nothing of it, her aunt might say. Free the mind of needless worry. Breathe deeply. You are prepared.

HER AUNT'S SHOP, Utopia Street Books, had seemed a magical place to Mildred when she was a child. Shelves of books reached so high to the ceiling that a special ladder had been invented to fetch them down. The plank floors creaked and groaned under her light step, as if whispering stories that only she could hear, and narrow corridors ended in cave-like rooms filled with books of all description. Hung throughout the shop were characterful portraits of some of the country's greatest writers, who watched with a tender eye those who came here to take down their books and breathe life again into their words.

At that young age Mildred believed her aunt must be as rich as a king in a fairy tale to own such a marvellous place, for to her child's imagination it contained all the stories in the world. The shop was indeed special, her aunt said, but she was not as rich as a king, nowhere near it, and for that matter she could imagine no such thing as a wealthy bookseller. That was not why she sold books. And besides, she was only a book's guardian until it was passed on to the person who would become its owner. What's more, she said, a book's true value was determined not by the amount of money that was paid for it but by the truth and beauty it contained.

In June of 1989, after Mildred's parents died, she came to live with her aunt above the shop, and here she learned to lose herself in stories of remarkable friendships between children and their animal friends, and fantastic journeys under the sea or back in time. Reading offered a merciful escape from her life, but grief was an eternal flame in her chest. The poor child was forever with her nose in a book, her aunt told the women in her circle; and her aunt, being a bookseller, said this with no small pride, though this was also said with great sorrow. She knew her orphaned niece would have chosen to vanish forever into one of those children's tales rather than face the world without her mother and father. When she wasn't at school or doing her chores around the shop, she sat reading in view of one of those old portraits on the walls or at the drop-leaf kitchen table in the two-bedroom flat upstairs. On her birthday she always got a special book, signed for her by its author, perhaps, or a rare first printing from another era with marvellous illustrations. These gifts were always wrapped in the finest silk. On her thirteenth birthday, which fell on the same year as Hong Kong's handover of sovereignty from the United Kingdom to the People's Republic of China, her aunt gave her a book of poems called *Remedies for Obedience.*

The author of this volume of poems was a young Shenzhen writer who'd been imprisoned on the mainland for his role in the reform movement that her parents had thrown their hearts into. The book was forbidden on the mainland, her aunt said, and people made special trips from there to Hong Kong to buy it and other books like it. They were beautiful poems that captured the optimistic spirit of the times before the violent clampdown began.

Mildred's fingers paused in their work of unfolding the silk cloth.

She knew her aunt's shop carried books like this, but she wanted nothing to do with any story or poem that touched on the events she'd always tried to clear from her mind, and so instead of asking more about the book, she remarked on the intricate pattern of the silk cloth that held it.

"Young people, including your mother and father, had been celebrating in the city square for weeks," her aunt said, ignoring the comment about the silk cloth.

They'd all believed a new openness was coming, freedom was on their doorstep. It was a time of great joy and celebration. And then word came that a violent turn was imminent, perhaps had even already occurred. The rumours were impossible to believe. The next day she saw the photographs published in the papers. The army had taken control of the city. Many people had died.

"After days of trying to call your mother and father, I journeyed to Beijing and found their flat occupied by strangers. And you, dear child, you were gone." She touched her niece's hand. "You'd been taken in by a friend of your mother. They were caring for you. I looked for your parents for days. I went to the university, to the faculties where they were studying. No one spoke to me. I had photographs to show them. Everyone was frightened, everyone suspicious. I found no trace."

Mildred stared at the cloth, afraid to fold it open, and felt the sharp sting of resentment for her aunt for forcing this terrible challenge on her. She rose from her seat and thanked her with a wooden smile and disappeared into her bedroom.

Still bound in its silk sleeve, the book of poems sat on her bedside table for weeks.

Weeks became months.

She ignored it as it sank deeper under a growing stack of other books until the autumn of that year, when she awoke from a dream in which her mother came to her and placed the book of poems on her chest. When she awoke, she brought her hand slowly out from under the covers and felt the book lying there, just as her mother had placed it in her dream.

She turned on the night light, pulled away the sleeve, and began to read.

MILDRED BEGAN HER apprenticeship in the bookseller's trade three years after she read the imprisoned writer's book of poems for the first time. Until then her duties at the shop had been limited to the mopping of floors and the dusting of shelves. Occasionally she'd unboxed and shelved books, but now she was introduced to the publishing representatives who appeared with their briefcases and satchels heavy with the unbirthed books they called galleys and advance reading copies. When authors came to give readings and to talk about their new publications, which was a great delight for Mildred, she was encouraged to speak with them not as the owner's niece but as a fledgling bookseller.

After school she worked the cash and directed customers to the titles she believed might be to their liking. She learned to select and to order next season's lists and to work with the publishers who supplied the books that visitors from the mainland could only find in Hong Kong, in shops like theirs.

At the age of twenty-five, in 2009, Mildred began her lessons in the dangerous art of book smuggling. Her aunt showed her the holes in the system, most often found in the fragile vanities of the guards who presided over these crossings. She introduced her to the likeminded booksellers on the mainland side whose idealism had survived that terrible summer so many years ago. After three crossings with her aunt, she carried her first box of contraband over the border, and with growing confidence she learned to move these dangerous books into the territories that had done so much to crush the memory of her parents and so many thousands like them.

NOW, WHEN INSPECTOR Duàn re-entered the interrogation room, Mildred asked if he could please explain what was happening. She was careful to appear unconcerned by this surprising delay, only mildly put out, but certainly she'd done nothing to warrant this inconvenience, she said. Her smile had no effect on him. He made no excuses for the bureaucracy that might have slowed her passage through customs. He offered no humble apology for staffing shortages.

"You take us for fools," he said, dropping one of her books

on the table in disgust. It was still camouflaged in its counterfeit jacket. The shift in the inspector's voice startled her. He turned on the camera and trained its lens on her.

"It's not great literature, I agree. But they'll sell in a week," she said, trying again to mask her alarm. "The housewives in Shenzhen are clamouring for this one. Yes, they'll sell out in a week."

Two other officials entered now, followed by a thin man whose funereal presence filled the interrogation room with the dread of a chilling omen. He wore the dark-blue uniform of the state security ministry and had the cold, intelligent eyes of a man who'd learned to manoeuvre well in the bureaucracy he served. The creaking leather of his shoes disturbed the brief silence when he crossed the room and picked up the book. He gave it a quick glance and set it down again with a smirk.

"Phone and wallet," he said.

She retrieved these from her pocket and handed them over.

"I have nothing to hide."

He slipped the identity card from the wallet and read out her name, and then said, "The book lady, our trafficker in popular romances."

She heard the mockery in his voice but did not react to it. He handed the wallet to one of his colleagues and slipped the ID and the phone into his breast pocket.

"Yes, that's right, romance stories," she said.

"Devoted to your customers, I see."

"I carry these over the checkpoint, yes, for different booksellers in Shenzhen," she said, attempting to regain her composure. "The publisher does not have a distributer on the mainland. That's quite common. This new one will fly off the shelves. I'm a go-between, an importer. I have my own shop, yes."

"You're a businesswoman," he said.

"We all need to eat, isn't that right?"

She had rehearsed the scripted calm she would invoke in such a situation, the distracting flirtations, the shock and disbelief, but she felt it all unravelling now. It was this man, and not the interrogation itself, that had her so unnerved. His eyes were dead, his manner condescending and ironic. She leaned back in the chair, heart racing, and tried to collect herself. Finally, she turned to Inspector Duàn, the man who'd pulled her from the line and now stood at the door watching this.

"The inspector will tell you. I have never caused a problem here. Not once. No one's ever accused me of anything. My deliveries are often checked, verified. They're very thorough here. And a good thing. They know I'm a distributor of legitimate books. Please tell this gentleman who I am."

Inspector Duàn looked on and said nothing.

She turned again to her interrogator. "There has been a mistake, you see."

"You're just a little bit cleverer than us, is that what you think?" the man said. "Pulling this charade for so long."

"There's no charade."

"You're trying to dismantle everything the People believe, isn't that right?"

"I'm just a bookseller."

By some miracle, this delay might be on account of some unpaid import tax or other minor breach in protocol, she thought, or maybe just staged to get a rise out of someone on a day of numbing routine. She closed her eyes briefly, attempting to wish the thought to life. It was all a harmless misunderstanding. Perhaps they hadn't even found the truth hidden under those false dust jackets. *Charm them. Distract them*, she decided. There was still a chance. Or maybe it was a bribe they were after. Corruption ran like a river through the bureaucracy, and men like these waited at its banks to take a sip or two when the water was sweet enough.

"Well then, we'll leave the bookseller alone for just a little while to reconsider her selfish lies," the interrogator said, and in a moment the men filed out, the door was closed, and now she sat in the empty space, wondering what would come next.

She watched the red blinking light of the camera and the banned novel on the table in front of her. It was still camouflaged in its brassy decoy jacket, the racy depiction of entwined lovers a lewd mockery of the fear that was growing inside her. She didn't dare touch the book or get up to test the door. The camera recorded everything. For hours it watched her with unwearying patience.

By now, the booksellers she was to meet in Shenzhen would

have messaged her aunt to report that she was overdue, something had gone wrong. She wondered if the police had already paid a visit to the bookshop and begun searching for offending titles. They would say nothing to her aunt about her missing niece. To them, she'd already never existed, disappeared like a ghost in their campaign against the city's booksellers who'd defy the edicts of the General Administration of Press and Publication. They would tear apart their bookshop and their lives, and Mildred Chen, at the age of forty, would become the latest of the vanished booksellers of Hong Kong.

TWO

THE GHOSTWRITER NAMED FARON JONES WAS ON HIS WAY UP TO his suite after checking in at the Hotel Metropole in Hong Kong when a girl from the mainland holding a Rubik's Cube stepped into the elevator and spoke to him in Mandarin. Faron earned his living with words, a very good living, really, but the language he worked in was English, not Mandarin.

He was fifty-one years old, had twelve books under his belt, and was one of the most sought-after memoir ghostwriters in the business. He was keenly perceptive, fast, reliable, and well-loved by his publishers. His prose was clean and direct and tinged with characterful nuance, yet it did not shy away from the occasional flourish. Each of his books was written with the sort of trade ventriloquism that managed to hide his own voice while articulating the voice of his famous subjects. He was paid handsomely to write about his clients and to hold his tongue when it came to the authorship of his books. Such information was on a strictly need-to-know basis. The people he wrote about were most often unreasonably wealthy public figures who required silence regarding his role in composing their lives for them, wanting as they did to live within the sphere of illusion he created for them and about them. In that quietly select world of ghostwriters, he was one of the most celebrated. He could tell almost anyone's story better than they themselves could. He'd written his own story once, years before, but he found ghostwriting much more to his liking. He did not enjoy including himself in the stories he told.

As for other languages, his French was good, his Spanish passable. He had no others beyond those until the moment the girl holding the Rubik's Cube spoke to him, and Faron Jones quite magically, and without knowing it, responded in perfect Mandarin.

HIS MOTHER WAS dying.

Her condition had been stable two months ago when he accepted the invitation to come to Hong Kong to meet the subject of a new book project he was thinking about taking on. Since then, a grim new diagnosis had been declared. He'd been on the verge of cancelling the trip when he recognized the chance to confront the single sad issue that had troubled his family for years.

His only sibling, a younger sister named Jana, lived with her Chinese husband and their daughter on the other side of the border crossing from Hong Kong, in Guangdong province. Instead of cancelling on his potential client, he tacked a week on to the front end of the trip, during which he planned to visit his sister on the mainland in order to share the distressing facts as they stood regarding their mother's rapidly declining health. He would use the visit to deliver a message, which was this: Come home and make peace with our dying mother before it's too late. The clock is ticking. His sister and mother had been at war for as long as he could remember. It was high time this unpardonable state of affairs was put right.

The woman he'd come to interview was an Iranian who'd sought refuge in the Japanese consulate in Hong Kong after a court in Tehran had found her guilty of something they called "corruption on earth," which was the regime's unconscionable attempt to deify the death sentence brought down by its courts. Her name was Lamya Khajenouri. She was now exiled from her homeland and facing extradition if she set foot outside the consular grounds. Ms. Khajenouri had entered the consulate just over three years ago now, on the afternoon she'd very nearly set herself on fire in front of the Iranian Consulate General in protest of her sentencing. Faron had watched clips of the terrifying incident, taken from numerous vantage points by horrified onlookers, and gasped in astonishment when instead of touching the flame to her gasoline-soaked clothing, she placed the lit match on her tongue and swallowed it whole.

Ms. Khajenouri's work as an auteur and actress had been little known abroad before a Cannes film festival jury declared her a miracle to behold. By now Faron had watched all of her films and read everything he could find on her—mostly appraisals of her career in the French and American movie industries and her work as a human rights activist, to which she'd dedicated her life after her journalist husband was murdered by agents of the regime in 2016. Since then, her campaign for justice would stop at nothing until the theocrats and the clerics responsible for her husband's death and the death of so many others were held to account. The death sentence that had been brought against her in absentia was an indication of how seriously the regime considered her a threat.

Faron observed the endless list of human rights violations around the world with the muddy compassion of a man who, while feeling deeply about these injustices, stayed like so many of his peers within comfortable reach of his limitations. He was no political animal by any stretch. Street protests and rallies or any other sort of overt political statement were not for him. Nor had he ever taken on a political book or a cause célèbre or a client with a political agenda. In fact, he hadn't formally accepted the proposal to tell her story for this very reason. He'd agreed only to meet with her at the consulate, where she'd been confined to three rooms and the small rooftop balcony garden that in the correspondence between them she'd described as her oasis. He certainly felt for her cause. The details of her husband's murder and dismemberment were exceptionally gruesome, and her confinement in the consulate was distressing, to say the least. If she left the premises, she would be detained and handed over to representatives of the regime, who would kill her. But as for Faron calling out the human rights abuses of an entire theocracy—not a chance. He just didn't know enough about it. It wasn't in his writer's DNA. If anything, this would be a study in character, not politics.

Ms. Khajenouri's management had contacted Faron's literary agent in London, a man named Hoggs, who felt this might be just the project for his most sought-after writer. The Iranian film director was certainly high-profile enough. Six years earlier, she'd been awarded the European Parliament's Sakharov Prize for her work in human rights, not to mention the Cannes award and the string of critical hits that followed. The advance he was looking to secure was guaranteed to be substantial. Faron resisted. Politics, and Middle Eastern politics at that, while disturbingly relevant, was far beyond his expertise.

He agreed to review the file that Hoggs had prepared and sent to his Toronto home. In the file was her email address. He studied the file and watched her films. Finally, he sent her a note, if only to remark on her courage and to wish her the best in her fight for justice. There were other writers better suited to the task, he said, people who knew something about the region and the important cause before her. She responded almost immediately. Only he could tell her story, she said; it had to be him. He was puzzled by the urgent tone of her messages. She insisted more than once that he was the writer she needed. He was intrigued and drawn to the mystery about why it could be no one but him. The correspondence between Ms. Khajenouri and the ghostwriter went on for two months before he finally agreed to come over and meet with her.

THREE

JUST PAST SEVEN IN THE MORNING, SIXTEEN HOURS INTO HER detention, the bookseller raised her head from the tabletop and saw the funereal man leaning over her on his knuckles. He seemed in a superior mood, like a man who'd just witnessed his arch-enemy's last rites. The satisfied smile, suggestive of something he hadn't known only hours earlier, crushed the faint hope that he'd come to tell her this was their mistake, apologies and you're free to go.

"You will stand now," he said. "It's time."

"For what?" Mildred said.

"To come with us."

"I will report you. You're illegally detaining a citizen with no cause. I've had enough of this," she said.

"We'll take you to where you can report us all you want."

"I'm just a bookseller," she said again. "You have no right."

"You will come with us now," the man said sharply, his tone shifting.

"This is a mistake. I'm simply going about my business. You kept me here all night long. I have no idea what I've done."

"Your business is undermining the People's will."

"I fail to see how a simple romance can threaten the People's will," she said. "I want to know who you are. I demand to know by what authority you've detained a law-abiding citizen."

"By the authority of the People," he said. He folded his hands behind his back and waited for her to stand.

Do not leave with them, she thought. *Do not leave with them. You will disappear like the others. You will not be heard from again.*

She heard her aunt's voice in her ear. *Do not move, do not move.*

The man gestured to the book lying on the table between them, and his voice shifted from mocking patience to anger. "Open it then. Open this steamy romance that all the housewives of Shenzhen can't wait to get their hands on. Please."

She crossed her arms.

He picked it up and with elegant fingers he retrieved a pair of reading glasses from his shirt pocket and read the first paragraph. It rolled off his tongue with the authority of a judge passing sentence. He shook his head in disgust, snapped the book shut, and stared at her over the rim of his glasses.

"Well?" he said.

"I don't know anything about that. I don't know anything."

"This is very unfortunate for you. We'll know everything soon enough. We have what we need for now."

She shook her head. "A packing error," she said. "Nothing more. It's just the wrong cover."

"An innocent mistake, of course," he said.

He produced a pen and notepad and placed them on the table. "Go on, then. Start writing. I will have the names of your colleagues and your customers. And the password for your phone."

She was not interested in politics or causing trouble, she insisted, not in the least. She was sorry for this mix-up. Of course they had her full cooperation, but they must see this was a terrible mistake. She loved her country and would do nothing against its best interests.

"And what country is that?" he asked.

"One country, two systems," she said obediently.

He put the pad and pen back in his pocket and straightened the cuffs of his jacket. "It's no matter to me if you play stupid. This will go badly for you now. This arrogance will only make things worse. It's no matter to me. Soon you'll regret ever learning to read in the first place."

When he told her they'd raided the offices of the illegal press that had published the book they'd found her with, she knew it would not be long before they understood they had more than a bookseller on their hands. They would learn that she ran New Light Editions, the most reform-minded press in Hong Kong, and publisher of the most dangerous books in China.

He spiralled a finger in the air and the two agents took Mildred Chen by the arms and stood her up and placed her in handcuffs.

"Let's go, let's go, let's go," they said.

A blindfold was secured, the knot turned tight like a screw at the base of her neck, and she was placed in the custody of a warder, who marched her through a series of corridors and out into the busy concourse where she'd been detained the day before. The woman gripped her arm and led her forward, walking with a bull-legged gait that caused her to lurch her shoulders violently from side to side with each step.

In the echoing concourse, Mildred heard the voice of a child ask why the lady was wearing handcuffs and a blindfold—"What's she done? Has she killed someone?"—and an adult voice reprimanded the child and told them to look away and mind their business.

Frightening waves of adrenaline coursed through her veins. The slow gathering of fear that had simmered in her during the night rose now to a suffocating panic. She resisted the impulse to break free and run; how and to where, she had no idea. When she planted her feet, the warder's grip on her arm tightened severely and the woman told her in the fewest possible words what was expected of her, which was complete and silent cooperation. If she resisted or tried to call out or make a fuss, she'd be shackled at the ankles and gagged as well—don't think for a moment she wouldn't. And so, bound and helpless, Mildred Chen was disappeared into the mainland through a gate reserved for VIPs and criminals, swiftly, no waiting, no questions. She asked the warder, quietly, "Where now? Please. Where are you taking me?" There was no answer.

FOUR

FARON HAD CAUGHT A DIRECT BUS FROM HONG KONG INTERNATIONAL to the Luohu border crossing only days before the miracle of perfect Mandarin visited him in the elevator at the Hotel Metropole. Through that checkpoint he'd entered mainland China and continued by cab to the bustling railway station in Shenzhen, where he was to catch a train to Guangzhou, his sister's adopted hometown. He'd been in transit for more than twenty-four hours by the time he arrived at the station, and so, too exhausted to utter even an irritable sigh, he found a seat in a concourse busy with travellers and boarding-call announcements, and wearily monitored the departures board for updates. For a moment he considered getting a hotel in Shenzhen to sleep off the worst of the jet lag, but he was eager to deliver the news of their mother's failing health to his sister. He took note of the local time, half a day in the future in relation to back home, and imagined his return journey two weeks from today, with his sister's promise to come home with him to make peace with their dying mother, and his own final decision, made one way or the other, about the Iranian dissident.

He was moments from slipping into blissful unconsciousness, slumped there in his uncomfortable seat, when an unusual sound caused him to open his eyes.

Seated directly across from him was a woman, blindfolded and handcuffed, dressed in grey slacks, a quilted blue riding jacket, and red sneakers. The sight was as startling as it was distressing. She was a slight woman, and in her shrunken posture and trembling hands he saw submission and fear. He was an experienced traveller, and far from naive, but in his surprise he was troubled by what he saw before him, a helpless soul so cruelly bound. The individual sitting beside the blindfolded woman seemed to regard her with casual indifference, though the empty seating around them suggested that they were travelling together. This second woman held a canvas satchel in her lap and looked much older than her companion. She wore a dark-blue blazer and slacks and boots suggestive of some sort of officialdom, a corrections officer or prison guard, by the look of it. Everything about her was round and dull, her fingers short and stubby, her eyes untrusting.

Equally disturbing to Faron was the indifference he observed in the commuters who strolled by without pause, as if a shackled and blindfolded human being was the most common thing in the world. The fact that his niece was growing up in a country where distress and suffering such as this failed to raise the slightest concern in anyone but himself came as only the most recent challenge to his troubled optimism. He did his best to avoid staring, but he couldn't help himself. Here was the very definition of the underdog, a helpless soul deprived of her liberty, and in such a publicly humiliating way. He was wondering if he shouldn't try to confirm that the older woman wasn't in fact the bad guy here—maybe she was a kidnapper or broker in some arranged-marriage or forced-organ-donorship ring—when a drone appeared out of nowhere and came to a hovering stop above the women's heads.

It was not a surveillance drone; nor was it the sort of toy children flew in his neighbourhood park back home. This one was a fairy drone, a sort of flying pink Barbie doll, its propellor blades disguised as a tutu at the midsection. Unnoticed by the strangers below, the device performed a boastful pirouette, and then flew off in the direction of a group of schoolgirls, who shrieked with pleasure when they saw it and jumped up and down trying to capture the fairy, which bobbed playfully just out of reach. Faron welcomed the diversion. For a moment their youthful enthusiasm unbound him from his nervous worrying for the woman in chains, and for his young niece's future in China, and for the news he was delivering to his sister. They seemed, at least, like normal kids. Finally, when the fairy shot up to the rafters, leaving them far below, they waved it goodbye with theatrical exaggeration—all of them but one, who separated herself from the group and approached an old woman standing a short distance away.

This was the drone's master, a street vendor of trinkets and games and flying dolls, it seemed, selling what she could to eke out a living. She was an old woman whose face was so deeply lined with age that she looked to Faron neither Chinese or Caucasian nor any other race, for that matter, as if her advanced years had graduated her to some unique realm of pure humanity. If it wasn't drones, it was wristwatches or pocket calculators or whatever else she managed to get her hands on to sell at some small profit. She was dressed in what Faron would soon recognize as the uniform of the working poor—in her case, green sweatpants, a black Adidas track jacket with white stripes, and a blue Nike baseball cap—sporty knock-offs that no longer had anything to do with training or exercise but were simply so mass-produced and abundant as to be rock-bottom cheap.

The girl handed the drone seller a few bills and in return the old woman produced a shiny pink box from the duffel bag lying at her feet. When the girl accepted the box and bowed to the woman, it occurred to Faron that a flying fairy, and a pink one at that, might be a nice extra something for his niece in addition to the other presents he'd brought from back home.

He rolled his suitcase over to the woman after the girl had rejoined her friends and pointed to the duffel bag. She rubbed her middle and index fingers over her thumb to indicate *money*, and he produced a small wad of bills from his pocket, out of which she deliberately plucked her price. She slipped this into a pouch fastened around her waist and withdrew from the duffel bag another toy identical to the one she'd just sold to the girl and the one that she herself was operating, which patiently hovered over their heads as they conducted their exchange. When their business was concluded, the lady offered Faron a toothless smile. He thanked her in apologetic English and turned and wheeled his suitcase back to his seat and looked up again at the departures board. There was still time yet.

His niece's new fairy was held in a state of suspended animation behind an oval plastic window cut into the pink box. She had pretty blue eyes and purple hair, and wore a tiara and pink ballet slippers that matched her frilly tutu propellor. It was a clever little device, he thought. He was pleased he could add this to the gifts he was bringing his niece; she'd get a kick out of it. As he thought this, he looked up and saw the older woman seated across from him remove a book from the canvas satchel in her lap. She opened it and began to read. The prisoner beside her sat as still as a statue, her cuffed hands resting on her thighs.

When the boarding call for Guangzhou began flashing on the departures board, he packed the gift in his suitcase, which required a quick bit of reorganizing, and when he finished this task, the blindfolded woman shifted delicately in her seat and turned her head, as if to face him. She paused, and then he saw her lips move, and for a moment he almost believed she was attempting to communicate some silent message directly to him.

He checked himself.

It was absurd to think she was aware of him, blindfolded as she was, much less to believe that she was trying to tell him something. No, what he'd seen was nothing more than an idle fantasy conjured of a professional ghostwriter's imagination too readily given to the re-creation of other people's lives. It was an occupational hazard that might get the better of him one day, but not today, not while he was en route to deliver his difficult news.

The warder wet a finger on her tongue and turned a page. Again, the prisoner fell as still as a statue.

Suitcase in tow, Faron proceeded to his gate, took the escalator down to the platform, and boarded the train for Guangzhou.

FIVE

THE REGIONAL TRAIN TRAVELLED THREE HOURS NORTHWEST OF Shenzhen, though the prisoner on board had no reliable sense of the direction they were moving in, and with every passing minute the shallow flesh of her wrists ached more in the grip of the handcuffs. In the talk of the passengers around her she listened for the name of a town or station stop but heard only tired refrains and coughing and complaints about the costs of living. Every time the train slowed into the next station, she felt the quickening of her fear, and she sat forward in her seat sharply as if readying herself to flee. Here at this station she'd be vanished, disappeared like the other booksellers. But the warder remained seated, and the prisoner waited and listened to the coming and going of passengers as they boarded or departed, and then the train lurched forward again and the prisoner settled back into her seat and the agonizing journey resumed.

At the eleventh stop, the warder prompted her to stand

and led her down the narrow aisle. When the carriage door was opened, she believed for a moment that she'd been released from a vivid dream, and she felt a breeze lit with the smells of spring growth and woodsmoke brush over her face.

The fantasy vanished in an instant when the woman dug her fingers into her arm and together they stepped down and walked through a rural train station loud with voices and out to where a cargo van was waiting for them.

With a nudge she was pushed up into the hold and a male voice directed the prisoner to lie down. "Here," the voice said, and she heard knuckles rap on a hard surface.

When she asked where they were taking her, she was pushed down roughly onto the retractable shelf, the side of her face was pressed against the metal surface, and finally she understood what was happening.

The Supreme People's Court had declared the practice a humane and cost-effective means of delivering sentence. This was an execution van. She turned her head violently with the realization and with her teeth she grabbed the hand that was pressing her head against the metal surface and bit down hard. Her executioner swore and leaned an elbow hard into her throat until she let go. Straps were pulled tight at her ankles and hips and chest, and a soiled cloth was pushed into her mouth. The van was moving now, and the prisoner's shirt sleeve was pulled up to the elbow, exposing the veins of the right forearm. A tourniquet was applied and pulled tight, and she felt the distinctive prick of a needle. She writhed and fought, but the straps held fast, and the rush of terror emptied her bladder as the syringe was drained into her arm.

THEY WERE STILL driving when the cooling dampness on her thighs woke her. In a daze, she turned her head and began a hard, choking cough that didn't stop until her head was steadied and the cloth was pulled out of her mouth. She vomited and coughed again until her throat burned but she was breathing freely now, and then the shapeless confusion that had seized her took over once more and the vehicle continued over the empty road in a hushed, deadly silence.

WHEN SHE REGAINED consciousness a second time, she understood that she'd been drugged but not poisoned, merely silenced on her way to some more prolonged agony. The vehicle was stopped now and she heard the driver's side door slam and the sound of gravel underfoot, and then the side-panel door was rolled open and the straps were undone and she was pulled out of the cargo van and the blindfold was removed. She blinked hard and spat the sharp taste of bile from her mouth and coughed, the pain still there from the elbow that had been pushed into her throat. The vehicle drove off, leaving the prisoner and the warder standing at the top of a narrow lane before an old stone building surrounded by farmland.

"Please help me," she said.

The warder marched her forward and into the building and up a flight of creaking stairs to a small room with a single bed and side table, a chair and desk, a dresser with a mirror, and a window that looked out to a landscape of greening hills. Shirt, pants, and underclothing were set on the bed. The warder unshackled the prisoner's hands and a small woman with grey hair and a hard sideways twist in her bent back appeared at the door. In her hand she carried a canvas sack.

The desk chair was placed in the middle of the room and the prisoner was told to sit. From the sack the woman removed a tool and plugged it into a wall socket and the tool stirred to life with a tired hum. She angled it at the back of the head, sharp and effective and cold, and the prisoner felt the small tremors in the bone rattle the inner ear. The tool followed the curve of her skull, and the first helpless bolt of hair fell to the floor.

When she opened her eyes and saw the wide strip of stubbled scalp in the mirror, the clarifying defiance of hatred blazed up within her. The machine carved away the rest of it, and when they were finished, she drew her hands over her naked skull and felt the rough grain of her humiliation.

The warder told her to get herself cleaned up. She'd find water and soap in the adjoining room, and clothing on the bed.

The door was closed and locked from the outside and she was alone.

She stripped down and stood over the drain in the tiled floor beside the squat toilet and uncoiled a grey hose from the spigot it hung from. She opened the faucet and sprayed herself with cold water and scrubbed away the sweat and vomit and the dried urine of her soiling. The defiance that had steeled her a moment ago was gone, and now she felt exposed and vulnerable and wondered about the weeks or months she might spend here, deprived of everything but her jailors' cruelty.

To dry herself, she used the blackened rag that hung from the spigot, but the rag was so foul that she washed her body again and dried her chest and legs and back with the pillow from the bed.

She put on the fresh clothing and again she looked at herself in the mirror and saw the face of a frightened stranger staring back at her. Her eyes were wide and haunted by the undeclared threats that awaited, but the pounding rush of the events that had brought her here seemed for an instant to belong only to that terrified face. It looked back at her from such a hopeless and pitiable remove that she almost lifted her hand to caress its cheek and say softly, "It can't be as bad as that. Don't give up just yet," and then with a sort of violent, crashing horror she recognized herself and quickly turned away.

She gathered up her hair from the floor and dropped it out the window, and then turned when the door opened. The warder appeared again, now in the company of a man of about sixty carrying a black leather doctor's bag.

He placed this bag on the dresser and asked the prisoner to disrobe.

"I will not."

The warder's face betrayed no compassion. "You're wasting the doctor's time," she said.

"I want to see a lawyer. You can't do this. People will know I'm missing."

"Think carefully," the warder said.

"I want to see a lawyer," Mildred repeated.

"You are missed by no one. There are no lawyers. Do as the doctor says."

"I will not."

"A superior attitude will not go well for you here," the warder said. "You mean nothing to anyone. You are nothing. Do as you're told."

The man stood by, embarrassed, perhaps bored. He looked at his watch. He was a local man thrust into this world against his nature, obligated by compromise. He had an apartment and a daughter, interests to protect. He was a regular man cowed by circumstance.

"There are men downstairs to cure you of this arrogance," the warder said. "It means nothing in the end, your small defiance. You are nothing."

AFTER THE EXAMINATION, the doctor washed his hands and stepped back into the room and slowly packed his bag. He wore shame on his face. It was the expression of a man who did not know what he'd become.

"You're not pregnant," he said quietly. "They can be sure now. I'm sorry."

The bolt being set in place on the other side of the door sounded, and Mildred sat on the bed, arms wrapped around herself, and worried through what the doctor meant when he told her they could be sure now. She didn't need a physician to confirm that she was not pregnant. She did not sleep with men. But the statement haunted the room and seemed to take on an absolute presence, and then she understood. She could be beaten, or worse, without the fear of causing a miscarriage, and her imagination sped off in vivid and terrifying directions for the cruelty of a world that could orchestrate its tortures with such chilling and deliberate forethought.

HOURS LATER, AFTER dark, the heavy bolt on the door was drawn back again and two men entered the room. They informed the prisoner she must sign a series of papers waiving her right to consult with a lawyer or communicate with family. Both of these men wore trainers on their feet and reading glasses and collared shirts with no neckties. They looked like country lawyers, but they were not lawyers. They were functionaries in this wicked industry of coercion and fear.

One of the men set up a video camera in the middle of the room while the other stared at her, waiting for her to comply.

She signed the papers, fearing what they would do if she refused.

The first man slipped the signed documents into a folder and checked with the second man. When the camera was ready and the questioning began, she knew the entirety of her adult life had led her to this sacred moment. It would define her forever. If she provided what they wanted she would be released back into her life, and condemned to live with the burden of shame. She could choose to save herself by offering the names of the booksellers in Shenzhen and the names and whereabouts of the writers she published and the names of her regular customers. She could do this and be free.

She cupped her hands over her face and breathed deeply and felt the powerful urge to tell them everything.

The man asked again.

"Begin with the names of the booksellers you supply in Shenzhen," he said.

She looked up and smiled sadly and nodded, and then something was summoned from within her, some perfect clarity in knowing not who she was but who she could not be, the person she refused to be, and with a floating confidence that surprised her, she relaxed finally into the artful lies that for this night, at least, would keep these dogs at bay.

SIX

LESS THAN AN HOUR AFTER BOARDING IN SHENZHEN, FARON spotted his sister and niece waiting for him beside a shimmering advertisement for Cartier watches as he came up the escalator at the station in Guangzhou. His train had arrived on time, punctual to the minute. Jana waved and smiled as he stepped off the escalator, and he came through the crowd and gave them both a good long hug.

"Go on, Peanut, don't be shy," she said, and gave the child a soft nudge.

Her daughter, whose name was Chloé more often than it was Peanut, was wearing what appeared to be a school uniform—a grey knit sweater, a blue skirt, grey knee-high socks, and shiny black shoes.

"Welcome to Guangzhou, Uncle," the girl said in unaccented English.

Her mother wore a green wool peacoat, blue slacks, and brown Chelsea boots. She looked healthy and happy and confident, and but for the few early strands of grey that marked the passage of time, her hair was as he remembered it, only slightly more stylish, worn without bangs and long to the shoulder.

"Come, you must be dead on your feet. Let's get you home," she said.

He was beyond exhausted, it was true, but he merely nodded and smiled and said it was great to see her again, it had been too long, and in his sister's self-conscious smile, which hesitated to reveal the toothpick-thin gap between her upper front teeth, he saw, as he always did, a younger, prettier image of their mother. He knew better than to say as much, however, not for the shy smile or the humbling space it revealed but for the difficult feelings between mother and daughter that he'd come in the hope of repairing.

The mission that had brought him to Guangzhou—to broker a truce, maybe even an everlasting peace—would take some doing. He needed to find his moment, which clearly wasn't now, in the middle of a bustling train station, his six-year-old niece hovering. When the right moment came, the news of their mother's declining health would soften the grievances that had ruled his sister's heart for so long, he was sure of it, and she would agree to his proposal to come home to say goodbye.

They took a cab to the Liwan district of Guangzhou, and in his sister's apartment building they rode the lift to the seventeenth floor, where they were met by Faron's smiling brother-in-law. The man offered a deep bow. Faron returned this antiquated formality, bow for bow, before the two men gave each other a back-slapping hug.

"It is exceptionally fine to see you again after so long," his brother-in-law said. "*The pain of parting is nothing to the joy of meeting again.*"

Yìchén Li, a professor of literature at the university, was an enthusiastic linguist. His spirited use of the English language was cleverly inventive and packed with literary references. He'd been studying it for more than thirty years and loved everything about it. He used words like *unbeknownst* and *kerfuffle* and quoted Dickens the way some people quote the Bible.

Faron, now reminded of this, said, "Let me guess. *Bleak House*?"

"*Nicholas Nickleby*, okay?"

THE GIFTS FOR his niece were unpacked soon after Faron emerged from a rejuvenating shower, hair still damp, wearing a change of clothes and the pair of house slippers his brother-in-law kept for overnight guests. He settled on the sofa and watched her open her presents. She bounced up from the floor, where she'd sat in a happy mess of wrapping paper and savaged boxes, and threw her arms around him and then sat down again and began learning the controls for the fairy drone.

The spacious three-bedroom flat wore its owners' distinct cultures and tastes with ease. Its old Chinese-style lamps and tapestries and rugs blended warmly with a British colonial feel of turned dark woods and deep, rich fabrics stretched luxuriously over sofas and chairs. The large tapestry hanging on the wall above the heirloom dining room table showed a finely manicured landscape of pagodas and gardens and a bridge spanning a river and figures gathering in a graveyard. The scene depicted something called the Pure Brightness Festival, his brother-in-law explained after he noticed Faron's interest. It was also known as Tomb-Sweeping Day, he said, when family members gather to tidy the gravesite and bring flowers and food and incense and burn paper symbols of the things that had been dear to their departed loved ones.

"The smoke of the burning travels heavenwards, you see," Yìchén said, "and touches that person in the afterlife. We are a *devilishly* superstitious culture, we Chinese."

Chloé had managed to launch the fairy while her father explained this curious tradition to her uncle. She flew the delicate machine toward her mother, who'd just then entered the dining area carrying a platter of steaming dumplings, and in a moment a rapid-fire exchange of Chinese sparkled between them. It was an odd and thrilling blur of sound to Faron's ear. He'd never heard his sister speak the language and he felt a deep sense of admiration and happiness for the fact that she'd made a life for herself in a part of the world that was so vastly different from the one they'd started in. She'd done well for herself. Here before him was a portrait of a successful life that had been chosen, pursued, and fully realized. He was happy for his sister, and then hard on this feeling of contentment and good will came the dreary thought that he'd soon have to rattle the harmony he'd found here with the news of their mother's sharp decline. He watched the fairy hover above the dish, as if it were trying to cool the evening meal with its spinning tutu, until Jana waved the drone away with her hand and calmly reprimanded the child. The fairy withdrew and settled obediently in Chloé's lap.

Shortly after their meal, barely managing to stifle yet another yawn, Faron thanked his sister and brother-in-law for their warm welcome and gave his niece a good-night hug. He could hardly keep his eyes open. He retreated to the guest room, which had already been prepared, and changed into his sweatpants. The pullout couch was open and spread with fresh sheets, the bedside table set with a small bouquet of fresh flowers, a clock radio, and a recent issue of *The New Yorker*. He slipped into bed and checked his phone, where he found two unread messages. The first was an update from home, punctuated by three heart emojis. The second message was from Ms. Khajenouri, the woman at the Japanese consulate in Hong Kong. She was looking forward to their meeting next week, the message said. *I hope you arrived safely and in good spirits.*

AT BREAKFAST THE following morning, Jana cross-questioned her brother about the reason for his coming visit to Hong Kong. He'd told her about his scheduled meeting with the possible subject of his next book. She was aware of the fact that he was not able to reveal the identity of that person in case he actually committed to the project, and when she took a few guesses, naming the various international personalities she knew of based in Hong Kong, he only smiled and shook his head and said he was sorry, he couldn't talk about it. Besides, it wasn't even a sure thing, he reminded her. He'd signed a non-disclosure agreement but not the book contract itself.

She tried a few more names in the car as they drove Chloé to school, looking for a crack in his armour, but she found none. They dropped her daughter off and drove on to the lake that was one of the first places her husband had taken Jana when she came to Guangzhou in 2012. Still within the city limits, it was the setting of a fable written centuries ago, she said, about an immortal snake that turns into a man and marries two women, sisters, each marriage a secret kept from the other, and how the one sister murders the other when she discovers the truth. It was odd that they should not conspire to murder the husband, Faron thought, but he did not raise the issue, and besides, it was just an old story after all.

The parkland around the small lake was lined by walking paths and ancient trees and fabulous pagodas that loomed eerily in the heavy fog that morning, all of which cast a mood of introspection over Faron. Wooden rowboats emerged and disappeared in the mist, and over the water voices floated, untethered to this world, as if hinting at the news he'd come to share.

When he finally told Jana the purpose of his visit, a tense silence held between them as they continued walking, and only the sound of their footsteps on the gravel and the distant crying of a baby could be heard, and then she said, "I don't know why you thought coming here would change anything."

It was the resistance he'd expected. This would take time.

"People change," he said.

They were two ghostly figures aswirl in the mist.

"You always *were* more sentimental than realistic when it came to Mother. I'm sorry. The woman's a pathological narcissist. I'm done with her."

"She's old now. She has her regrets."

"Did she put you up to this?"

He wanted to lie and tell her yes, but he didn't lie. He was incapable. Their mother had not asked. She would never ask.

"It's good of you to take this on," she said. "But no. Let's just have our time here. I'm glad you came. And I'm sorry she's dying. But there's nothing to say."

The sharp physical likenesses they'd shared as brother and sister had blurred as they'd aged into adulthood. More than this, the intervening years had confirmed for her their mother's lifelong lesson that trust, once betrayed, could not be regained.

Jana was dug in. She would not yield to her brother's request. The passage of time had only widened the distance between mother and daughter.

As they walked through the mist, it seemed to Faron that there was little chance he'd be able to say or do anything to solve the problem between them. She was determined to move forward, as far from the past as she could; and here he was, still willing to fight for what, to her mind, was irretrievably lost—nobly or perhaps foolishly sacrificing himself to the doomed project of saving his shrinking family. Her manner was not scolding or dismissive or sarcastic, though; it was instead almost apologetic, and in this he placed his hope.

An electric moped bearing two young people, a brother and sister, perhaps, came up behind them now and rolled silently by. The moment offered him a glimpse into their past—siblings clinging to one another, as they'd done so often in the shared solitude of their youth—and without a sound the image slipped back into the fog of memory.

"And you, my good brother, are you happy?"

He hesitated before answering. His personal life was not unlike that of many of his friends and acquaintances. He was of a generation defined by fractured marriages and noble second and third tries. He'd enjoyed and suffered through a modest number of mid- to long-term relationships, each ending in a confusing haze of amicable heartache. In his professional life he'd fared considerably better, which to his mind was the lesser win. At heart he was an idealist who believed that souls could match, that certain people were meant to be together. He believed in love. So, rather than settle for the next available relationship, something present and waiting, he endured in solitude those infrequent though lengthy periods of time when he found himself romantically adrift. He lived in the two-bedroom penthouse suite of an east-end luxury condo that featured a sky garden and waterfall on the rooftop, an on-site stress relief centre, and a generous full-sun balcony off the living room, which enjoyed a wide view of the lake. He played squash three times a week at the Mayfair Racquet Club, where he was known among his fellow squash enthusiasts as a devoted player with a love of the long rally, a stubborn disdain for the sidewall boast, and a decent drop shot.

When he had a project on the go, which was most of the time, he worked every day from early morning to mid-afternoon, researching his newest subject, conducting interviews, or writing, and then read a novel or enjoyed a film or met a friend for a drink at one of their preferred downtown haunts. He enjoyed arranging the twist or gratifying plot point to befall the lives of the clients he turned into characters, but carefully avoided such twists in his own life. At the end of the day, after a full writing session, he returned peaceably undisturbed to his own life. Seated at his desk every morning by six, he was disciplined by the pull of routine and dedication. Always there was the satisfaction of control, of shaping the lives of others while minimizing the unpredictable in his own. The careful optimism that carried him through his days was a marker of his good sense and testament to this cautiously deliberate life. Choices were made and decisions stuck to. He followed through. He was attentive, smart, and steady. Fools and cynics operated at the fringes and paid the price accordingly.

"Yes, yes, I suppose I am happy," he said.

She linked her arm in his as they continued through the rolling mist, past an old man wearing a blue hat crouched among the reeds with a fishing pole balanced on his knee.

"And is there anyone new in your life?"

Faron almost blushed.

She knew about the end of his last relationship, already three years gone, but had received no updates since. He wondered what she'd think of his current romantic situation. No, he didn't wonder. He knew clearly enough.

"Oh, please, do spill," she said, tightening her locked arm around his. "I'm going to abandon you here if you don't . . ."

The sister razzing her brother about a new girl was an old routine from high school.

"Yes, yes, there's someone. You'd like her."

"Good for you," Jana said. "You deserve to be happy."

He wondered if anyone *deserved* happiness, but he didn't burden the moment with a contentious remark. "As do you," he said.

"And does this mystery woman have a name?"

The woman in question was indeed a mystery to him, but a thrilling mystery he was in no rush to solve. She was a book translator—her name was Setareh Azad—and she was the only Persian he'd ever met before his correspondence with the Iranian activist and film director began. It was almost two years ago now that he'd received the query about the Farsi language rights to the single novel he'd written, published well before his reincarnation as a ghostwriter. He'd googled the sender's name and found that she'd translated an impressive handful of novels he greatly admired. The email contained no easy flattery or generic observations regarding the romantic struggles of his novel's young protagonist, so often the tack readers and reviewers had taken in discussing his book, which he'd written, like no few self-regarding first novelists of his day, while living in a grenier in, yes, Paris.

SETAREH AZAD HAD introduced herself in that first email as a translator connected to a small Los Angeles publishing house. SouthBook Publishers specialized in bringing English-language books to the Persian diaspora and was interested in acquiring the translation rights to his novel. They mostly sold into the American and Canadian markets, but many of their books ended up in Iran itself, one way or another, either carried in one or two copies at a time or in e-book format.

The translator articulated various interpretations of the themes she'd discovered in Faron's novel, some of which hadn't occurred to him, and the reasons she believed his book would be of interest to their readership. She mentioned that she too had lived in Paris as a young woman—she'd taken a year at the Sorbonne—and was lit with nostalgia by his tender portrait of the city. She loved the novel and was looking forward to hearing from him.

When he looked up the publishing house, and then the translator herself, he found no picture of her on her LinkedIn profile, just a photograph of his book at the top of what was called the "wish list pile." He had no idea where she was based—he presumed LA—until a handwritten letter arrived five days after he signed the contract. It turned out she lived not far away at all, he was surprised to learn, just a short hop from the city by ferry or water taxi, on one of the Toronto islands that on any clear day he could see from his condo balcony.

Faron spared his sister most of these details as they toured the lakeside that morning, sticking to the broad strokes. There were many things he left out, of course, chief among them being the fact that Setareh Azad was already in a romantic relationship with another man—not married to him, no, but committed to him in a life-long partnership. He'd anticipated the position Jana would take on such an entanglement—a homewrecking distraction with no future, surely. But the relationship was no mere distraction, and there was no homewrecking involved. Setareh's partner not only knew about Faron, but encouraged the two lovers, to the point that the three shared the same bed, and more often than not they shared it at the same time.

BY VIRTUE OF their respective roles as writer and translator, Setareh Azad knew more about Faron than he did about her. She'd read his novel twice, which she always did before contacting an author she was interested in translating. She admired his portrait of the young man who falls in love with the woman he sees every day for a year at the bookshop on rue de Verneuil in Paris but cannot summon the courage to speak to, so daunting and powerful was his love for her, and fearful that this love, if realized, might one day end. It was, essentially, a story about the enduring power of unrequited love. Underlying this storyline was that of the protagonist's sister, who as an eight-year-old suffers a fall that results in a severe brain injury. Physically healthy, she is forever locked into a state of innocence.

To some extent, the love story reflected Faron's life as it was at the time, lived too much in his head, inexpert at anything other than timid self-doubt and fascinated by the young woman he saw browsing in the bookshop called La Porte Rouge across the street from his Paris attic. The sister in the novel whose tragic life he so gracefully rendered served as a subtle counterpoint to the protagonist's failed movement toward experience. With the skill of a master, he'd captured the romantic paralysis of a generation, and all this at the ridiculous age of twenty-four. He was, and he admitted it openly and with no shame, unequal to the novel he'd written those many years ago. It was quite beyond him now, as it had been quite beyond him at the time, written as if in a trance in his cold-water flat in the 7th arrondissement of Paris.

UPON ITS PUBLICATION the novel was met with praise from the most influential critics, at home and abroad. The young writer was welcomed onto the literary scene as the golden boy of the season, celebrated in fawning profiles, and compared favourably to Bellow, Gallant, and Chekhov. Sales were brisk for a time and then fell off to an inglorious trickle, as did the interview requests and the piecemeal book reviewing he'd taken up. Ideas for another novel were scattered and fleeting. There was nothing he could sink his teeth into.

Two years after the book came out, he was house-sitting for an old professor of his near the downtown campus of the University of Toronto, wondering why he'd ever come back from Paris, when the first ghostwriting offer came in. He accepted in a heartbeat. For three months he immersed himself in the life of a Montreal entrepreneur and inventor of a technology that reshaped the global telecommunications industry. The first of five equal installments of the advance from the Montreal mogul alone was three times more than all the earnings for his novel put together. Faron had never seen money like that before, and here it was, piling up in the bank account that had always and only registered in the near negative. It would have been beyond foolish to walk away from this new opportunity.

Over the next eight years he wrote the life story of a Formula One driver with a dark secret; a Real Madrid forward with a golden right foot and a taste for rare automobiles; and a member of the Royal House of Windsor. By the age of thirty-eight, Faron Jones was among the most sought-after in the business. He had no interest in writing another novel.

Setareh Azad knew nothing about this other side of his writing life until he mentioned it months later. He was relieved to see it did not threaten her interest in him or his novel. He'd worried that his career as a ghostwriter might be at ideological odds with the author whose work she wanted to translate—that she might now see him as a writer who'd traded a clear artistic vision for a comfortable paycheque. He was proud of his work as a ghostwriter; that wasn't the problem—they were smart books, however flattering of their subject they were. But he always knew that the brisk sales had more to do with the wider societal ill of celebrity culture than they did with the elegant character profiles he delivered.

There it was, then, writing to size, writing to market—realities he felt not exactly happy about but accepted as necessary conditions for the life he'd chosen. He was well-off, more than comfortable, and felt no need to make excuses. Yet on those afternoons they met, he listened to Setareh's adulation with wistful regard as she praised the writer he'd once been those many years before, capable of writing a novel so true in its artistic ambition that now he hadn't the first clue how on earth he'd done it. He'd lost something of himself in the interim, it seemed to him, his perspectives skewed by money, first too little, then vastly more than enough. The future had approached at full speed and delivered him to the tipping point year of fifty-one, where life at once became more subtraction than addition. The downslope was here. And now, peering through his lover's eyes into the heart of that naive and beautiful book, he felt the first stirrings of regret sounding deep in his soul.

SEVEN

IN THE TIME BEFORE HE BECAME A HUNTED MAN, JIANG MING had been a teaching assistant and doctoral student of classical poetry at Peking University, a poet and a student leader. Now he didn't know what he was in the days immediately following the massacre at Tiananmen Square.

He moved constantly between Beijing safehouses, sometimes barely hours ahead of the men who pursued him, and with each move followed the dreams he could not outrun. In the daylight hours they lingered at the outer edges of his waking mind, and in the darkness of night they woke him in fits of terror. He tried writing them down, hoping this would weaken their hold over him. His tattered notebook was filled with desperate attempts to articulate these dreams, but they remained untamed and the men who pursued him were never far behind.

His academic work had always been exceptional, and the essays and poetry he contributed to the student newspapers and literary journals of the day were hotly discussed by many of the reform-minded campus literati, among them his numerous academic referees. His writings distinguished him as a compelling voice in the movement that was sweeping the country. It also brought him to the attention of the commissars of the University Committee and the Beijing Municipal Public Security Bureau. The arguments and metaphors he'd composed in the high spirit of the times had since become a punishable offence.

He rarely stayed more than a single night at a safehouse and dared not return to the building where he'd lived for three years with doctoral candidates from the same department, both of whom had already been picked up and questioned. He was running out of options. He needed to get home to Shenzhen, in the deep south. From there, the people who called themselves Operation Yellowbird would smuggle him into Hong Kong and move him on finally to somewhere in the West. He knew of a number of student leaders who'd already made the trip successfully. He tried not to think about those who'd vanished without a trace.

Throughout that late spring he disappeared during the day into the comforting anonymity of the city's cluttered hutongs and waited until evening to call the telephone number he'd memorized to confirm the location of the next safehouse. He stayed well away from the university and the square where police and soldiers still maintained a heavy presence. He rode his bicycle for hours, one young man among millions, nameless, invisible, the fear that presided over him hidden in a face wiped clear of expression. Often he listened to music on a Walkman as he cycled. The cassette he preferred was a pirated tape of a

British pop group whose singer he found irresistibly handsome. The name of the band stumped Jiang Ming absolutely, but that did not matter. The music was a merciful distraction from the glowing embers of the dreams that haunted him.

ON THE LAST day in June he awoke confused and disoriented, as he often did in the weeks following the massacre. For a moment he didn't know where he was or why he was there, the room dark and unfamiliar, and then he remembered. He quickly gathered his things and exited the flat shortly before sunrise, once again trailing behind him the dying embers of an unnerving dream.

He descended to the vestibule, where he'd stored his bicycle under the overhang of stairs, and carried it out to the street. Light was breaking and the new day was already rushing with pedestrians and bicycles and pull carts and scooters. He placed the headset of the Walkman snugly over his ears and pressed play. The music started, immediately scattering the dream. He straddled the bike and was about to push off when a plainly dressed man walking toward him met his eye and lifted a finger as if to say, *Hold on for a minute, please, a question for you, is this the right way for . . .*, and as Jiang Ming lifted the headset from his ears, he was torn from his bicycle by two men who came out of nowhere. His wrists were cuffed behind his back, a sackcloth thrown over his head. He was hustled into a car, face pushed violently against the floor, and delivered to a bleak industrial zone of factories and slag heaps where a sour wind carried the chemical spirits of burning coal and turpentine and the woody smell of death.

JIANG MING WAS chained to a metal chair on the tenth floor of an abandoned flour mill works and questioned for eight sleepless days and nights about his co-conspirators and his involvement in the drafting of the document called Manifesto 89, which demanded that the members of the Politburo Standing Committee face arrest and trial for the crime of mobilizing the People's Army against the civilian population. He attempted to reason with his abductors, but he discovered they were ruled by a gluttonous appetite for cruelty that had no interest in reason. He told them they'd mistaken him for someone else. Whomever they were looking for, he was not their man; a graduate student and teaching assistant at the university, yes, but he was interested only in the study of poetry. He had no political inclinations whatever.

It was an easily disproven lie.

In his backpack, along with the notebook and a few items of clothing, they found his published volume of poetry. The men flipped through the pages of *Remedies for Obedience*, but seemed more interested in the music on the Walkman they'd removed from his belt than they were in the book, in which he'd paid homage to his favourite foreign novelist by depicting the Beijing leadership as a barnyard of bloated hogs who fattened themselves on the sacrifices of the People. They passed the headphones amongst themselves and listened with dangerous curiosity. The man in charge returned Jiang Ming's belongings to his travelling bag and left the room. The two men who remained stripped him of his clothing and produced a car battery from the wooden box in the corner of the room.

On the day of the massacre, he'd locked eyes with a soldier as the man aimed his weapon at Jiang Ming's heart, and he'd watched in frozen terror as the soldier angled the rifle upward and fired over his head. He was spared that day, whether by the man's shame or mercy he could not know, but on the morning of his abduction, his captors showed neither shame nor mercy, only a hunger for violence and a mastery of the picana attached by a black cable to the car battery.

They wanted details of the organizational structure of the Beijing Students' Autonomous Federation and his role in the chaos it had created.

They wanted names and addresses.

Most of all, they wanted the compliance and surrender of a broken spirit.

HIS TORMENTORS USED electricity on him many times that first day, and still he didn't talk. They showed him a copy of the manifesto he'd endorsed along with eighty-eight other members of the Students' Autonomous Federation, most of whom they claimed had already been rounded up and were at this moment begging forgiveness for their anti-revolutionary hooliganism.

When the prisoner lost consciousness, they slapped him awake and continued their questioning.

The man who'd left with the travel bag returned near midnight and told the prisoner that a floppy drive had been seized in a raid on the university's Student Activity Centre three days earlier. The drive contained a detailed map of safehouses across the city. All the names and addresses they needed were spelled out in that directory. Jiang Ming was one of the first miserable souls they'd detained, the man said. Raids were being carried out as they spoke.

The prisoner was held in that diseased room the whole of that first summer of the purge. The great silencing had begun. At night the man whom his torturers called the Chaperone sat with his threatening moods by the door, smoking and playing cards against an imaginary opponent who, out of nowhere, sometimes provoked the man into a sudden fury. His captive crouched silently, spine pressed to the wall, steadying himself for the next sharply jagged outburst as he watched his jailor descend deeper into his foul humours.

DURING THE DAYLIGHT hours, for seventy-eight days, Jiang Ming stood ankle-cuffed at the window ten storeys up and watched the bleak factory landscape of brick and blacked-out and broken windows roll far off into the distance. The window was kept wide open, but that did not help the rancid odours that brewed here. Debris from boxed lunches soured the air with a bitter musk that grew acidic and sickly as the days passed. Sometimes he leaned out the window so far he thought he might slip and break his body on the stonework below. He saw men and bicycles and pull carts and queues clocking in at a grey steel door behind an iron fence far below and looked upon them with respect and envy and then bitterness, and finally he tried not to look upon them at all and forgave himself for knowing that he'd condemn any one of those men down there to his own miserable fate if only it brought him a taste of freedom.

After the first days of his detention, they no longer came with their brutal questioning, yet with every creaking sound of a floorboard beyond the blighted walls that held him, or when the Chaperone looked at him with his slatey eyes, he expected the torture to resume at any moment. Suspicion and fear was general in the city now. His friends were being picked off one by one, he knew, the great purge well underway, and here he sat, helpless and beaten in this nest of terrors. When the floorboards moaned overhead, he wondered if this abandoned mill wasn't a torture chamber filled with young people bound and bloodied for their involvement in the student movement. He clenched his teeth and balled his fists in anticipation of the next round of electric shock that would burn holes in his flesh, as if they'd housed that electricity in his very bones and might open the current at any moment.

More days passed and still they did not come to pick up where they'd left off. His job now was to wait and to survive, but even breathing became a monumental task. The will to live was slipping. Uncertainty became the new torture. The sun poured its daytime heat into the small space, rousing with it the hot stink of garbage, and in the evening filled it with spectacular colours as the sun set dramatically over the city and finally the colours faded to a lengthening cascade of warm ochres, but the room was always sour and hot and the waiting never changed. The Chaperone smoked without pause and mumbled inaudibly to the cards spread before him, counting and arguing and banging his beringed knuckles against the hard table. He hacked up gouts of phlegm into his fist and smeared them absently into his trousers as he studied his card game, focus unbroken.

No options remained to the prisoner. There was no pity or compassion or sense left in the world. All that was left for him was to close his eyes and chase his beaten spirit out through the open window in search of a memory that would keep him alive.

JIANG MING HAD devoutly attended the lectures of the most venerated scholars of the day in his first year at Peking University in 1982. Always in his satchel he carried a notebook and pen, and in his heart he carried some keenly imagined future in which he stood shoulder to shoulder with these great men of letters. More than this, it was his dream in those innocent days to become a poet equal in stature to the poets he admired, and on many days he believed this was destined to be. He felt he'd been chosen, by whom he could not say, but the belief was there, and so powerful that it had to be true.

This was also the year he lived on the third floor of a residence with dozens of other ambitious young men who made it impossible for him to ignore the unfortunate condition that haunted him. In the quiet of the study hall, when the afternoon sun drew shadows on the faces of his classmates, he was filled with such a poisonous yearning that he thought he'd go mad. He wrote poems in praise of his desire to be with these young men, but wisely tore them up immediately after committing each to memory. Using the open showers in the company of his floormates became an agony he could not bear. He feared his shame would present itself as he stood naked among them, dripping wet and helpless, and so he began to shower in the middle of the night when the facilities were deserted.

It was in his third academic year in Beijing when he was welcomed into a small group of young men who sought pleasure in the same way he did, and with them he found relief but no peace. Always, in the wake of his spent passion, he returned to his lonely room to brood over the problem of his sickness, which grew yet deeper and more pronounced when he was introduced to a beautiful Cuban named Gabriel Ochoa, who'd come to China at the age of nineteen to study its language and the writings of its political thinkers. This young revolutionary did not suffer under the affliction that ruled them both, as Jiang Ming did. He rejoiced in it. They were different in every respect but for the hunger they shared for one another and for the other men they took into their beds. The Cuban had mastered his understanding of who he was in a way that surprised and thrilled Jiang Ming, who'd never considered that a freedom such as the one he observed in Gabriel Ochoa was there for the taking, if only the courage was summoned to do so. There was no hesitation or self-loathing in him, just pure joy and lust in the young man's embrace. Jiang Ming recognized the envy and wonder he felt for one who seemed so casually able to dismiss the dangers that surrounded them, even aspired to the example, but he enjoyed no similar release that year from the ugly phantoms that haunted his secret life. Shame was the shy sister to the desire that consumed him.

In the first naive months of their passion, he believed Gabriel Ochoa's interest in his day-to-day activities was a sign of his devotion. It seemed he'd found a possessive lover of the sort described in the mythology and literature of the ages, a relentlessly passionate soul who still carried the warmth of the Caribbean sun on his cinnamon skin. What he began to fear, but failed to understand, was how this beautiful revolutionary was able to sing the praises of Castro and Mao and Marx with the same tongue that brought him such pleasure. They could fuck for hours but talk of politics and ideology for no longer than a minute before another scorching argument was set alight; these worrying clashes visited them more often, and soon they lasted longer than the fucking did, until they overshadowed all the good things altogether.

He was alone with the Chaperone for such a long stretch of days that Jiang Ming began to wonder if his jailor too wasn't a prisoner, so desperate in their suffocating confinement that he sometimes spoke over his games of chance in the voice of a child. Night and day, as often as he could, Jiang Ming closed his eyes and drifted off into the tender arms of childhood. He left his body behind, empty as a hollowed-out tree trunk, and visited his dear mother with her scented herbs and classical poetry and their long walks hand in hand at the edge of Shenzhen Bay. He conjured the sound of her voice and her laughter and the way she called him up into her lap when he was little and how he liked to trace his finger along the top of her ear while he sat listening to her stories.

She was known in their neighbourhood in those days as the unfortunate widow of the young tradesman who'd disappeared after leading a labour action at the machinist shop of his employ; eventually thereafter she was known as the eccentric mother who recited Mandarin poetry to her quietly luminous son as they trod the boardwalk at the edge of the bay. In Beijing she'd been an eager student of poetry before moving to Shenzhen, where she met and fell in love with the man she would marry. By day she worked at the dispensary she ran in the city's Luohu district, selling herbal cures for the body and soul. In her free time, as on those pleasant strolls by the bay, she recited the poetry she'd learned in her student days to the boy, who burned with silent delight at this magical gift of language.

It was the sound of her voice as much as it was those poems that thrilled him, and it was due to her that the language of his art would be Mandarin, not Cantonese, though they spoke both languages at home. Sometimes as they walked along the promenade she dropped his hand from hers and he closed his eyes to help sharpen in his mind the verbal colours she shared with him and followed the sound of her voice like a balloon on an invisible string. He was careful not to lose her in the crowd—he was a boy yet, after all, and afraid of the uncharted world and this wide, dark bay that was said to be a watery tomb for the city's lost souls.

His mother never spoke about those unfortunates who'd been claimed by the bay's sad history, but he knew it was the resting place of countless drownings, suicides, and killings, this according to the rough talk he'd heard in the schoolyard. He wondered if he might hear his father's name spoken in the rumoured tales of dangerous migrations across the bay to the free city of Hong Kong. The rumours were general in the neighbourhood, spoken of in quiet tones by those who came to his mother's dispensary with their pains and unending sorrows. They spoke of the dangerous boats piloted by human traffickers who threw you into the black sea at first sight of a Chinese gunboat patrol and let you sink like a stone.

It was just a bay, after all, water and boats and fish, but to young Jiang Ming it was the hunger at the end of the world that had swallowed his father whole, every bit as treacherous as the jailor who held him into the waning days of that first burning summer of the purge.

ON THE FIRST day of autumn, the prisoner was collected from that place and allowed to clean up and given a change of clothing for the first time since his detention. He was brought before three magistrates and read the charges laid against him, which were thirty-seven counts of inciting the inversion of state power. Presented before the magistrates were his published essays and poems and the document entitled Manifesto 89 that bore his name and signature; also brought forth was the directory of safehouses contained on the floppy drive and witness statements from a dozen classmates and various faculty members testifying to his counter-revolutionary statements and activities. One of the informants was the Cuban named Gabriel Ochoa. The defendant was not invited to speak at his trial, but he rose and spoke regardless. He denounced the court as a sham and a disgrace, and pardoned his torturers and accusers, including the Cuban, whose secret passions he would not betray, and declared that history would pass final judgment on the criminals responsible for the tragedy of June Fourth. He was silenced, but not swiftly enough, by the bailiff and guards. Doubled over under their blows, he was taken aboard a plane and flown to Qingpu Prison, in Shanghai province, where he was condemned to seven years of forced labour.

THE CONVICT JIANG Ming was among the hundreds of men forced into the hard labour of operating the industrial press that supplied the nation and select territories of the wider world with catalogues and phone books and greeting cards and endless miles of pamphlets of no-gloss two-tone propaganda. The only political prisoner in a hive of pickpockets, embezzlers, burglars, con artists, and murderers, he was of a special class, singled out for the corruption of his beliefs. He was forbidden to interact with other prisoners beyond the necessities required in the performance of his duties at the printing press. He had no access to newspapers or books or pen or paper, his cell had no window, his slippers no laces. The things he did not have were too many to count. The things he did have were too few to matter.

Twice in the first weeks of his incarceration he met with a lawyer in the yellowing vault of an old room where water dripped from the ceiling and a camera waited with the patience of a riverside crane. When the man failed to appear on the day of their third scheduled conference, Jiang Ming sat watching the camera watching him and understood that he'd become the bait and his counsel had fallen victim to the state security apparatus and was likely now handcuffed to a metal chair, just as Jiang Ming had been in that forsaken flour mill works. So it went, the system tirelessly consuming one soul of conscience after the next in its bottomless hunger.

THE BUILDING WHERE he carried out his duties was attached as a wing to the central prison block, and the thunderous machines on the shop floor were said to have swallowed a man whole only days before Jiang Ming arrived. In the warehouse behind the printing presses were grey boxes, piled high to the ceiling, and in these boxes were greeting cards containing the encyclopedic breadth of all human emotion. Once a week a dozen forklifts loaded these boxes onto a fleet of trucks, making room for the stacks to grow again. Pallets of greeting cards were driven to Pudong International and flown to distributers around the world. In this way, the press and the prison itself earned its keep in the Deutsche Marks and British pounds that were paid for its shipments.

Jiang Ming worked alongside a young man who was serving a sentence of twenty years for robbing a German executive of 500 yuan after prostituting himself in the penthouse suite of the Shanghai Crowne Plaza. He was a slight creature who, at the age of sixteen, had fled the poverty of his rural upbringing in search of employment in the big city. He lived on the street for six months before learning that foreigners carried in their back pocket more money than he saw in six months of selling trinkets at the city's riotous intersections. He was a country boy, beautiful and naive, another despondent soul in this asylum of the damned. Twenty-two years old now, he was friendless and mortally resigned to the fate that had condemned him for the sin of being born poor. It was six months before they spoke to one another about anything beyond the functions of the great machines they operated, another three months before they conferred, and two more after that before Jiang Ming proposed what he'd been ruminating on since the day he laid eyes on him.

He would give over a portion of his meals to the boy, whose

prison name was an unutterable slur, in return for books borrowed from the library. As a regular inmate rather than a political prisoner, the young man benefited from borrowing privileges that were denied Jiang Ming. Though he had no inclination toward books, and in fact could not read, the proposal seemed to him the first stroke of good luck his life had ever known.

Once their exchange began, Jiang Ming fed his starved soul late into the night in the dim glow of the electric bulb that hung in the barren corridor beyond the barred cell door. He lost ounces and then pounds, but the pains in his shrinking stomach were forgotten when he opened these books and began to read.

At first he read gardening books and tawdry romances and adventure tales for children—anything the boy managed to secure. His accomplice's selections were piecemeal and random. He had no idea what sort of books he took down from the library shelves. Jiang Ming was resolved to accept whatever he was brought, so comforted by the holy act of reading. Soon, though, he learned to question his conspirator about the library, and began to coach him accordingly, until finally he found the shelves that offered the poetry of the Yuan and Ming dynasties, popular mysteries and detective stories, and even a few age-old classic novels. And when on three consecutive occasions the young man delivered stories of love and romance, this subject, on a sharply personal level, was raised again in Jiang Ming's own heart. He remembered his lustful dreaming and the instinct that had seized him when he saw this boy for the first time, his fine hair and delicate features, and he knew again that this dangerous yearning would prove to be his death or his salvation.

He began to study the cautious hesitation he noticed in the young man's behaviour. It was a sort of nervous pause, an embarrassed glance they met one another with, the lowered eyes when they secretly carried out their exchanges. He believed it was the reluctant love that he himself had known before the beautiful Cuban had offered his cure, and then his betrayal, and now he saw it in the silent young man who carried books to him with the tender care of an unrequited lover.

ONE DAY HE removed a greeting card from an unsealed box and saw that the card was a celebration of marriage. On its face was a glossy photograph of a bride and groom splendidly happy in their new union. He slipped it under his waistband, and in it that night he wrote a single line of thanks to his accomplice, using the pen he'd stolen from the shop floor that day. *The books you bring me have lifted my heart.* It mattered nothing to him that the boy knew not a word of their written language. He pressed the card between the pages of the book that he returned to him the next morning, and over the months that followed, a fresh note on a new greeting card was always there, tucked lovingly between the covers. These, to Jiang Ming's mind, were his secret tutorials in the language of love.

Though the unlettered boy said nothing when they exchanged books, the embarrassed hesitation grew only deeper.

He gave not an inch, no sign that anything had changed or ever would between them, but as the months wore on, and Jiang Ming patiently coached him in recognizing various book titles and the names of the men and women who wrote them, he believed that his accomplice was acquiring some rudiments of literacy and that he'd begun to understand the forbidden messages he wrote in the Anniversary and Christmas and Get Well and Condolence and Birthday cards printed out by the great machines for the European market.

He composed these love notes in the simplified Chinese that could not be mistaken. Every new day, when he saw the young man in the breakfast cafeteria or on the shop floor where they worked, he hoped that in the misery of this place they might find happiness together. Fate at last had offered Jiang Ming a kind turn. The certainty began to beat within him like a pulse.

He was triumphant as he walked through the echoing hallways to the cafeteria one morning and sat with a smile on his face across from the man whose shy and hesitant demeanour crashed in a dizzying instant. He pushed the extra helping of food back to Jiang Ming's side of the table and said the deal was off; he was lucky he didn't report this degeneracy to the bulls who ruled their lives. The violence of the reversal was stunning. Jiang Ming remained seated, the expression on his face unchanged, but the chaos in his heart nearly split open his bony chest. The soaring fantasy he'd created was destroyed. Afterwards, for five bleak months, he stewed in the torment of his loss. He doubted he'd ever come out of it alive. So it went in the lonesome pattern of his days, month after month, until he finally understood that death was in no rush for him, there would come no sweet relief, and finally he set to the campaign that would change his life forever.

EVERY OTHER DAY for three weeks he slipped a small clutch of greeting cards under his waistband and secreted them back to his cell, and in them he began to tell his story. He wrote of forced labour at Qingpu Prison, to which he'd been condemned for seven years for the beliefs he'd expressed in his essays and poetry; he wrote about forced sleep deprivation and beatings and torture in the Residential Surveillance at a Designated Location program; he wrote about the disappearance of his lawyer and the political oppression in the country he so loved, and about Manifesto 89, in which he and the other eighty-eight writers and filmmakers and academics and student leaders and editors had called for an independent investigation into the Tiananmen massacre, already six years ago now, and about the sham trial he'd received after his illegal detention. He wrote about the men who touched electric currents to his genitals and held him bound in a chair for days at a time, and about the corruption of those who were intent on destroying the Chinese soul. He filled thirty-nine greeting cards with the blue ink of the ballpoint pen he'd stolen from the shop, providing dates as far as he remembered them, names of disappeared lawyers and activists, and sketches that depicted the positions he'd been forced into while his torturers did their work. The last three cards he smuggled back to his cell were quartered, opening with the conceit of an enormous square flower, each panel offering as much writing space in his delicate script as five manuscript pages. Each morning, he returned these stolen cards, filled with his writings, to their original packaging, and there they sat, concealed and ready for shipping to their foreign destinations.

THE GREETING CARDS began turning up in England a month later, first in London, then Manchester, then Leeds, fanning out across the land on Tesco and Sainsbury's lorries headed west and north from the port of Felixstowe, Suffolk, to wherever a birth or a death or anything in between required a sentimental note. With a bouquet of flowers, a retired dentist in Swindon brought a card home for his Chinese-born wife, who after reading the strange message alerted the BBC, which posted the story the following day. Many of the earlier-purchased cards, initially identified by non-Chinese readers as the work of a lunatic vandal, were tracked down and retrieved from trash bins across the country. Tesco and Sainsbury's scoured their stock. Of the thirty-nine cards sent out, only five were lost. The story was in the English papers for weeks.

Forced Labour and Political Detention in China
Dissident Reaches Out from Prison
Cry for Help in Greeting Cards
From China Without Love

The country followed the story with intense curiosity, including a literary agent named Maggie Yan, who read the transcripts as they were translated and pieced together by English PEN, then tracked them down in the original after they appeared on a Chinese-language dissident website called China Watch. Ms. Yan was a British national born of Chinese parents who'd laboured in a work gang in Jiangxi province, shovelling up dead and dying sparrows in the time of Mao's Four Pests campaign, before crossing into Hong Kong and travelling onward to London with their daughter, Maggie, then six years old, in 1970. In Jiang Ming's messages she heard a unique and exciting new voice. The story of his struggle against the authoritarian regime was inspiring. She also recognized an irresistible pitch and a golden marketing opportunity.

She'd hung out her own shingle after five years at a mid-level agency on Paternoster Row, quickly gaining industry recognition for her keen eye for new talent. Her list consisted of politically aware, marginalized, or queer artists with a story to tell. This dissident writer had it all. After she learned of his ingenious cry for help, she sought out and read and admired *Remedies for Obedience*, a tattered copy of which she found in the front office at the PEN Centre at 24 Bedford Row.

She'd heard much from her parents about the regime when she was a kid. The tragedy of the Four Pests campaign had sealed itself in her brain, with the image of dead and dying sparrows fallen from the skies after days of non-stop pot-banging and bush-beating and banshee cries, creatures grounded by the weight of exhaustion in a country-wide mobilization that aimed to kill the creature believed to be fattening itself on the People's grain. For months after, she couldn't look at a bird in the London sky without thinking of her mother as a teenager shovelling heaps of sparrows into the bed of an open-back truck.

Along with the near complete eradication of the other three pests—rats, flies, and mosquitos—the end of the Eurasian sparrow in the skies over Mainland China gave rise to the frightening swarms of locusts that blackened the sun and equalled the plague that had blighted the land of the Pharaohs. In the two years that followed, tens of millions of people starved to death, including six great-uncles and -aunts of the Yan family in Jiangxi province. Maggie knew she had to meet this writer, this brave man who'd defied his incarceration with such ingenuity. The clincher came in Greeting Card 17—identified as such by English PEN after it surfaced in Dedham, Essex County—in which the writer referred to himself and every other man and woman of conscience in China as "the fifth pest."

ON A TUESDAY afternoon dull with rain, Maggie Yan greeted the dissident writer at Heathrow with a bouquet of flowers and the promise to make him famous. Also present were representatives from English PEN, Amnesty International, and Hostage International. An empty wheelchair piloted by a nurse and physician from the National Health Services rolled up, as well as three local politicians and camera crews from the BBC and Sky News.

Forced exile abroad was a tried-and-tested strategy used by the regime to appease international human rights observers when it came to high-profile dissidents such as Jiang Ming. The greeting card fiasco had caused headaches for the CCP, which welcomed the chance to rid the country of the counter-revolutionary poet the very day his sentence was up. Beijing managed to appear benevolent while permanently exiling another annoying pest.

Jiang Ming hadn't wanted to leave. He resisted. He didn't want to be anywhere but home, where he'd intended to intensify his role as an emerging leader of the reform movement. Two men from the Security Service, wearing dark slacks and mirrored shades, escorted him onto the plane at Pudong and flew over with him, napping between games of mah-jong and telling Jiang Ming to cheer up, friend, consider yourself lucky we're not tossing you into the bay, like our fathers did your old man.

Maggie Yan brokered a deal with Bloomsbury to publish a novel based on Jiang Ming's experiences as a leader of the student reform movement and his agonizing years as a political prisoner. He'd never written a novel before, but his volume of poetry, along with his high profile as a political exile and spokesman for the democracy movement, had earned him more than a little good faith. Big things were expected. They didn't crowd him; his new agent made sure of that. In the meantime, instead of writing his big prison book, he wrote a second and third volume of poems, which the publisher agreed to sign and publish in simultaneous translation, left page in Mandarin, right page in English. These two volumes were contractually distinct from the prison novel, and not what they were hoping for, but they received strong reviews in Britain and in the US and were picked up by a small publisher in Hong Kong called New Light Editions that made beautiful books and knew how to sell them.

He was not long in London before he became a sought-after and influential voice regarding the political and cultural affairs of his homeland. His commentary and essays were published in translation in the British press. He lent his backing to the organizations dedicated to the cause of Chinese democracy, and every June Fourth he marched in front of the embassy with the thousands that collected there to remember their dead.

But he wrote no fiction. That first contract, stalled four years in, was in danger of lapsing. Maggie began to enquire, gently, as to how things were going. The book she was originally hoping he'd write, the one she believed he was destined to write, existed in some hopelessly scattered form in his head. It was an absurdist dreamscape of night terrors held in the frozen sea of writer's block until the spring day he met the exiled Egyptian painter Narouz Gamal standing in front of the David Hockney called *A Bigger Splash* at the Tate Gallery. Five months later they got their three-bedroom flat on Surrey Lane and filled it with books and paintings and four languages, and Jiang Ming, like a pearl diver braving the sea monsters of lore, dove into writing his long-awaited prison novel.

It took him six years to discover the voice and story that would contain all that he knew and felt about the human spirit. In the intimate portrait of his mother, and in a childhood haunted by his father's disappearance, he found a hero for whom love and sorrow were intimately and forever linked. He would learn that in the ecstasies of love lay buried the seedlings of betrayal and that madness or death were always nearby. His was a portrait of an artist in the making where the streets he walked teemed with magic and despair. He saw rats emerge from a storekeeper's sleeve and fields of locusts drift as clouds over the bay and sparrows fall from the sky in a story that whispered its political allusions and themes in the softest breath. His hero's perceptions were powerful and frightening to him—why was he like this, why did the world thrum so in its high fury? The artist as a young man was held in a perpetual state of heightened fear and longing, and when he finally understood that his father had been disappeared for his beliefs, he measured his suffering and his anger in the verse he heard in the lonely chambers of his heart.

He wrote with beautiful intensity of his coming of age in Beijing and of the hope he found in the reform movement he discovered there. His interest in men and the many small moments of love he pursued in that secret world were as pure and subversive as the meetings he attended with the young women and men who would crash the corrupt halls of power and bring a new openness to the People. He wrote of the bright horizons that awaited his generation and of nights of song and celebration in Tiananmen Square and the belief that they were marching at the front edge of history. Theirs was the generation that would change the world. It was nothing less than that. His search for love and freedom as a man who slept with men in a world that measured his every move drove Jiang Ming's hero through the furious pages of his novel. These were elusive but always within reach, appearing in sharp moments of anticipation and hope and progress and then stolen away again. As if by cruel design, the betrayal by the Cuban named Gabriel Ochoa preceded the massacre that emptied the city of its dreams. And then came the safehouses and his arrest and torture under the Residential Surveillance at a Designated Location program that almost killed his spirit. Here his hero learned to set free his soul to wander in the bardo of the middle world between death and life, and then came his jailing and forced labour and falling in love with the beautiful boy convict who finally kills his hero with the cold denial of love.

On the morning of the editorial meeting, nine days after Maggie Yan submitted the novel to his publisher, Jiang Ming descended the steps of Bloomsbury House as if floating on a cloud. They were mad for the book. It was an unqualified triumph, both timeless and crushingly urgent. He felt, after so long, the unalloyed joy of promise fulfilled. Maggie cradled his elbow as they descended the stone steps to the sidewalk.

"I know it almost killed you to write this," she said. "You've done for Qingpu what Solzhenitsyn did for the gulag."

Jiang Ming was accustomed to professional flattery, but he appreciated the sentiment all the same. And she was right. It had almost killed him to write the thing, reliving the years of torment he had to tell about.

"Solzhenitsyn," he said. "Nineteen years in exile. Is that what I have to look forward to?"

"Be proud. You're changing the world."

He didn't reveal to her that on certain days the smell of steamed egg-white-and-milk pudding brought tears to his eyes. He didn't tell her that his desire to return home had become unbearable. Instead, he smiled ruefully when she kissed his cheek, still holding his elbow, and she reminded him that she'd collect him and his partner, Narouz, this evening at eight and together they'd head to the Groucho Club to celebrate properly with the acquiring editors, the publisher, and the translator, whose rough translation had assisted his British publishers in making their determination. He thanked her again and turned and walked the short distance along Bedford to Bloomsbury Street. The high mood seemed general throughout the city. Across the street he saw two children bouncing a ball between them. The tops of trees were coming into a heartening springtime green, and a ripple of swallows, now returned from their sub-Saharan wintering grounds, cut musical arcs in the sky.

Still levitating, he raised his hand to an approaching taxi and glimpsed the faces of the young and the old in the cars that passed—women, men, and children driving or ferried along in their pursuit of commerce, school drop-offs, romantic negotiations, domestic errands. It was still a wonder to him to live among those who considered their liberty with such casual regard, or didn't think about it at all, as if it were as free as the air itself; yet it was the muscle fibre that held all the city together in its maddening, glorious tumble.

He'd come to admire the English capital in the ten years it had been his home. He could hail a cab as confidently as any bowler-hatted Londoner, straight-backed, palm up and out, eyebrows raised; take a pint at the pub down the street from his three-bedroom flat on Surrey Lane, where he lived with the Egyptian painter to whom he'd dedicated his life, as well as his new novel—*For Narouz, my love, my heart*; and even, with his uncertain command of English, sing along with a song about paradise glimpsed in a Waterloo sunset.

Yes, all this, but love it here he did not.

Here he was free to live as he needed to live, as a man who slept with men and as a dissident writer who was to this day observed by Beijing's foreign security services and would be even more so once this new novel was published; but when a fog settled over the city, as so frequently happened here in the early-winter season, he walked London's streets for hours as he'd done in the Shenzhen of his youth and felt the powerful arms of nostalgia carry him weightlessly home.

He was waiting for a cab to draw to the curb when one of the children darted into the street in pursuit of their dropped ball, causing the approaching blue Peugeot sedan in the opposite lane to veer suddenly. At that moment Jiang Ming saw his lover, Narouz Gamal, walking toward him, come to help celebrate this moment of triumph—or to offer his loving hand if the publisher's reaction had not been favourable. They took real joy in each other's successes—artists could be such competitive fools—and now more than anything Jiang Ming wanted to share the wonderful news that his novel had been well received. Narouz would understand like no one else the deep sense of relief and the purest joy that came at a moment like this.

He raised his hand and waved and nodded yes, yes, and Narouz smiled and understood immediately. The news was good. He did a playful dance as he approached, a skip in his step and a flirtatious swagger in the hips, and the child pursued their ball, and the blue Peugeot crossed lanes and jumped the curb with a hard bounce.

Jiang Ming's heart did not fill with terror or pain in the instant the car struck him down. It was flooded instead with such a powerful feeling of nostalgia and love, for Gamal and for his mother, that he felt some odd light move through him, and his soul came away, as it had done years ago in the torture room, and he saw his body travelling through the air and landing at the siltstone steps of Bloomsbury House, four doors up the street from where he'd been standing, and he felt the truest part of him rising like a balloon. Soul unbound, he blew a farewell kiss to his partner, who was running now, and to the others who were at that moment rushing to the accident scene, his agent, Maggie Yan, among them, and to the astonished child who stood dumbstruck, ball in hand, in the middle of Bloomsbury Road.

EIGHT

THE GHOSTWRITER AWOKE BLURRY-EYED AND DISORIENTED ON that early fourth morning in his sister's guest room. He slipped out of bed and sat in his pajamas at the kitchen table next to a window looking out over a city that sparkled in the pre-dawn darkness. The house was quiet. He brewed himself a pot of tea, and in the blue light of his device he composed a message to Lamya Khajenouri. He hoped her spirits were high and her health was good, he said, and perhaps there was some slow but sure progress in the difficult matter before her. He'd been keeping up with the news, of course, but wondered if there were any developments that hadn't made the papers yet.

Ms. Khajenouri was a true artist and fully committed to her cause—he knew this from her films and from the messages she'd written him—but the celebrity angle was easier to sell, and so sell it the news sites did. Headshots and movie stills of the glamorous activist accompanied every new update. Even the serious websites spent too much time on her life as a director and actress rather than on the issues she was risking her life for. People were rotting in prison back home for speaking their mind, she reminded the press whenever she could. The morality police still terrorized the streets. The criminals were still in power and bleeding Iran of its very soul. That's why she was here, she said, trapped in this consular asylum. She implored the press to focus on the fact that women in her country were dragged off the street for the unpardonable sin of wearing their hair down, and if they were still young and a virgin, they were forced into a jail-cell marriage and raped before they were executed because the execution of a virgin was unacceptable. It was this barbarism she was fighting against, she said every chance she got; instead, the news sites offered stories about her film career and profiles in courage of the woman who struggled heroically on following her husband's murder. The coverage only grew more sensational after the ultimatum was announced. The clock was ticking now. If the Japanese caved to the Chinese demands, she would be dragged from the consulate and disappeared into the murderous halls of Evin Prison in Tehran. The reporting was not wrong in that regard; the situation was grave. But to Faron's mind, much of the coverage was maddeningly voyeuristic and tailored to an obsession with celebrity.

Since landing, and after he learned of the ultimatum imposed by Beijing, he'd offered to meet earlier than they'd originally agreed, and now, seated in his sister's kitchen, he asked again if he shouldn't come sooner. He could be on the train today. Within minutes his phone pinged with her reply telling him they could meet as originally planned, to enjoy time with his family.

He sipped his tea and set to thinking about the book he'd write about her, if he decided to take on the project. With some shame he wondered if using the consular standoff as a structuring device for the story didn't put him in the same league as those cynical newspaper editors who did their best to turn Ms. Khajenouri's story into a celebrity drama rather than a fight for change in her country. It was a narrative strategy that any storyteller worth his salt would consider using. With it, he'd create an undeniable tension (would they or wouldn't they break down the consulate door?) on which he could hang the backstory of her early years in Iran and her evolution as an artist who learned to manoeuvre quietly within the system, her marriage and rise to fame, and then the murder of her journalist husband that thrust her so violently into the activism that now defined her—all the while teasing the reader with the approaching standoff at the consulate. It was his training and instinct to think this way, as it had been to wonder what was happening to the blindfolded woman at the train station. But he was more than a storyteller in search of the right structure for the book. He was not a callous or opportunistic writer and never resorted to narrative trickery. He would capture what was unique about his subject. It was always the truth that he was after, only just lightly buried under a dusting of biographical detail. He already felt that Lamya Khajenouri's story would be like no other he'd known, though he couldn't say yet why he knew this, or if in fact he would accept the challenge of writing her story.

Day was breaking when Jana joined him in the kitchen shortly after six. She sat with him at the table, also in her pajamas, and poured herself some tea. Of the three prevailing concerns on his mind at that moment—the Iranian dissident, their dying mother, and the manacled woman—he chose to speak about the woman at the station.

He'd dreamed about her now four nights in a row, he said. In his latest dream, hardly two hours ago, she was being escorted home to visit a dying family member. He'd wanted to rescue her but felt powerless without the language.

Jana set her cup on the table, gave it a half turn, and sighed.

"What?" he said.

"I don't think it's necessary to guilt me like that."

Surprisingly, the connection between the dream and their mother's failing health hadn't occurred to him. "Jesus, no. I'm sorry. I honestly wasn't thinking that."

"Alright, you're forgiven. But enough already about that woman," she said, by which she meant their mother, and so he turned the conversation to lighter matters. He was not so eager to talk about their mother right now either, or about the compromises his sister might have made in deciding to raise her daughter in a country that had learned to look away when in the presence of a helplessly blindfolded woman. He considered his own compromises. He knew he wouldn't have to dig deep to find the remnants of a decimated people and way of life where he lived, on the north shore of Lake Ontario. The vanquished were underfoot anywhere you stepped, it seemed, but now was not the time to consider such uncomfortable truths. Instead, he steered the conversation to their plans for the day and she spoke about the neighbourhood and the art gallery she wanted to show him, and the fun restaurant she had in mind for lunch, and then she went to wake up her daughter. It was another school day.

Faron had come to expect certain things here since arriving—his brother-in-law's frequent Dickens references, which ranged from impressive to humorous to annoying; the delicious smell of steamed buns and rice porridge that filled the apartment every morning; the bright burst of cheerfulness that was his little niece; and exploring the city with his sister, who'd been gracious enough to take time off from her position at the university, where she worked as director of communications in the international students office. What he'd not expected was her defensiveness.

Her reaction to his dream was predictable enough, considering the purpose of his visit, though predict it he had not. She might have even believed he'd made up the blindfolded woman, or at least padded the dream to land the point that even thieves and murderers needed to say goodbye to their mother. He'd noticed this defensiveness a few times now since arriving, and had begun to tread lightly, but not lightly enough, it seemed. He was honest to a fault and inept at calibrating his mood to fit a certain social occasion or emotional dynamic, in any believable way, at least. His face gave him away at every turn. He had even less control over his dreams than he did his social niceties. His sister was otherwise generous in her welcome during his stay. They'd found in their shared pool of memories a few fond ones to dip into, and enjoyed one another's company. Yet the spirit of their difficult mother, even at this great remove, reflected their differences back at them.

Jana spoke to him over her shoulder after she returned to the kitchen and began preparing her daughter's breakfast porridge at the stove.

"But you can't judge an entire country on a single anecdote, of course," she said.

"Sorry, what are we talking about here?"

"That prisoner. The woman in handcuffs and whatever."

"I'd be surprised if the same thing didn't happen back home now and then," he said.

"Somehow I doubt that. It *is* different here. That's not what I'm saying. But who knows what she did. Maybe she's a killer. Maybe she spat on a policeman's shoe. They can be pretty heavy-handed sometimes."

Silence fell between them as she plated her daughter's porridge, and then he heard the sound he'd learned to expect in his sister's home at this time of morning, just before seven.

It was coming from the living room.

"I hardly ever dream anymore," Jana said. "I can't remember the last time. Is that a growing-old thing?"

"With Sigmund's permission," he said, "dreams are the detachment of the soul from the fetters of matter."

"It's way too early for that, thank you very much," Jana said.

The sound grew louder, and then the fairy flew into the kitchen and hovered over the table like a pink swarm of bees.

"Chloé!" her mother called out. "Would you *please*!"

"So we meet again," Faron said to the fairy.

"*Please* stop horsing around and come eat your breakfast!"

"I'd like to hear you say *horsing around* in Chinese. If you can say that in Chinese, there'll be a prize involved."

She repeated the idiom in Chinese.

"My sister, the genius," he said.

"Chloé!"

In the few days she'd had the gift, the child had become expert at the controls. How she manoeuvred the fairy with such impressive accuracy without so much as being in the same room was a mystery to Faron and perhaps testimony to the electronics savvy of all children her age. The thing held steadily in front of him for a moment longer, then reluctantly heeded Jana's rebuke and retreated. A minute later Chloé appeared, wearing a big smile, pink pajamas, and green Shrek house slippers. The grounded drone in hand, she took a seat at the table.

"Good morning, Uncle," she said.

"Good morning, Grasshopper."

He saw by the expression on her face that the reference was lost on her. Suddenly he felt his years. She set the fairy down on the table.

"Maybe we should slap the cuffs on *this* one," her mother said, setting the bowl of porridge in front of her. "Not even dressed yet. *Eat*."

"What's a prisoner?" Chloé said.

Her English was unaccented but full of holes.

"It's not polite to eavesdrop," her mother said.

"What's eavesdrop?" she said.

"An eavesdropper is someone who listens to other people's conversations," her uncle said.

"Eat," her mother said.

"*Eavesdropper* rhymes with *grasshopper*," Chloé said.

"It certainly does," Faron said. "A prisoner is someone who goes to jail."

She nodded gravely and ate a small spoonful of porridge.

"Girls who eavesdrop instead of finishing their breakfast go to jail," her mother said.

"But they let them out of jail in time for recess," her uncle said. "You have recess here, right? Do kids in China have recess?"

"Yes!"

"That was your mom's favourite subject when we were kids."

Chloé shot her mother a wide-eyed look of amazement. "It was not! It was *drawing*."

"And you know who lets a prisoner out of jail for recess?" he said.

She shook her head slowly and hunched her shoulders.

"Kids who eat up all their breakfast."

FARON JOINED HIS brother-in-law at an on-campus faculty dinner that evening in honour of a visiting American academic named Maynard Beenhouwer. The scholar was in Guangzhou to present a paper on semiotics and the art of translation, which, according to his brother-in-law, the professor had done earlier that day in excellent Mandarin Chinese. He was a tall, bearded man with a slight stoop and a quietly handsome face, and polite enough that evening to ask Faron about his work as a ghost-writer and one-time novelist.

"I imagine not a lot of outside influences are tolerated in Iran," he said when Faron mentioned the new translation in the works. "Maybe even worse than here."

"The novel's more love story than anything," Faron said. "Probably safe, as far as politics go. But it's a Persian-American house that's doing it. Based in California."

"I see. For the diaspora, then."

"That's right."

They were seated now with nine faculty members from the university at a large round table loaded with a spectacular selection of regional dishes. The various specialties were introduced and explained to Faron as his brother-in-law slowly spun the circular floating tray in the centre of the table.

"Oh yes, *Lazy Susan*," Yìchén said. "Isn't that marvellous? Here we just say *dinner table turntable*. Such an expressive house of metaphors is the English language!"

Faron selected a few items and pushed his ceramic cup forward when Professor Beenhouwer suggested he try a colourless liquor called baijiu, which he said was something like an Italian grappa or Portuguese aguardente.

"Wonderful, thank you."

Beenhouwer filled the cup and pushed it back to Faron and asked if he was familiar at all with Chinese literature. Faron confessed that he wasn't much of a sinologist.

"So the work of the Chinese novelist Jiang Ming?"

"I'm afraid not," Faron said.

He sipped the liquor and tasted the items on his plate as the scholar proceeded to tell him about the novel he'd translated that was at this very moment charting on bestseller lists in the States. The first translation had been woefully inadequate, he said, rushed as it had been after the novelist was struck down and killed by a car in London, where he'd been living in exile.

"Oh, seventeen years ago now. A brilliant writer, really. Gone before his time."

It was a novel of ideas, a dazzling crossbreed of gritty realism and political allegory, the professor said, but it wore its themes with a remarkably light touch.

"His use of the language is extraordinary. He began as a poet, you see. After the Tiananmen massacre, his protagonist is hunted down and ends up in a penal colony. That's where the novel is composed. From there he sends it out into the world chapter by chapter. There're quite a few similarities to the novelist's real life. Which I find fascinating. Sadly, it's hard to find the original on the mainland. Copies trickle in from Hong Kong now and then, so I'm told. Less so now, of course. Beijing's got its eye on Hong Kong like never before. They have something called the General Administration of Press and Publication. Their purpose in life is to harass booksellers to extinction. If a speedier death is required, the government just buys the building they're housed in and drives them out."

"And they just let him mail those chapters off like that from prison?" Faron said.

"Oh no, he writes his chapters in the greeting card stock they make in the printing press where he works. Forced labour. Gruelling. Horrible. That's from his real life. He steals greeting cards and writes his novel in them, and then they're shipped out into the wider world. Entire chapters appear in different cities, São Paulo, Caracas, Leningrad. It's really brilliant. Each is discovered on the specific day that corresponds with whatever the greeting card was meant to celebrate or honour—a kid's birthday or someone's graduation or wedding. A marvellous conceit. The greeting card themes become less literal and more metaphysical, let's say, as the novel progresses. *Our Sympathies on the Birth of Fear,* that sort of thing. As ingenious as it is gutting. No small touch of magical realism there too. It all works splendidly."

The translator paused and sipped from his ceramic cup.

Faron selected a green vegetable sprinkled with sesame seeds. "You're something of a cultural ambassador, then. A bridge between languages and people. That's exciting, I imagine."

"A dangerous bridge," Beenhouwer said. "The eyes and ears of the government are everywhere. Talk about Big Brother. So, yes. I'm being monitored. They put it in polite terms. I've been assigned a *guide*, you see. She takes me around and keeps her eye on me. I've been allowed to speak here only because an English translation of the novel has about as much effect here as a Klingon translation would. There's no impact. It doesn't bother them, really. Mind you, it's been getting worse the past few years here with"—he lowered his voice—"Chairman Pooh still at the helm."

"You've lost me," Faron said.

"Xi Jinping," the professor said. His voice was quietly conspiratorial. "Winnie-the-Pooh. It's a meme. Surprised you haven't seen it. He finds it particularly annoying. It really is delicious how similar they look. The president takes exception. They're trying to scrub the internet of it. Good luck with that."

Faron had assumed the professor was exaggerating the Orwellian interest in his presence here for the benefit of the story he'd just recounted, characterizing it as perhaps a brave political act simply to add some intrigue to an otherwise quiet academic life; but now the worrying thought of his niece growing up here returned, and he felt yet another small but measurable crack in the careful optimism he'd been doing his best to preserve since arriving. His niece was not only growing up in a country where no one looked twice at a blindfolded woman in a train station, but in a society where writers and booksellers were harassed to the point of exile or extinction.

"Well, gentlemen," his brother-in-law said, leaning forward from his seat beside Faron. He gave the serving wheel a gentle spin. "*As fate would have it, Mrs. Bedwin chanced to bring in, at this moment, a small parcel of* . . . dongpo rou."

The plate of deep-fried pork cubes wrapped in twine slowed

and landed in front of Faron. This latest Dickens challenge was the easiest of all.

"*Please, sir. Can I have some more?*" Faron said.

"Very good, Mr. Jones! And perhaps, my esteemed friends," Yìchén said in his brave nineteenth-century English, "you did not know that this sumptuous delicacy was the Chairman's favourite dish. It was banned in the kitchens of the official residence by Madam Mao herself, so afraid for her husband's alarming girth was she." His voice dropped to a whisper. "So here we must think of Joe, the fat boy," he said. He puffed out his cheeks like a little chipmunk.

Beenhouwer and Faron waited for it.

"*The Pickwick Papers*, okay!"

NINE

EVERY MORNING THE BOOK SMUGGLER UNTWINED A LOOSE FIBRE from the curtain over the window and tied it to the short length of thread by which she counted her days as a prisoner. The filament was now the length of her middle finger and represented the five days she'd spent locked in this room, watching the view to the hills as she waited. She was provided no books, no pen and paper. She had only the window to stare out of, which at first provided some solace, but soon the view became a cruel reminder of the outside world, which seemed content to go about its business without her. The anxious monotony of her days was interrupted at the noon hour and in late afternoon by a man who came with a small bowl of food for her, but the long hours of solitude were nothing compared to the unease that grew in her heart as the sun set and darkness began to push through the window.

The nights here were a diseased garden where fear grew its deep roots and tendrilled up into her troubled dreams, and at the same hour every night some unknowable thing approached in the blind dark and hung over her bed before entering her chest as a shimmering blue light.

She was never awake when this happened, but she was aware of it nonetheless—her body filling with a presence that wanted to hold there—and she was wrenched from her dreams and sat bolt upright and the strange light left her again, scared off like a startled bird. The faintest trail of illumination crackled in its wake, evidence of a shooting star.

She rose from her bed at such times, heart racing, and peered through the window into the darkness, wondering if she wasn't finally losing her mind. She wasn't normally given to the augury of night illusions, but she couldn't ignore the recurring dream. In her agitated state, she'd pace the room, replaying what she knew of her family's history. There were no rumours of mental unrest or whispered talk of insanity on this side or that. Was her mind falling backwards into the past, regressing as an old person's might into the childhood fairy tales she'd read at her aunt's bookshop? Hardly possible for a woman her age, just forty and otherwise strong of mind but for these disturbing fantasies. Wasn't there always a faerie or some such magic to comfort the heroine—or to lure her to her doom—in the books she'd sought out for consolation as a child? Which, then, was this, the comfort or the bewitching?

She got out of bed and paced the floor again when the dream woke her on that fifth night in a row. The torment of sleeplessness would magnify the troubles of any ordinary soul, but her life was ordinary no longer, and hers was no ordinary soul. She wondered if she shouldn't follow that trail of light out through the open window the next time it appeared. *Follow me*, it told her. *Close your eyes and take the air under your arms and fly home.* It was only a matter of believing. Why not throw herself from the window, finish it now or take wing—one or the other—before her jailors did it for her? The waiting would become the greatest agony, otherwise, and the slow insistence of time would crush the mirage of hope that remained. She wondered how the Iranian in the consulate had survived her three years of uncertainty, bless that woman's brave heart. Only five nights of her own detention had brought her as close to madness as she'd ever been. Her old aunt too would be sleepless with worry at this wretched hour, pacing the floorboards in the bookshop, marking time, as the Iranian in her gilded cage would be, all three women waiting in unison for the spark of first light to grace the horizon.

THE PRISONER WAS handcuffed and led out into the bright morning of the sixth day of her confinement, the length of thread pinched between her fingers. For a moment her spirits lifted when she felt the sun on her face, and she breathed deeply, almost gratefully, and then she saw the cargo van.

It was over, she thought.

Everything she'd said to the camera was a lie, they'd discovered, the bookshops and people's names she'd conjured in a smokescreen of courage that was now instantly dispersed.

The blindfold was secured over her eyes again and she was put into the back of the vehicle and they started to move. She sat on the wheel hub and listened to the crunch of gravel beneath the tires and felt the curves and the tilt of the road. She didn't allow herself the fantasy that she was being returned to her life or transferred to some other holding site. They'd passed sentence. She was useless to them now, a waste of time with her bold lies. This was the last hour of her life.

The warder and the executioner, whom she sensed hovering as he lit and smoked one cigarette after the next, sat without speaking, and with each new cigarette came another precious increment of time to remember and to dream, and under that black blindfold sparkled the racing emotions of a terrified soul awaiting its end.

They drove on like this, the man smoking, her terror hung at an impossible pitch, until the van slowed and came to a stop.

She was removed from the hold and marched back through the same station they'd arrived at six days earlier and put on the train that had brought her here. She was to be kept alive for at least another day, it seemed, a second confession video would be required, and she realized she was still holding the thread between her fingers, dampened now from the sweat of her fear.

The clatter of voices quieted to a murmur as the warder led

her through the carriage and seated her, and then herself, and the train began to move. The warder shifted, her hips pressing grotesquely against Mildred's in her narrow seat, and then came the sound of pages being turned and the pained whisper of the jailor reading to herself like a child, unpractised, the dangerous novel resting in her lap as the train bumped noisily forward. Mildred closed her eyes and listened and felt the novel take hold of her, and quietly it unlocked the cuffs at her wrists.

In this waking dream she rose and walked down the length of the carriage and opened the door and stepped off the train into a field of wild sunflowers whose heads turned and bowed in greeting as she drifted among them. *Come*, they said, *you're almost there*, and in the middle of the field she found a deep well and peered down into its endless dark and felt the cool air rising from below. There was no hesitation. She stepped forward and dropped like a stone and opened her arms and began to fly. The walls of the well shaft dissolved and the shaft became the blue oceanic sphere of a horizon lit far below and all around with sprites and spirit creatures who seemed not to notice her at all, and finally it became clear to her that she was one among the millions.

The jolting of the train roused her from this vision and she turned her head to the sound of boarding passengers, the clatter and heft of their bags and the whispered comments, and she wondered if there would be a woman or man among them who'd step forward to ask what this was all about, a young woman blindfolded and bound like that; this wasn't the Middle Ages here, what were they thinking? But the travellers passed in silence. Suspicion and fear and self-censorship ruled every heart on the train that day. The warder read on in her quiet, halting voice and cast the soft breath of turning pages over the prisoner's arm as the train crawled slowly onward to the bookseller's fate.

TEN

FARON HEADED BACK TO HONG KONG A DAY EARLIER THAN planned, his sister's rejection of his proposal tucked unhappily away in his heart. He'd failed to move her off her position and so he thought it best to leave now rather than force a confrontation he knew he'd regret. She drove him to the station and waited with him for his train. The fact that their mother would die estranged from her daughter cast an indelible stamp on this last day together, and when he felt her sigh as they embraced, as one sighs when an unpleasant task is finally done with, he understood that for her the matter was closed and she could finally get on with her life.

As his train approached the outer reaches of the rail yard at Shenzhen station an hour later, he awoke from a shallow slumber and saw an old man sitting on a stack of railway ties, king of his little mountain. The man shook his head vigorously and raised a fist at Faron, or perhaps at the train itself for disturbing his peaceful ruminating. It was an odd sight, this man protesting the intrusion into his privacy in such a way. Why anyone would choose to curse at a train in a rail yard—if anywhere the place where trains most certainly belonged—was beyond Faron. He collected his suitcase from the overhead rack, wondering about the surly mood of the man on the mountain of railway ties and the irony of his dissent—a train-gazer angry at trains, of all things—and made his way up to the concourse and farther along to the glass-walled food court on the upper level, which he'd noticed on his outbound journey six days earlier.

He studied the menu pasted at the door of the first restaurant in the long line of eateries, in no rush to get to the border crossing for Hong Kong. His first meeting with Ms. Khajenouri was set for the next day, and he had time yet before the room he'd booked at the Metropole was ready. Inside, diners bobbed over their meals with intense devotion, spoons and chopsticks aflutter. Faron felt the delicious stirrings of hunger. It looked to be a small family establishment, just ten or so tables, a place where he couldn't go wrong.

A woman at the food-prep counter sectioning a roasted duck with a large pair of catering scissors glanced up and met his eye. She smiled pleasantly and waved him in, and then turned back to her work. She wore her hair tucked up in a bun and a red polka-dot apron over a yellow sweater. In that pleasant smile he'd recognized the simple moment of human connection that was his favourite part of travelling. He decided to acknowledge this goodwill with his own simple kindness. He pushed through the glass door and she looked up and smiled again and he mangled the few Chinese words he'd learned since arriving. She didn't laugh at the attempt, as his niece had done, practically splitting her gut when he tried to imitate the sentences she taught him. Instead, the woman nodded vigorously and said something incomprehensible, and then, out of words, he pointed to the menu taped to the wall by the door and held up four fingers to indicate the Guilin rice noodles. She confirmed his order by holding up the same number of fingers, then laid her shears on the cutting board and scooped a generous portion of noodles from a large pot and drained and deposited them into an aluminum bowl.

His hunger grew as she doused the noodles with oil and added thin slices of grilled meat. She smiled to herself the entire time she did this, looking up at Faron again and again with a shyly exuberant grin. He imagined that she saw few foreigners come through here, despite this being one of the busiest transportation hubs in the country, and even fewer who were willing to stumble through a bit of Chinese. She sprinkled scallions and spring onions into the noodles and meat, then peppers and pickled beans, and topped it off with fried peanuts and white radishes bathed in chili oil. He resisted the temptation to take a video of her preparing this small delight—he already felt more self-conscious and conspicuous than was good for him. She transferred the finished steaming noodles into a white ceramic bowl, stepped out from behind the counter, and led him to a table at the glass wall overlooking the wide concourse below. She set the bowl down and held up four fingers again, confirming his order, and pointed to the bowl. He thanked her and took a seat.

The noodles were perfection. The simple experience of taking a meal in this indistinct locale was, he reluctantly admitted to himself, the most gratifying moment of his trip so far. His niece had been lovely, yes, but the unscripted moments he stumbled upon while travelling always brought the simplest and most intense pleasures. Once, in Colombia, a stingray wound on his left ankle led to a hospital visit during which he met, seated beside him in the chaotic emergency room, a professor of etymology to whose home he was later invited. There he met the man's family and stayed for the next three days, so warmly welcomed by the entire family that the man's small daughters cried when Faron finally had to return to Toronto.

He'd begun to accept the fact that he'd done his best but failed to summon his sister's spirit of forgiveness. There was nothing left for him to do. Now he would turn his attention to the Iranian at the consulate, to whom earlier that morning he'd sent a brief message to say he was returning to Hong Kong sooner than expected and he was available now at her convenience.

As he dipped again into the bowl of noodles, he looked up and saw a fairy drone of the same type he'd purchased six days earlier. Hovering outside the restaurant window, just an arm's length away, it was the same model and make, as far as he could tell, with its spinning pink tutu, purple nylon hair and tiara, and pointy ballerina-slipper toes. It rose in a perfect vertical and dropped down again a moment later, like it was coming in for a second look at him, and as it did so he considered the fairy's race for the first time. Of course, racialized dolls were not unusual, so how then to explain such a strident incongruity as this pink-skinned fairy darting around the Shenzhen rail station rather than one that looked a little more like the people it was being sold to? It was odd, he thought.

A message from back home popped up on his phone as the fairy, still paused, hovered before him.

Burning the midnight oil here. Hope you're well. Any progress with Jana?

Was there still hope? As he began to type his reply, he almost believed there was, though his sister had been clear. She wasn't coming home.

Heading back to HK now. Empty-handed. Can't sleep?

It was still the middle of the night back in Toronto.

Their messaging had been off and on since his touchdown in Hong Kong. He'd forwarded half a dozen pictures of his sister's home and neighbourhood in Guangzhou and a selfie with her and his niece standing on a bridge over the Pearl River. There'd been a couple of food and cityscape pics, two or three voice messages, and a few simple *Good mornings*. Since arriving, he'd not found time to think about Setareh in the way he wanted to, unrushed while strolling alone through a new neighbourhood, say, but now he remembered her quiet confidence and grace and kindness and the moody curve of her breast and the way she smiled and nodded when she wanted him to do certain things for her when they made love. She was a bashful lover, which was an odd and thrilling contradiction in a woman who invited two men into her bed. He sat thinking of her, vaguely frustrated now, wondering what she was doing up so late.

ON A CAUTIOUS afternoon in the early days of their meeting, when a strand of hair came away from behind Setareh's ear as she leaned over his novel and read aloud a curious turn of phrase that she had some questions about, he'd struggled against the urge to touch her hand and tell her something that he could not take back. There was a sharp alertness and instinct that had begun to draw him to her as early as that. When she smiled, which she did often and easily, he'd felt strangely moved, connecting to the moment in a way he hadn't done in years. When she excused herself to use the restroom—they were at the Tea Room in the Windsor Arms Hotel—he wrote on a napkin, *Her voice danced between them as incense sweetens a room,* and then, cued to the embarrassing schoolboy sentiment, tore it up and dropped the pieces under the table.

She spoke little about her life back home. He imagined it was too painful for her, an anxious and unrelenting reel of the theocracy's miserable greatest hits. Nor did she speak much about aunts and cousins and uncles, all of whom had left Iran long ago for Stockholm and Los Angeles and Berlin. The subject of her past was a dead end to which Faron deferred with respectful silence. It was not his place to ask. How she'd become whoever she was after whatever trauma had befallen her he had no idea, though he wanted to know this about her more than anything.

She mentioned only in passing the war that had lobbed Iraqi rockets into the heart of Tehran, her bedroom window criss-crossed with masking tape, and playing with other children in the underground parking while the rockets fell for days.

Hers was the first generation of girls to come of age after the Islamic Revolution, but she spoke little of that too. She would share her past with him at a time of her choosing, if at all. He didn't expect more detail in this regard, not even after they became lovers. She'd spent her childhood in a quiet state of siege, he imagined, and then in her teens the thugs who roamed the city looking for young women began to take notice of her. She didn't suffer from any direct attacks by the morality police, but the fear was always there. To this day they prowled the streets. The murder of Mahsa Amini was only just the latest vicious reminder of what she'd left behind. The country's prisons were filling up with young people who'd never see the light of day again. It was as it always had been.

Instead, she spoke often about the man in her life in those early days when she and Faron began meeting. His name was Mikkel Austerlitz, a Montrealer whose parents had come over from Denmark in the seventies, when he was a boy. He'd spent years with Médecins Sans Frontières before settling in Toronto, and now served as chief thoracic surgeon at a downtown hospital. He'd been with Setareh Azad for more than two decades and was the love of her life. Faron took note, believing that she told him this in order to avoid any embarrassing missteps or misunderstandings. He was grateful for it. Their meetings were always professional in nature and focused on the novel that had so moved her, and her desire to bring to it a new readership. By now she'd changed her LinkedIn profile to show his book as a translation in progress. He didn't ask how long she saw the process taking, or when the book would be published. Nor did he fail to recognize the parallel between the reawakening of his out-of-print novel and the renewed pleasure he found in the company of an attractive woman. He was one year out of a relationship that had not ended soon enough, and on any given afternoon or evening they were set to meet, he felt his slumbering desires awaken with the promise of a slow drink with a woman he found both beautiful and fascinating.

They didn't need to meet as often as they did in those early days; in fact, they didn't need to meet at all, and not once did he ever propose getting together—it was always Setareh. And so it wasn't long before he concluded that her interest in him was more than professional. Still, he had no delusions about this going any further. He enjoyed her company immensely, simple as that, and he was happy to accept yet another invitation to meet. The plague that had stolen two years of their lives was winding down then; the city was finally opening up again. She was a friendly new face after nearly two years spent in the small social bubble he'd occupied during the pandemic. He was eager to embrace the world once more, and grateful it was Setareh he could spend time with.

One early evening, as he waited for her at a restaurant table, he saw her across the street through the window and knew immediately that the man walking beside her was the husband he'd heard so much about. His heart collapsed in a shameful spasm of jealousy. What a fool he'd been to lie to himself so boldly, hiding even from himself how this woman's presence had captivated him. He admonished himself for the self-deception, and then conceded defeat to the better man. The couple were not holding hands or speaking to one another as they walked, but the energy, the force that held them together, was clear enough, even at that distance.

He'd heard too much about the man—his work in Haiti and Bolivia and Rwanda and at the hospital here in the city, and about their January migrations to Buenos Aires (his favourite writer was Julio Cortázar, his favourite music, tango)—not to have conjured some noble image of him in his mind's eye. Now, seeing him beside Setareh, he felt not only the fool but an uncharitable and selfish fool. He sighed audibly, admonished himself again, and stood to greet the happy couple as they entered the restaurant.

He was pleased, for Setareh's sake, that the man, in addition to being accomplished, was handsome and trim and wore a generous smile that matched hers in radiance and sincerity; he was greying debonairly at the temples and bore the beginnings of characterful age lines. His eyes, intelligent and blue, hinted at a depth of character worthy of a woman like Setareh Azad.

They invited Faron to their island home a week later. It was a fine meal they shared with him, the conversation effortless and wide-ranging. The following week it was Faron's turn. He was a good host, but his cooking could not touch Mikkel's. Their dinners became a regular occurrence he looked forward to, and it was not long before he began to consider the man a good friend and more than deserving of his trust and admiration.

As a couple, they'd struck Faron as traditionally minded, serious in their professional goals, and almost old-fashioned (Mikkel brought her flowers every weekend, and Setareh had a near-maternal regard for the rituals and traditions that were dear to her culture). They were the last people in the world Faron might expect to summon a third party into the intimate heart of their relationship, which, five months into their friendship, when Setareh's hand found his lap and stayed there, and she leaned in to kiss him, happened in the way that life-changing experiences sometimes begin—innocently, spontaneously—and everything about it was right and natural once the three of them got over the initial shock of it. Faron became their regular overnight guest.

Sometimes the two men coincided at the Queen's Quay terminal on the evenings Faron caught the ferry over. Mikkel had a pied-à-terre downtown, close to the hospital, but he could reliably count on coming home two or three nights a week. On those occasions when Faron spotted him at the launch, he was struck by the thought of how, in this public space, the most important and urgent things about people were as unnoticeable as starlight on a summer's day, burning but invisible. More and more over that spring it seemed to him that this duality was at once a saving grace and a curse. Not everyone was in the throes of such an unusual love affair, of course; yet it was curious to consider that inside everyone burned some silent urgency or blinding crisis or defining passion, and that humanity was destined to live in this schizophrenic state of dual realities, the public and the private, the declared and the unspoken, and it was only in the rarest and most finely balanced relationships that these worlds might peaceably coexist.

The three of them shared this unusual lifestyle without subterfuge or jealousy. Faron wanted the best for Mikkel and Setareh as genuinely and as desperately as he wanted the best for himself and Setareh—and what's more, he wanted this for the three of them. They didn't spend time puzzling over the nature of love or analyzing the dynamics of their relationship; perhaps a touch at first—such was their surprise when it unfolded—but soon this new turn felt perfectly in sync with their lives as they should be. The absence they'd not been aware of before, as individuals, or as a couple, was in an instant perfectly filled. Two men who respected each other were in love with the same woman, and the woman they loved moved between them with the playful hunger of a fallen angel.

While they were doing the washing-up after a pleasant meal the night before Faron travelled to Hong Kong, the subject of Setareh's translation of his novel came up in conversation. It had been a mighty struggle for Faron not to ask about her progress on his book. She'd been working on it now for almost two years, and though he knew nothing about the art of translation, this seemed slow by any measure. It wasn't a terribly long book, after all. Mikkel had read it twice by then, Setareh countless times, and that night as he dried a serving dish, Mikkel asked if she'd treat them to a bit of her translation read aloud. Faron seconded the motion, saying that a page or two would be a nice going-away present.

"That's right," Mikkel said. "Something to take away with him. The poor man's got a hell of a trip ahead of him."

Of course they knew what was taking Faron to Hong Kong and China, both the professional and the personal reasons. They had been nothing but supportive since his mother's diagnosis came in earlier that year. And with reference to the identity of his next possible commission—the Iranian auteur whose films Setareh would almost certainly know—he said nothing at all. They'd made their direct and indirect entreaties, curious to discover whom he'd be meeting in Hong Kong, and he was bursting to tell them but resisted, citing the obligation of secrecy.

"I'll read it to you both when you get back," Setareh said, kissing Faron lightly on the mouth. "The whole heartbreaking thing."

He was unable to push aside thoughts of his mother's illness that night as he lay next to Setareh, worrying beyond any reasonable hour about the countless things that could go wrong while he was away. He'd arranged for daily living support from the Victorian Order of Nurses, and yet he was unable to take comfort in knowing that she'd be well looked after in his absence. He rolled out of bed and stretched out on the living room sofa, afraid his tossing and turning would disturb his bedmates, but sleep wouldn't come there either. Growing more anxious as the night slipped away, he got up again and looked through the bookshelves for something that might divert his restless thoughts. He sat at the kitchen island with a glass of milk, staring out the window at the black lake set majestically under the canopy of starlight, and listened to the wall clock eating away at the dwindling hour. Nearing four o'clock, he entered Setareh's writing studio.

The pale moon shone down through the skylight and cast a shimmer of blue over her translation-in-progress as it sat there on her desk. This was not the first time he'd seen the manuscript, of course, but he'd never had the opportunity to study it as he did now. He picked up the first page and drew his eye over the mysterious script, as beautiful and remote as a distant galaxy. He didn't even know which way to read it, left to right or right to left, but in his hand was the story of his young life, back when he'd only dreamed about love, retold now in the voice of the lover who slept soundly in the next room. He felt the echoes of his youth drifting ever further into the irretrievable past for the curious layering of emotions and languages and perceptions that would be Setareh's translation. Would the story even be his anymore, he wondered, once her work was done? He would have no way of knowing. His novel in her voice would be hidden from him forever for his ignorance of the language. He returned the folio to its proper place, closed the studio door behind him, and lay down again on the sofa and waited for dawn.

NOW, AT THE railway station restaurant in Shenzhen, he watched the fairy drone move away from the window and fly off into the wider space over the concourse. A new message from Setareh did not come in. He returned the empty bowl to the counter and left the restaurant.

As he rode the escalator down to the main level of the concourse, an update from Ms. Khajenouri pinged on his phone. He stood to the right and read the message: She was looking forward to seeing him at two o'clock tomorrow. The consulate would send a car to collect him at his hotel. After he replied with a quick confirmation, he looked up and saw the old drone seller standing at the bottom of the escalator.

It wasn't so odd that their paths should cross again, he thought. People had their routines, and this would be a preferred location for its heavy traffic at this time of day in the Shenzhen commuter's life. Of the tens of thousands who passed through the station on any given afternoon, how many were grateful for the opportunity to buy a last-minute birthday gift or transistor radio or pack of batteries? He gave her a smile as he stepped clear of the escalator, and then, as he turned in the direction of the metro entrance at the far end of the station, he saw the drone again, this time approaching over a field of heads.

He wasn't so intrigued by this odd little toy anymore, having lodged in a small flat with just such a device for six days, but it seemed that the old lady was having some fun with him now, perhaps inviting him to come in for a repeat sale. The drone zoomed in close and circled him with some intent, and then flew off again.

As he weaved his way among the bustle of travellers, he turned for a quick glimpse at the digital clock flashing over an advertisement, and the fairy came into view once more, this time at a great height. It stopped for a moment up there, as if hesitating, or waiting, and then it dropped steeply at such a sharp angle in Faron's direction that he was forced to duck to avoid being hit. It zipped past and up again with an impish swirl, and as he turned his head to shoot the old lady a cutting look, he stumbled and tripped over a foot.

The person he fell into raised her hands in a blind defensive manoeuvre—he saw in that instant that the wrists were cuffed—and the awful crack of bone meeting bone made such a frightening sound that the fairy, which had appeared again, flew up and away once more.

When the prisoner lifted the blindfold from her eyes, she was too startled by the rapid unfolding of events to think clearly. The warder was slumped helplessly to her right, a thin streak of blood tracing down from her forehead, and before her on the polished floor lay the man whose foot she'd felt clip hers when she'd extended her leg. He was a foreigner and a stranger to her, but the concern she felt when she stood and removed his sports coat from where it hung over the handle of his suitcase caused her to lean down to the unconscious man's ear and tell him she was sorry, she hoped he was alright, but she'd had no choice but to force the situation.

She draped the coat over her cuffed hands and took the stairs down into the metro, where she saw three schoolgirls huddled near the turnstiles. They frowned and turned away when she asked if they could help her, so she stood next to the fare vending machines, her hand reaching out from under the foreigner's coat, careful to obscure the cuffs, and solicited travellers as they streamed up and down the stairs.

Her escape was doomed to failure, she thought. At any moment an officer of the transit authority would appear and take her away for panhandling. The handcuffs would be revealed. She reproached herself now for not checking the warder's pockets for the keys, but she couldn't return to the scene; it would be too dangerous.

As she thought this, she turned to the stairs and saw the drone seller, one hand on the railing as she descended, the duffel bag filled with her wares in the other. She was a pitiable sight, the sort of street person Mildred would normally offer a few coins to, but now she herself was the pitiable one, brought low by this frightening change in her circumstances. Only days ago she wouldn't have given a second thought to something as basic as a hot bath or a clean bed, much less her own freedom.

The street vendor would know something about hardship and stern reversals. Or perhaps she'd known nothing but deprivation in an indigent life defined by unrelenting poverty. She was smiling though, Mildred noticed, as she came down from the last step and approached through the crowd, as if she knew something much more than the chains that bound her to this hard life.

She stopped in front of Mildred, hiked her bag to her shoulder, and clasped her hands together as a beggar might plead for money, or mercy. Mildred told her no, she was sorry, she had no money to give—"We two are in the same boat, you see"—and the old lady again smiled her toothless smile and shook her head to indicate that Mildred had misunderstood.

She opened her hands and revealed a modest roll of banknotes. "Go home," she said, and pressed it into Mildred's hands, and then she turned and walked slowly back up the stairs.

SHE SPENT HOURS changing trains in the Shenzhen metro, first riding north, then east and west and south again. She was marking time, waiting for night to come. In an unexpected kindness, the woman had given her enough money for a full-day metro pass and two, maybe three meals. It was an intervention that seemed so unlikely that she checked her pocket for the bills after every transfer to make sure she hadn't imagined the encounter.

As she rode the trains, she attempted to disappear into the tireless jostle: wearied faces, bored teenagers, prophetic office workers already numbly resigned to the commuting routine that would swallow the expanse of their adult lives. Finally, she exited at Fumin station and emerged into a cooling night lit by neon signs and traffic lights and the whirl of a neighbourhood eager to leave behind the day's worries. The coat still draped over the handcuffs, she walked until she saw the shop sign she was looking for.

The hunched old man behind a worktable looked up when she entered his establishment.

"I'm closing now. How can I help you?" he said.

She came forward and cinched up the coat. He took her two hands in his and raised the manacles to eye level.

"How much do you have?" he said.

She told him a price and he released her hands and stepped to the door. She wondered if he was asking her to leave. Or worse yet, he might call out to the street that he had a lady in handcuffs in here and someone should get the police.

She waited a moment, wondering, and then he turned the latch and pulled the blind down over the glass.

Without a word he directed her to his workbench, and there he removed a leather wallet from a drawer under the workstation and laid it open. He selected a double-sided #4 pick and told her to place her hands palm up on the bench. He slipped the pick into the keyway and began feeling for the spring-loaded bar that must be lifted from the teeth of the ratchet.

She watched the rootwork of veins in his hands under the translucent parchment of his skin as he interrogated the lock, wondering what secrets this locksmith had discovered in his decades of opening safes and sealed rooms and strongboxes. She wondered if he carried his secrets quietly or if he would speak with some pride at the tea house tomorrow of how he'd released a lady felon back into the world last night, a young woman so frightened that her hands trembled and she said nothing at the sight of the raw skin on her wrist when the first cuff finally came off.

She didn't remove the freed hand from the workbench after the pawl was released from its hidden ratchet, though she was desperate to take it in her other hand, still cuffed, and soothe the burning flesh with a gentle massage. The wrist was red almost to the point of bleeding.

The second cuff opened soon after and the manacles fell to the workbench. She paid the man his modest fee, and after she left his shop she walked in the direction of the Shuiwei border crossing, through a neighbourhood of beauty salons and red neon lights and restaurants and taverns and karaoke bars filled with middle-aged men who peered out at her as she passed, the night loud and drunken and cold. She pulled the foreigner's coat tightly over her shoulders and wished for the safety and comfort of her home and the kind reassurances of her old aunt. She had no phone and not enough money to buy one. Her head was shaved, her wrists red and burning. The hunger and thirst in the cold night grew worse and the road was dark as she gained the empty gravel route that led to the edge of the bay. And there she stood, watching the lights on the other side.

ELEVEN

HOW LONG HE LAY UNCONSCIOUS ON THE POLISHED FLOOR OF the railway station before three strangers lifted him and set him upright in a seat was the least of the mysteries that would confound Faron Jones leading into that second week of his travels. The first surprise that met him was the fact that no one had made off with his suitcase or rifled through his pockets while he was out cold, though he did notice his sports coat was missing. He didn't know that a small crowd had gathered and puzzled over what to do with the foreigner until they decided it best to pick him up and leave him slouched in a seat and go about their business; nor did he know that the woman he'd collided with had come to soon after and recognized the calamity that had befallen her—an escaped prisoner would prompt an inquiry that would surely lead to her dismissal, if not worse—and so she too had disappeared into the teeming rush of commuters. Where the blindfolded woman had gone he had no earthly idea.

He touched his face, expecting blood, but his hand came

away clean. The pressure at his temples was intense. He gave himself a minute before attempting to stand. Head in hands, elbows on his knees, he cast his eye down to the floor and saw the book lying under his seat. He picked it up.

It was the book the woman had been reading the first time he'd seen her with the prisoner, some florid romance, judging by the cover.

He opened his suitcase and withdrew the bottle of Advil that Setareh had reminded him to pack. He dropped the book on a pile of shirts, cracked the seal, and dry-swallowed three tablets, then slipped the bottle into his pants pocket. He sealed the suitcase again, waited impatiently for the pills to take effect, and then, his head still pounding, got up and continued on his way.

HE CLEARED CUSTOMS at the Luohu crossing, got a cab on the Hong Kong side, and arrived at the Metropole just as the pain in his head began to come down. He paid his driver while a young man in a red bellman's uniform retrieved his suitcase, rolled it up the ramp, and stood waiting for Faron, who was distracted by the beauty of what he saw before him.

The view of Victoria Harbour from the main entrance of the Metropole was fit for a painter's brush. Fog was general over the city that afternoon, but colourful notes emerged from the muted greys and blues that moved over the promenade at the foot of the bay just beyond the porte cochère—a woman twirling an orange umbrella on her shoulder, a yellow backpack, a child's sweet face—and when he saw three fully battened sails of an old-style junk emerge from a rolling gap in the fog out on the water, he felt a delicious sense of freedom and wonder for the humbling gift of travel.

He turned and admired the building that loomed before him. The Hotel Metropole was, to his eye, the most impressive architectural statement on a long and densely packed shoreline of soaring office towers and skyscrapers, the tops of which all vanished into the heavy cloud cap that hung over the peninsula.

Adventure awaited him somewhere out there in this great city, he thought. The dreary obligation of trying to persuade his sister to come home with him had been lifted. He'd done what he could. Now he'd enjoy his only free night before the work commitments that had brought him here began. His meeting with the Iranian would call for his full professional attention.

Ms. Khajenouri's story, if he decided to tell it, did not require a happy ending, as such, but it did want for hope, and now, with Beijing's ultimatum, hope looked to be in precious reserve.

Hope was as integral to his storytelling as character or setting or structure; without it, he would be unable to tell her story. He was no longer the sort of young and fearless writer who could blindly pursue an idea regardless of the direction it took him. As a professional, he accepted the convention that insisted on a clear resolution for a character who bravely confronted the challenges that awaited and won in the end. But if, in Ms. Khajenouri's case, those challenges were insurmountable, they would overwhelm Faron as well, and defeat any chance he had to write successfully about her life. He needed the golden key that would unlock her story in his mind and help turn her life into one he could share with the world.

He caught up with the bellman now, apologizing for the delay, and followed him into a vast marble foyer crowded with guests—most of whom seemed to be in their teens, or even younger—huddled over something of great interest in small groups of three or four. The faint whirring and clacking sounds here and there and the murmur of their excited voices suggested some experience or event was being shared throughout the lobby. His first thought went to the sad dominance of video games. The days when young people played in the real world were long gone. This was what they were doing, clustered around dozens of shiny screens, he thought—oh, how dismal Hong Kong suddenly became—but then one of these youthful groups opened and he saw the bright colour-burst of a Rubik's Cube in a pair of small hands, and then another cube, and another. There were a hundred kids and more in the lobby that afternoon, assembled in their happy constellations of adolescent zeal, all of them madly spinning away at one of those cubes. Over the reception desk, a red digital banner announced, *The Hotel Metropole Welcomes the 2024 Asian Pacific Rubik's Cube Championship*.

He tipped the bellman and checked in, then bought a bottle of water and a box of Smarties at one of the hotel shops on the retail floor. His headache glowed briefly at his right temple. He swallowed another Advil and washed it down with a sip of

Evian, and waited at a bank of elevators until the *ping* sounded and the doors to the left opened.

He rolled his suitcase in and pressed the button for the seventy-seventh floor. The doors were closing when a hand holding one of those multicoloured cubes reached forward and the doors bounced open again.

"Sorry, thank you," the girl said as she stepped in.

"No problem," he said.

A tight little ponytail of black hair sprouted up from the back of her head like a fountain. She was maybe twelve years old. She gave Faron a funny smile when he said that, *No problem*, as if she was surprised, and then she pressed the button for the seventy-eighth floor. As the lift started to move, she began spinning the cube's squares in the way he'd seen in the lobby, and with what seemed impossible speed, the cube was solved. She sighed and mumbled something under her breath.

"Excuse me?" Faron said.

"Sorry. Nothing. I'm usually faster than that."

"That *was* fast."

"You should see some of the other Cubers," she said.

"I saw a few in the lobby. You'll give them a run for their money."

"*A run for their money*," she repeated. "Fantastic. Where did you—"

"In my humble opinion, anyway," he said.

She shrugged. "You're here for the competition?"

"I'm just a regular civilian. I'm hopeless at that. Total mystery. I've tried it a few times."

Nodding, she returned to her cube and solved it again with a spinning flurry.

"The average age for top-level competitors is thirteen," she said, looking up again. "I'm only eleven. It has to do with a young person's uncluttered neural pathways. Our brains are basically faster than old people's brains. No offence. And this is the cream of the crop here. You understand that? *Cream of the crop*?"

"Sure," he said.

"Anyway, you're way too old to compete. I mean, maybe you have a kid competing here?"

"No, no kids," he said.

"My mom's doing a spa treatment downstairs. It's like a whole city in this hotel. You wouldn't have to leave for a century. She thinks I have a chance this year. She's very focused on me placing in the top three." She turned again to the puzzle in her hands, re-scrambled now, and nailed it in a heartbeat. "Where are you from, anyway?" she said, looking up again.

"You know where Canada is?"

"My uncle lives in Vancouver." She kept on spinning the cube.

"I'm no expert, but I'm thinking you have a pretty good chance this year. That's seriously impressive."

The lift slowed and drew to a stop at the seventy-seventh floor.

"My uncle says there's lots of Chinese in Vancouver."

"He's right. Good luck, this is me."

As he stepped off the elevator, she said, "I guess that's where you learned your Chinese."

He turned to her, puzzled, but the doors closed and she was gone.

He stood there for a moment, working his jaw from side to side as he attempted to un-pop his ears, and pondered the girl's odd comment. He'd felt the pressure building in his inner ear as the lift had ascended. That was why he'd misheard her, he decided.

Suitcase in tow, he followed the room numbers down the long hallway, relieved now that he was moments from a shower and a fresh change of clothes.

THE SUITE WAS spacious and pleasantly fragranced with a warm touch of sandalwood and citrus. The bathroom looked fine, in white and blue ceramic, with a large pattern-tiled walk-in shower. He drank down the rest of his water as he stood in the middle of the main room admiring the decor. The bed was a king and set with grey linens and crowded with the overabundance of pillows he could never understand. He removed all but one and placed them on the floor on the far side, and then he pressed the remote on the night table and watched the blinds over the wide window rise slowly and the suite fill with full sun. He was above the clouds up here. For as far as he could see, the upper storeys of the highest buildings of the city floated on a brilliant sea of white.

He still felt the insistent pulse of his heart beating in the exposed tenderness where he'd knocked his head, but now an unusual sensation crept upon him. He became aware of another presence in the room. It was such a powerful feeling of otherness that he was suddenly sure he was not alone here. Perhaps he'd interrupted cleaning staff at their duties. He called out, "Is anyone there?"

He checked the bathroom again and found nothing. Returning to the main room, he dropped to his knees and looked under the bed. The closet was empty too. He pinched himself to make sure he wasn't dreaming. He was quite awake, he was certain, but knowing this did not dispel the feeling that he was being observed. *Jet lag and plain old exhaustion*, he thought. He'd still not managed to settle into the proper time zone, so inverted were the hours of day and night. The persistent dream of the blindfolded woman hadn't helped either, unsettling him from any short nap he was able to catch. Yet now, oddly, he had no desire to sleep, despite the dull ache in his head. In fact, he felt marvellously awake and energized.

After showering under a pounding jet of water so hot the bathroom mirror steamed up completely, he returned towel-wrapped to the main room and opened his suitcase in search of a fresh change of clothes, and there he saw the book he'd rescued from the train station floor peeking out from a stack of pressed shirts. As he reached for it, the phone beside the desk lamp began to ring.

"Good afternoon, Wystan," a woman's voice said.

"I'm afraid you have the wrong room."

"Oh, I'm sorry. Isn't this seventy-seven sixteen?"

She had the right room but the wrong person, he told her. He glanced out the window again. Way off in the distance, a glowing vapour trail chased after the speck of an airplane. Below, the blanket of cloud over the city was turned white in the unfiltered sun above.

"I'm sorry," she said. "Goodbye."

He returned to the suitcase and was reaching for the book once more when the phone rang a second time.

"Hello, Wystan, I was just—"

"Sorry, wrong number again," he said.

There was a pause.

"I'm sorry for bothering you," she said, and hung up.

He stood by the desk for a moment, waiting for the phone to ring again. When it didn't, he dressed quickly, deciding to ignore the book—a real bodice-ripper, for sure, with a cover like that, he thought—and brushed his teeth in the fogged-up mirror.

In the one free day he had to look forward to here, he was determined to get out and see a bit of the city. It was already 5:37 p.m. local time, still pre-dawn of the same day back home. He collected his wallet and passport, secured the door behind him, and rode the elevator down to the lobby, ears popping again.

When he saw that the crush of teenagers was gone now, he decided such an impressive space warranted more than a passing glance.

The lobby's design might have been called industrial Gothic for its rough concrete arches and buffed-nickel columns and soaring windows. The reality-bending angles and vaulted arches drew the eye upward, as the Notre-Dame Cathedral had done on his many visits in the time he lived in Paris. A few guests of the hotel quietly came and went, trailing behind them lovely church-like echoes. He turned in the direction of the soft clatter of a bellman's cart, heavy with tuxedos swinging leisurely on their brass bar, and then beyond that he saw, recessed like a transept into a cathedral wall, a blue-lit passageway and a small neon finger pointing the way to Bar Verneuil. He'd lived on rue de Verneuil in Paris the year he wrote his novel. There was no reason to resist.

He walked down the corridor and through a set of leather-padded doors, and inside, behind the bar, he saw three large windows cut in the shape of teardrops. On the other side of the windows swam the restless inhabitants of an enormous tropical reef tank. He was as delighted as he was curious about this unusual space.

A bartender greeted him in English. He took a seat on a barstool and ordered a dry martini and watched the bright corals and fish and wondered about the ironic spirit that had thought to situate a reef tank in such an unusual setting—for those given to drowning their sorrows or wetting their whistles. But this was more than a play on words. It was a shimmering work of art in which a painter's pallet swam and nature played on in her glorious abandon.

He'd loved aquariums as a boy, especially reef tanks, and had dreamed often about life at sea, inspired by the Jacques Cousteau specials he and his sister watched when they were kids. No one could take him out of the grey world he lived in back then the way Jacques Cousteau could. When he'd intoned in that septuagenarian voice of his, so French and wise and infused with the sea air of the ancient Mediterranean, *Octopus, octopus, your babies are dying*, young Faron had felt such beautiful despair for those baby octopi that he'd almost cried.

The bartender delivered his martini, stemless and suspended in a glass bowl of ice, garnished with a sprig of rosemary.

"This is fantastic. Everything here is," he said, gesturing to the teardrop windows.

She told him he was most welcome.

The hotel had spared no detail or expense in putting the aquarium together, it seemed. The martini too was perfection. He sipped at it slowly as he admired the view before him. It was all as the sea itself would have made it, sculpted by millennia of crashing storms and rolling tides. Schools of clownfish and orange grammas swam their ceaseless circles, passing from one window to the next on their lazy patrols. A nurse shark and lionfish nosed the glass to the left and right and dipped again out of view. The names came back to him as he enjoyed his drink, in no rush at all now, so delighted by the scenes in the windows before him. He was about to snap a couple of pictures for Setareh and Mikkel when a woman appeared in the middle window, scattering a cloud of angelfish like a brilliant new idea.

She wore a mask and a light wetsuit, blue with yellow lines down the sides, and carried a single tank on her back and, in her hand, a small net bag of tools. She was engaged in maintenance or repair or feeding, it seemed, though he noticed no fish trailing her, as they might a source of food. Her black hair feathered about her head as she swam, angled head down, concentrating on the base of the reef. She looked young and fit, the sort who lived on the ocean and wrestled drift nets from troubled sea life and shared the deed on a popular Instagram account. A vigorous trail of bubbles issuing from her respirator followed behind her as her work brought her close to the glass window. There she stopped and looked up and out into the dry world where Faron sat on his barstool, watching her. Her smile grew at the edges of her respirator. She placed an open palm against the glass and blew him an underwater kiss through her breathing apparatus.

He was the only one at the bar. Even so, he looked left and right, and made the universal *Who me?* gesture, hand to the chest, at which she nodded and blew another kiss.

He smiled, blushing only slightly, and raised his martini. He decided this was part of the hotel's public relations policy—warm greetings for all guests at all times.

The blennies and gobies nosed up alongside her as she continued her work, startled only occasionally by the stream of bubbles that issued from the regulator and the push of the flippers that held her in place. *The ancient Mediterranean, indeed*, he pondered. The nurse shark appeared again at the glass, and then returned to the bottom.

He sipped and spun slowly on his swivel stool. Another patron had now positioned himself at the far end of the bar top, where he sat reading a paperback. The fellow looked up as he turned a page, and nodded in Faron's direction. Hanging from the lip of the bar was a cane with an eagle-shaped brass handle. Faron nodded in return, still spinning slowly, and looked again at the centre teardrop window. The woman had vanished.

"May I?" a voice said.

The man, standing beside him now, hung his cane on the edge of the bar and set down the paperback and the glass of whatever he was drinking.

"Impressive, isn't it?" the stranger said, looking up at the fish in the window. He spoke with an American accent and appeared to be in his late forties, more or less Faron's age. His face was deeply worn, handsome, and friendly.

"I've always loved aquariums," Faron said.

The bartender approached.

"I'll have another one, thanks," the stranger said, seating himself. He turned to Faron. "I hope I'm not pushing in. Gideon Kastner," he said.

"Faron."

A slight palsy caused the man's hand to tremble in Faron's grip when they shook hands.

"Faron. Like Faron Young?"

"That's right," said Faron. His phone pinged.

"One of the greats. Born and raised in Shreveport, Louisiana. Same as me. That song 'It's Four in the Morning' still makes me weep." He sipped his drink, the hand atremble. "Your kid here for that Rubik's Cube convention?"

"No kids. Here or elsewhere. You?"

"Same. Big hotel. Cubers one day, Trekkies the next."

Faron waited to check his phone. He was hoping it was Setareh. He reminded himself to send a picture of the reef tank. Maybe she was up by now. She was an early riser, as Faron himself was. He glanced at the teardrop window again, wondering where the diver had gone.

"A Trekkie convention would be more my speed for sure," Faron said, turning back to the man.

"*Where no man has gone before*," the stranger said.

Faron was starting to regret coming in here when the city was waiting to be explored. He recalled the view of Victoria Harbour and the busy promenade and the spectacular sight from his room of buildings poking up from the clouds. He would make his apologies and push off soon. The bartender removed the man's empty glass and set down a full one.

"Pineapple and ginger ale," the stranger said. "I don't drink alcohol."

"That makes one of us," Faron said.

The man sipped at his drink, then gestured to the bruise at Faron's hairline. "That looks fresh."

"An unforced error earlier today."

"You don't look like a conventioneer. Here on business?"

"That's right."

"I'm here myself with a small gathering of like-minded souls," the man said. "Nothing like that Cuber convention. There's just five of us." He paused to reconsider, and raised his glass. "Well, six now. Cheers."

"I'm not sure I'm following."

"We don't go around advertising the fact, mind you. The idea's all hocus-pocus, a bunch of nonsense to most people."

"Okay."

"We're interested in a pretty unique sort of person. There aren't many of us around."

"And what sort of person is that?" Faron asked, peeking over his rising wall of skepticism.

"People who come to the aid of others. Those who give of themselves, completely."

When a short pause landed between them, Faron resisted the urge to check his phone. "The world could use a few more good Samaritans, I suppose," he said.

"Matters of the lost soul concern us deeply."

"Maybe they're not even lost. Who's to judge, right?"

"Not that kind of lost," the stranger said. "I couldn't agree more. No. I mean lost as in *misplaced*. Dislodged. Set adrift. Unbound. We're keenly interested in matters of soul transmigration, to be specific. Do you know what that is?"

The pained smile that appeared on Faron's face might have suggested that yes, he got the idea, but he was the last person on earth who wanted or needed any illumination on the subject. Long ago he'd drawn his own conclusions regarding matters of the soul, which was, like any useful fantasy, something people reached for in times of personal crisis and then summarily forgot once normal times returned. He feared that the man was some sort of Holy Roller in the process of teeing up a shameless elevator pitch in praise of the promised land, and if only he could open his heart to Jesus . . .

"Listen, I don't want to be rude, but—"

"I'm sorry, sounds a bit hare-brained, I know. It takes some getting used to. I'm perfectly aware."

Faron nodded and looked up and watched the centre window, hoping the woman might swim into view and distract the stranger from his purpose.

"I'd never given it a moment's thought until"—here he mimicked a mind being blown, fingers exploding outward from his head—"wham, the world's a completely different place." He touched the paperback in front of him.

"And these people you're with," Faron said, "they're the lost souls, I take it." He'd let the man say his peace and then he'd be on his way.

"The other way around, actually," he said.

"How's that?"

"We host the souls of the departed until they can manage on their own."

A smile grew on Faron's face as he sipped his martini. He hadn't needed to travel far from his suite at all to encounter the first thing he always wanted to find in a new city, which was a colourful bar or restaurant and a stranger with a good story to tell. It sounded like the soul collector beside him had a good one indeed, and was dying to tell it. The claim was delightfully absurd, but the poor fellow looked harmless enough.

"All five of you, you each do this soul management thing?"

"Six now," he said. "Yes."

"The bench deepens," Faron said.

"That it does," he said.

The stranger's hand on the paperback obscured the author's name. But the title was clear, as was the general idea of the cover art, which in blue-grey tones depicted a feathered quill held by a hand in the act of drawing itself. In elegant font, the title read,

Songs of the Blood Moon

a novel-in-verse

by

―――

It was barely seven o'clock on a foggy Hong Kong evening, with time yet to finish a slow drink in the company of this unusual man, Holy Roller or no. Seated here in view of the reef tank, lionfish and nurse shark nosing the glass, he'd listen to what the stranger had to say about lost souls, or whatever he was trying to sell him, and then finally be on his way.

The bartender slid a second martini across the bar top to Faron. He raised it to his lips, wishing the diver would reappear at the teardrop window, and Gideon Kastner began his story.

TWELVE

IT WAS IN A HOSPITAL BED IN RAMSTEIN, GERMANY, WITH HIS LEG raised on pulleys in a plaster cast, that Faron's companion at Bar Verneuil, in one miraculous burst of inspiration, wrote the poem that changed his life forever.

"I was embedded with the 10th Mountain Division out of Fort Drum, New York," he said, "when the vehicle we were travelling in hit an IED. I was with *The Washington Post*. I got this." He patted his left leg. "And then I wrote this." He pushed the paperback over to Faron. He was the author of a novel called *Songs of the Blood Moon*.

"Congratulations. But sorry about the leg and—"

"And everything else, yeah. Thanks," Gideon said. "The journey of a thousand miles begins with a single step, bum leg or no bum leg."

Until he composed that first poem after getting blown up in Iraq, he said, he was a young man who never failed to believe he was the smartest person in the room. His interest in books and showing off, two favourite pastimes, disguised the uncomfortable truth that he lacked anything by way of the talent required to do what he most wanted to do with his life, which was to write a novel that could stand in the company of *The Red Badge of Courage* or *A Farewell to Arms.* The young man he used to be could hold forth on these books in a way that made people think he knew what he was talking about, yet his observations were nothing but an empty parroting of what someone else had said about them. Even his professors at Baton Rouge fell for it. He wowed them with clever essays, quoting Bakhtin and Derrida and, to no one's amazement back home—least of all those who worked at the *Shreveport Caller*, where he'd interned in high school—he won a national essay award for a piece on the Afghan land mine problem, which helped him get into the journalism program at Columbia. He landed at *The Washington Post* not six weeks after graduating with his MA. His trajectory was brilliant. Every night for two years he did what he could to twist that long essay into a novel. But with all that, it was still just a stack of soulless manuscript pages that read like a UN report warmed over by a mediocre creative writing undergrad. He was frustrated and despondent, but he still had the ear of a certain New York editor he'd met at the award ceremony four years back.

Bethany Schneider-Hooks had taken to sending the occasional note to Gideon's DC home address, usually handwritten and always professionally flattering, once including a *Publisher's Weekly* clipping that spoke to the interest in the industry regarding his area of expertise. *The world needs someone to tell this story* was a typical Bethany comment. He knew the land mine issue wasn't going anywhere any time soon, but he grew so bored of the subject that he wished he'd chosen some other grave injustice to write about. The truth was, after all the concise prose and towering stacks of statistics, he didn't know what the hell he was talking about. He'd always felt like a fraud, but now he knew he was. He was an inch away from abandoning the project when the opportunity to embed with the 10th Mountain Division in Iraq came up.

He fist-bumped his way back through the office to his laptop after a meeting with his editor at the *Post*. Buoyed with confidence, he composed an email to Audrey Snopes, the brainy intern from Minnesota around whose desk he often found excuses to linger. This was the break he'd been hoping for, he wrote in the email. If the actual reporting gig wasn't enough, which it certainly was, he'd finally get some traction on his stalled work-in-progress. It was all falling together now. He emailed Bethany, too, about the positive development. She herself had hinted that the manuscript was missing a personal angle. *We all want human stories these days*, she said, *not just history, and not just facts*.

It wouldn't be fun or pleasant, but that wasn't why he was in the game, he told Faron. It was the truth he was after. He needed to feel the rattle of automatic weapons fire and breathe in the smell of cordite burning in the air around him. There were too many realities he knew nothing about to be writing the sort of book he wanted to write. He'd never even seen a dead body. Mentally he prepared himself as best he could, and three weeks later, on the December morning when the armoured vehicle he was riding in drove over a mine outside Baghdad, killing the four soldiers he was embedded with, he understood that he himself, and not his land mine book, was the real work-in-progress.

Faron wondered as he listened to the man's story where the facts ended and the myth-making began. He was a good storyteller, that he couldn't deny, but what any of this had to do with the hocus-pocus of transmutating souls he couldn't begin to imagine.

Five days after getting blown up in Iraq, he scribbled out a letter to the girl he hoped might be his girlfriend one day, this Audrey Snopes person he knew from the *Post*. There were large bouquets of flowers in the four corners of his room at the military base hospital in Germany, sent by the good people at the *Post* and by Bethany Schneider-Hooks in New York. But none had arrived from Audrey. The oxycodone helped, but the throbbing pain and ringing in his ears didn't stop. The faces of the soldiers he'd ridden with flashed before his eyes at the strangest times. He'd spoken to people back home about his ordeal—colleagues from the *Post*, his family, interviewers from ABC and CNN. He was, for a few days, a poster boy who spoke to the perils of the journalism trade. He was often forced to close his eyes and grip the sides of the bed for the pain that burned in his leg during those interviews, but he got through them. A number of mornings he'd woken up crying, and certain foods he'd once enjoyed now nauseated him. He'd known those four men for only three days before they rolled over that IED, but their memory haunted him day and night. Writing something, anything, he decided, might do him some good.

So he started in on a letter to Audrey. He needed to connect with her now, open a channel, but a love poem surprised him when it came off the tip of his pen instead of the simple letter he'd intended to write.

"I'd never written a poem in my life, much less a villanelle," Gideon said. "I read it over. It took me a while to understand what I'd done. You know what a villanelle is?"

"Yeah, no. Not really."

"Trust me. A demanding form. Stricter than a Victorian orphanage."

"It just came to you?"

"Five tercets and a quatrain over nineteen lines, two rhymes throughout. Seriously."

He'd stared out his hospital room window, thinking about those four dead kids he'd ridden with—his age, more or less, but he could call them kids now because it was right and proper to drill home the tragedy—and then he started writing another poem, this time about the things he wanted to un-remember. It was automatic, as if he was possessed. They just started flowing. Within weeks, he had a little folder full of verse scribbled out on napkins, get well cards, notepaper—anything handy when a poem came to him fully formed, like magic.

THAT FALL HE was shipped back stateside and did three months of physio at Ochsner St. Martin, outside of Baton Rouge; in the new year his brother took him on part-time at the flower shop he ran in Terrytown. After ten months he had the stack of poems that was his novel-in-verse cleanly whittled down to a sharp 190 pages. Come spring, he found Audrey Snopes on Myspace and boarded a bus carrying the finished manuscript up to New York City, where she'd been hired on at *The Village Voice.* He could hardly contain his excitement when he considered the impact the book would have. The scourge of land mines suggested so much more in a world where death waited so patiently underfoot. The metaphor was starkly poignant. He knew this as a man who struggled every day with the burden of that left leg.

On his third day back in New York City he visited the House of Ali Baba, where he used to go as a student once or twice a week. There was a new guy slapping the shawarmas together, but the place still had the student-dive vibe he'd always loved. *Some things don't change*, he thought. A ceiling fan pushed the stale air about, and day-old newspaper trampled to a brown smudge layered the floor. He ordered the chicken shawarma and ate it seated at the front window, the manuscript on the seat next to him. Today was the day. Bethany Schneider-Hooks's card, pressed between the damp skins of his wallet, was worn as thin as a wafer but still legible. He finished his meal and walked to Broadway and West 56th, ascended to the ninth floor, and announced himself at reception. Bethany Schneider-Hooks emerged from her office, arms outstretched, and gave him a hero's welcome.

"Where on earth has this prize-winner been hiding?" she wanted to know. She took him through and introduced him to everyone. Assistant editors and curious interns poked their heads up from their cubicles to get a look at the writer with the mangled foot. It was weirdly twisted, pointing forever eastward to his nose tip's northern orientation. He leaned on his cane and handed over the manuscript.

"As good as I've got," he said. "I hope you like it."

He knew he looked a little worse for wear, leaner, an altogether more drastic version of the boy she'd met years before at that award ceremony. He'd been through a lot. The monstrous foot and the hummingbird quiver in his right hand might put her off somehow. People had their prejudices. She promised that his manuscript was going straight to the top of her to-read pile.

He took a cab over to the Cooper Square offices of *The Village Voice* after that and lingered for a time, hoping, and finally he spotted Audrey locking her bike to a post beside a fire hydrant across the street.

"Hey. Wow," she said.

"Holy smokes."

"What are you doing here?"

"I'm just up for a visit." It wasn't a bad lie. "Congratulations on the gig. I've been following your work."

She glanced at his leg, which she'd been trying to ignore.

"Looks weird, doesn't it?" he said.

"Not really. I mean, yeah. Something's definitely going on down there. But I don't know. Maybe it's not that noticeable." She drew a strand of hair behind her ear. "Thank you for your service, I guess. You have time for a coffee or something?"

They headed in the direction of a nearby diner. She wanted to know all about it, every last detail about his time over there. He told her everything but the most relevant part, which was that he was frightened all the time now, practically jumping out of his skin when a balloon popped or a child shrieked. She linked her arm into his as they walked and told him it was wonderful they'd crossed paths again.

He found the note from Bethany slipped under the door of his room at the Matador Hotel three days later. It said, simply, *Call me.* He walked down to the booth on the corner, dropped a couple of coins into the slot, and waited for her to pick up. It was the last time he stepped into a phone booth. The following week, after he went in to sign the unagented deal, he got himself a cellphone. Eleven months later, the book was published.

GIDEON SLID THE novel closer to Faron, who picked it up and flipped through the pages. He read the jacket copy and the review pull quotes on the back. "Congratulations, this is amazing," he said.

Gideon quoted *The New York Times* from memory. "'Mysterious and compelling. . . . An eloquent, unnerving novel that illuminates the personal consequences of war.' I mean, you can't pay for something like that," he said. "Shit sales, though. Complete shit."

Comparisons to Vikram Seth and Alexander Pushkin were made, but these didn't help much to move the book. He didn't bat down the compliments. How else would he sell it? His publisher, after six weeks of perceptible enthusiasm, had all but let the work sink into oblivion. This was only months after the Bear Stearns collapse, and the novel-in-verse, good as it might be, appealed to no one but Pushkin scholars and hard-core Seth enthusiasts who were riled or enthused by the comparisons. He got a small place in Brooklyn and asked for a book tour, but was politely informed that no one in the business had ever heard of an author tour that paid for itself or deserved the writer's investment of time. He told Bethany he just wanted to put his book into people's hands. It was a book that needed to be read. To that end he'd sent a copy to the 10th Mountain Division at Fort Drum, where the four men he'd ridden with had been based. In honour of the fallen, he'd inscribed on the frontispiece. He hoped this might bring some sense of closure too, but he was still as jumpy as ever. He experienced night terrors and sometimes fell into brooding moods that held for days. He and Audrey were friends by this time, which was helpful, but being stuck in the friend zone brought its own problems. He wondered if he wasn't deluding himself.

The book still hadn't earned out its modest advance, and Audrey was dealing with a clash of personalities with a colleague at the *Voice*, so they'd get together and share their woes. He knew things had to change, and soon. He was living off the last nickels of his advance and the occasional cheque his brother sent him from the flower shop, but he swore he'd never go back to journalism. Pushing his book was practically a full-time occupation, besides. *Songs of the Blood Moon* had been out for a year now but had some life in it yet. He was determined to move heaven and earth to put it into people's hands, and spent most of his days going around to bookstores to offer his services—readings, poetry workshops, informal lectures on how to get published. He went to high schools and community colleges, libraries, and YMCAs. He carried copies of his book in a red gym bag to the five boroughs of New York City, selling it piecemeal to whomever he could. He left no stone unturned.

"In fact, I'm going guerrilla. I've got a new approach," he told Audrey one day.

"Onward, good soldier," she said. "Take the poetry to the people."

"A book doesn't exist unless it's being read, am I right? Plus, I'm broke. Wish me luck."

Bag hiked up on his back, he walked through the canyon of buildings along 7th Avenue and thought maybe he'd detected something in Audrey just now, a conditional surrender, maybe. He wasn't even sure she'd read his book—he was afraid to ask—but he was hoping he was slowly breaking free from the soul-sucking friend zone she'd placed him in too long ago. He imagined her taking his book down from her bookshelf tonight and reading it curled up in bed and feeling some deeper need growing inside her to know him, to love him.

He set up that same afternoon on a small square of sidewalk at West 45th and 7th, between a McDonald's and Planet Hollywood. He figured he'd get the tail end of the matinee crowd and the early-evening supper rush, who might be feeling generous after a drink or two. He unfolded the portable table and bristol board placards he'd picked up after leaving Audrey's company, and stacked twenty hardcover copies of *Songs of the Blood Moon* into four neat piles. He slipped the placards over his head, so that the two sheets of bristol board, inscribed with large black lettering and joined by lengths of birthday ribbon, hung suspended from his shoulders. On the back board, he'd stencilled, *Poetry Is the Bomb*, with a happy face drawn into an old-fashioned-looking circular cartoon bomb, wick sparkling with a red-marker flame. On the front, he'd written, *Explode with Me.*

He saw the superior grins of those who failed to understand the sacrifice of a man who chose to commit his life to the making of his art, including the young-looking cop on the other side of the street who was writing up a couple of teenagers for jaywalking. He watched the blank stares of men and women who spent their lives lost or hiding from their own thoughts, and kids pointing and grandmothers frowning and the beautiful young hipsters too cool to notice anything but each other's yesteryear hairdos. Tourists snapped his picture, charmed by his American freedom. Farm boys from Iowa eyed him suspiciously from the window at Roxy's. A pretty girl in a blue dress and yellow sneakers floated over and told him the world could use more poets nowadays. She bought a copy, had him sign it, and was absorbed back into the pedestrian flow along West 45th. The humanity of the city rose to its glorious heights. Throngs of people coursed by. He sold three more copies in under an hour, eighty dollars in pocket.

"Thank you," he said again and again. "Hope you like it."

Things were looking good.

A man wearing a Hard Rock Cafe T-shirt sidled up to the table and said, "A novel? Written like a poem? Man, why not just shoot off the other foot?"

But Gideon wasn't thrown from his sense of purpose. When three more copies went in under ten minutes, he wondered why he hadn't thought of doing this sooner. After he made yet another sale, he punched the air in an uncharacteristic gesture of triumph. Luck was on his side on this magical evening. He hauled out his cellphone and dialled Audrey's number. The hope of an artist in full flight was indestructible. He felt better than he'd felt in a long time. Even the pain in his leg disappeared as the phone began to ring. He'd do his best to stay cool, though; confidence was what he'd lacked this whole time, he decided. He shook out his bad leg and tilted his head skyward, as if in prayer, and then he heard a voice—not Audrey's on the other end, but a voice shouting, *Run, look out, he's got a—* And with that rose a sudden eruption of panic. At once half the street was yelling and running and the other half was pointing in the direction of the man with the cellphone and the bomb placards draped over his body. The uniform three months out of the academy who'd been harassing teenagers across the street took a knee and yelled, *Drop the phone*, and fired the first shot, which entered the cartoon bomb at the level of Gideon's lower abdomen.

"THEY SHOT YOU? The cop shot you?" Faron said.

"I was in a medically induced coma for ninety-eight days. Yeah, the fucker shot me. Four times." He took a slow sip of his pineapple and ginger. A scattering of yellow gobies floated past the middle window. He was quiet for a long while, sipping and thinking.

"I can't even begin—" Faron said. By now he'd forgotten why he was being told this story in the first place.

"Yeah, thanks. And then they pulled me out of it, and here I am," he said, tapping his chest. "Colostomy bag, the whole works. Addicted to every painkiller under the sun. I won't tell you how many operations I went through. You don't have enough fingers on both hands to count. But that's when I knew."

Faron waited. "What did you know?"

"That I had a migrant on board."

"I'm not sure—"

He tapped his chest again. "You wake up after a near-death experience and write something like this"—he touched the cover of his book—"so anything can happen, right? I felt him for the first time after near-death number two. Either I'm the luckiest guy in the world or the guy with the worst luck ever. Depends on how you look at it. But I realized he'd been in here for a while already. Since that IED in Iraq. Who said life is the ceaseless march toward the miraculous? Didn't someone say that? Maybe I'm saying that. I'm saying that I'm the luckiest man in the world to still be here. That's my take on it. *Miraculous* is my middle name. I pretty much died twice to get to where I am."

"I can see how you'd think that," Faron said. He didn't want to sound flippant, but he had to ask. "But this other thing you're talking about—this *soul* thing. I'm sorry . . ."

Gideon detected the mild patronizing tone that Faron's voice carried, but he took no offence. He'd heard it before from various other skeptics, and had endured much worse, so a touch of condescension was water off a duck's back. What he was asking Faron to consider required a serious suspension of disbelief, which, as a writer, he knew must be earned.

"Wild claims, I know," Gideon said.

"I'm afraid so."

Gideon pulled a silver chain out from around his neck and held it steady so Faron could get a good look. It was a grey lump of lead vaguely shaped like a baby's thumb.

"What doesn't kill you, right? This is the one that atomized my femur. The three others are in my desk back home."

Faron sipped his martini again and wondered at the scary inventiveness of it all. The man was mad, surely, but he had his story in place, as if he'd told it a hundred times before. It was a fantasy no less miraculous than that of the four archangels, the twenty-five prophets, or the single Holy Ghost. Who was he to judge?

"The leg still gives me problems," Gideon said. "I'm prone to rheumatism like you wouldn't believe. The liver was damaged. Hence the pineapple. I used to love drinking. God, I miss booze. Sitting in bars is torture. But it's something I do. Call me a masochist."

He motioned to the bartender and told her to put Faron's drinks on his room, then tucked his book under his arm. "Time to empty the C-bag. Sorry. Not a pretty sight when this thing overflows."

He prepared to leave.

"It's been a pleasure," Faron said. "Thanks for the drinks."

"Not at all. You know what day it is, by the way?" Gideon said.

Faron thought the question had something to do with jet lag and the disorientation of time zones. "Wednesday," he said.

"You know what sort of Wednesday?"

"Not specifically, no."

"It's the day before the Day of the Dead in this marvellously superstitious country. Otherwise known as Tomb-Sweeping Day or the Pure Brightness Festival. It's a nationwide spiritual orgy. April's the season of the dead here."

"My brother-in-law was saying."

"I've taken my passenger all over the world, looking for the final resting place where he'll be comfortable enough to leave me alone. A lot of countries celebrate All Souls Day. Same sort of idea. Mexico, Italy. Philippines. I tried Germany. I thought Berlin might be a good bet. He loved it there when he was a young man in the twenties and thirties. It was a libertarian paradise for poets like my guy, an escape from dreary old England. I was hoping he'd see it as an escape from dreary old Gideon Kastner. No such luck."

"Your guy was a poet?" Faron said.

Gideon downed the last of his drink. "That's right. Artistic souls often don't let go easily. So I'm told. But they're terribly nostalgic. Wystan spent some time here too, you see, so I thought we'd give it a try in the People's Republic."

"Someone called my room an hour ago looking for a Wystan."

"I imagine that would have been a member of my party looking for me. Sometimes we refer to one another by our stowaway's name. Sort of an inside joke. A misdial, I suppose. Sorry about that."

"Your guy was an English poet named Wystan who lived in Berlin in the thirties?"

"Right again."

So here it was, then. Better than Einstein. Better than Elvis. Faron couldn't imagine stumbling upon any religious festival or cultural curiosity or traveller's adventure more keenly unique than the one sitting before him at this fabulous reef tank bar, drink in hand. He was, deliciously, in no rush.

"Your guy is W.H. Auden?" Faron said.

"The one and only."

"Fantastic. I mean— Wow."

"Well, yeah, if you're into poetry."

"And you're here to . . . set free Auden's soul?"

Gideon nodded.

Faron smiled. It was as if this man had just claimed to be injected with alien DNA. He tried his best to calm his delight. He levelled his voice. He didn't want to mock the man, but couldn't help himself.

"So Hong Kong's the Area 51 of the soul?"

"That's good. I'll remember that one."

"Sorry, I didn't mean—"

"He wrote a book here. I'm giving him options. I need my life back. He always was a peripatetic soul. I'm holding the door open for him. It's like trying to shake a pit bull off a chew toy. Desperately to this mortal coil he clings. He doesn't want to let go. Poets are terribly insecure people. And stubborn. He died in Vienna in 1973. I was fourteen. In college I probably read one or two of his poems. I always wanted to write a novel. I was never interested in poetry. How life's perfect design masquerades as this abundant chaos is a mystery to me. There's a reason for all this, but I'm not the guy with the answers."

Gideon paused and looked at the middle teardrop window, teeming with sea life. The nurse shark bumped up against the glass and dropped out of sight again.

"And that's how you came to write those poems in Germany?"

"There is no other reason, alas," Gideon said. "I have no talent whatever in the field of poetry. He speaks through me. Spoke. He's been quiet for some time now, but he's rumbling around in there."

Faron couldn't resist the question. "Do you . . . do you *feel* him?"

"He's a presence. It's hard to say. Like someone's watching you from an unusual angle. It's not physical, no."

"You didn't care about poetry, you said. Why would he

choose you? Shouldn't he go for a poet, someone more like himself?"

"I have no idea. I had no idea about the transmutation until after I got shot." He touched the paperback under his arm. "I was clueless. He wrote this through me. I was just the vehicle. Once I realized I wasn't going mad, I tried to tell people I'd been inhabited by Auden's spirit when I wrote *Blood Moon*. At first they thought I was talking about inspiration. Every writer has their influences, they said. I told them I wasn't talking about influences or speaking metaphorically. Then they just thought I was a lunatic."

"I can imagine," Faron said.

"I was in the dark for a long time, just like you are now that—"

The bartender interrupted Faron's appreciation of this last comment when she appeared with the chit for Gideon's signature. She slid it over the bar on a silver tray and wished them a good evening. His companion seemed perfectly self-possessed now, fully returned from the memories he'd just shared.

"Alright, then," he said, extending his hand.

"A pleasure," Faron said.

"I'm sure we'll meet again."

"Clairvoyant too, I see."

"In the more immediate matters before us, yes, somewhat," Gideon said.

"I look forward to it. And congratulations on the book. I

mean, to both of you. And those great reviews. You'll have those forever."

"May great literature outlast us all, sir."

And with that, the crippled writer tipped an imaginary hat and limped his way out of Bar Verneuil, his book tucked lovingly under his arm.

THIRTEEN

FARON STAYED ON AT THE BAR FOR A SHORT WHILE AFTER GIDEON Kastner took his leave. He typed Auden's name into his phone and read briefly about the man's life and career. He called up the first pages of *Journey to a War*, the book Auden had written with Christopher Isherwood about their time in China just as Setareh Azad pressed send on a series of messages from back home. He tapped open their group WeChat.

The stupidly brilliant emoji-blown kiss that began the chat brought a smile to his face and filled his heart with light. Next was a flexed bicep and three champagne glasses and a photograph of manuscript papers stacked on Setareh's desk—his book, her translation—with the word *finished* followed by a big red beating heart.

Your masterpiece—and mine, she wrote.

Here was the reason she'd been up all night—*burning the midnight oil*, she'd said.

He sent out a barrage of hearts and champagne glasses,

and asked if she had time to chat, but no reply came. Perhaps she'd stepped into the shower or slipped into bed after working through the night. For years his novel had slumbered quietly in libraries and second-hand bookstores around the world, and now it had been awakened by her magic touch. It would cross a threshold into the consciousness of what was to him an entirely unknown culture. He wanted to give this moment its due, to mark the occasion with the sound of her voice in his ear, and wished deeply that he'd not travelled so far from her, that he could be there to celebrate this tremendous achievement.

He waited a while longer for her reply to come in, and when none did, he thanked the bartender and pushed off and walked down the hallway and out again into the echoing lobby. Two hotel employees speaking quietly beside a potted fern nodded politely as he passed them and caught a revolving door at the main entrance as it spun, and out he stepped into the humid Hong Kong evening.

The promenade between the hotel and the bay was alive with people, and beyond, the harbour was busy with brightly lit yachts shining their red and green side lights, cabins illuminated like pearls on a black cloth. On the far shore, the silver and gold cityscape rose up and cast its glow over the surface of the bay with spectacular exuberance.

In an instant Faron felt marvellously unburdened. It had been too long since he'd been anywhere that was completely new to him. He was a writer for whom routine was as crucial as language itself, and in Hong Kong he could rely on neither, which was precisely the point when he travelled. He was drawn to the glittering newness of the city, its vibrant exoticism, its loud and perhaps obvious target destinations; but the sort of travel that most interested him was not found in a planned itinerary or a famous museum. It was the unscripted flirtation with a city that would lead him to some brief but meaningful glimpse of life as it was lived here. Gideon Kastner had already delivered one such unexpected encounter, and he would remember it forever. Now he would tempt this city to offer up yet another. And just then, as he stepped out from under the porte cochère, he heard a woman's voice call his name. He turned and caught sight of someone emerging from the revolving doors behind him.

She was dressed in black cropped pants and a grey sweater, with a red shawl wrapped loosely around her neck. Familiar to Faron in a distant, dreamlike way, she wore her dark hair in a loose ponytail—she was not Asian—and began run-walking in his direction, with a bit of a skip in her step. When she came closer and smiled, he saw the faint impressions of the diving mask on her forehead and cheeks. It was the woman who'd blown him those odd underwater kisses.

"Hey, you," she said, sidling up to him. She tucked an arm into his.

"Sorry, do I—?"

"I'm so glad you're finally here! Welcome to Hong Kong."

When she kissed him on the lips, he was startled and confused.

"Well, *tell me*. How are you?" She was American, by the sound of it. "And what happened there? Did you hit your head?"

"I think you're mistaking me for someone else. How do you know my name?"

She met his resistance with an enthusiastic smile.

"You're adorable. Join me for something to eat. I'm *famished*."

Her widely set eyes gave her a feline appearance, and when she turned her head, the starfish tattoo on her neck moved ever so slightly, as if swimming over her pale skin. Her hair was still damp from diving, or from showering afterwards, and with this momentary image of her peeling off her scuba gear and stepping into the shower, Faron was alerted to the fact that she was attractive enough to be a ploy designed to separate a lonely tourist from his money. She could have found his name in the hotel registry—he was not born yesterday—but his idealistic nature opted for his first impression. She'd simply and quite honestly mistaken him for another man.

"I'm not who you think I am," he said.

"Who *is* these days!" she said with a smile. "A different vibe here from Paris, right? Don't you love it!"

"You know Paris?"

"Only what you showed me!" she said.

He told her again that she was mistaken to believe they'd ever met, let alone spent time together in the French capital. It made no difference what he said. She held his arm, and his attention.

"You can be whoever you want to be this weekend. Or for whenever," she said. "I'm perfectly fine with that."

As they walked, he pieced together that she was an oceanographer from San Diego on contract with the hotel chain that owned the Metropole. According to her, they'd met at a hotel in Paris last April and had explored the city together; subsequent to that, they'd arranged to meet again here, in Hong Kong, a year later. He was puzzled by the misunderstanding, and more so he was puzzled that she seemed to think his protests were some gambit they'd established long ago and had agreed to keep going. He attempted to put right the history between them, that there was no shared history at all here, but she met his efforts with a quip or a smile and a peck on the cheek, with such casual disregard of his objections that he decided this was in fact a game, an entertainment that he was willing to play until one of them grew tired of it.

After half an hour of determined wandering, she led him down a misty laneway lined with restaurants and hanging red fabric lanterns and small tables where the neighbourhood clientele sat eating and drinking and smoking. Steam and the chatter of voices rose from the colourful food stalls that dotted the lane and filled the busy air with delicious flavours. The red lanterns and small yellow and green neon signs placed above every restaurant door bled their colours into the grey night and turned the laneway into a narrow carnival of moody pastels.

"This is the one," Faron's companion said, hooking her arm in his again and leading him up a narrow length of stairs.

Inside the restaurant, two children were playing with plastic dinosaurs at the foot of a table where a man in his seventies sat dressed in a grey linen suit and black bolo tie with a silver metal clip and jade stone. The long whiskers on his chin matched his grey suit; his eyes were as green as the stone in his tie. He dipped his head in welcome and returned to the deck of playing cards spread out on the table before him. A young woman wearing an orange apron and blue Crocs emerged a moment later from the back room, menus in hand, and gestured for her customers to sit anywhere they liked. The restaurant was empty but for these two new arrivals. They took a seat at the table overlooking the misty laneway they'd just stepped in from. The waitress placed the menus between them and retreated to the kitchen.

The restaurant appeared to be family-run, a modest place with a few tattered posters on the walls and high, round-back chairs. The children playing with their toy dinosaurs belonged to the woman who'd just seated them, Faron imagined, and the smartly dressed gentleman sitting three tables over would be their grandfather.

He didn't venture the few phrases in Chinese that his niece had tried to teach him when the woman appeared again to take their order. As he'd done at the train station restaurant earlier that day, he simply held up the number of fingers necessary to indicate his order, which, in this case, was the sautéed crystal shrimp and the pork and vegetable dumplings. They were both famished, it turned out. The woman from the reef tank ordered three other dishes and a couple of "píjiŭ," she said, holding up two fingers. She had only slightly better language skills in this city than Faron, and the waitress, who'd been serving foreigners at these tables since the age of fourteen, nodded with a half smile and returned to the kitchen.

"You're a mind reader," Faron said.

The word for *beer* was one of the words he'd asked his niece to teach him, and very nearly the only one that seemed to have stuck. Chloé had loved his pronunciation. "*He-j-eo. He-j-eo,*" she'd laughed, and then buzzed him with her fairy drone.

The oceanographer's name was Ramona, he discovered, and as they waited for their order she seemed to drop the pretense of the game and told him about her job at the hotel and the master's thesis on anthropogenic habitat modifications in the Great Barrier Reef that she'd completed at the University of Sydney. He suspected she'd tired of her charade. On equal footing now, the pretense dropped, he told her he'd seen the ocean for the first time at the ripe old age of nineteen but had been mesmerized by it since the early days of Jacques Cousteau's televised adventures.

"And so goeth the lofty dreams of youth," he said. His face filled with the soft hues of embarrassment.

"You're so cute," she said.

She spoke about her girlhood in La Jolla Cove, the Pacific Ocean on her doorstep, and spending every free moment snorkelling or sketching sea shells, and summers as an assistant to the harbourmaster at the Sunset Marina down by the Stanley Bridge Pier. Sydney was a blast. She still had great friends there, she said.

The waitress came with the steamed crab and scallion pancakes and sautéed crystal shrimp. Faron snapped a picture of the table and sent it to Setareh and Mikkel, and then remembered he'd forgotten to snap a picture of the reef tank. They tucked into their meal, both of them falling silent as they ate, until he noticed that the elderly gentleman three tables over seemed to be observing him closely.

He'd already grown used to being the object of some curiosity here. One afternoon in Guangzhou two schoolgirls had stopped him in the middle of the street and asked if they could take their picture with him. It was not him they were interested in when he was spotted in certain neighbourhoods here, of course, but the fact that he was not an Asian man, and he'd felt in some vague and harmless way the responsibilities of an ambassador charged with the good mission of representing his people in these foreign lands. He was cheerful and accommodating when those schoolgirls produced their pink phones and snapped pictures of each other giggling and blushing as they stood at his side, and now he was equally accommodating when he heard the man speak of him and his new friend as if they weren't in the same room.

"Look at them go," the man said, addressing the children playing at his feet. "Finally tasting real food for the first time in their life. Poor devils."

The children angled their pudgy faces upward at their grandfather's remarks, then the lizard faces of their dinosaurs stared up too, and nodded, and then they returned to their play.

Faron cleaned his fingers and the corners of his mouth with a napkin. "Devils or not, compliments to the chef. This is delicious."

A look of shock and delight filled the old man's face. The waitress in her orange apron and blue Crocs looked up with a wide smile from where she'd been standing behind a counter.

"Thank you, I'm happy to hear that," she said. "Please forgive my father's impertinence."

The besuited gentleman placed the cards on the table and said, "My good sir, apologies, apologies. No offence. My daughter's right. I didn't know you understood—"

"Don't worry about it," Faron said.

Ramona kicked Faron's leg under the table. "Well, aren't we full of surprises?"

"How so?" he said.

The grandfather rose stiffly from his seat and approached. "Young man, I retract the 'devils' statement. A figure of speech, that's all."

Faron stood and shook the man's slight hand. His green eyes, striking in an Asian man's face, were kind and sparkled with curiosity.

"Not at all," Faron said.

"It's just that we rarely hear a foreigner speak Cantonese or Mandarin," the man said. His smile raised the thin whiskers on his chin. "Both of which I speak."

"What's he saying?" Ramona said.

"Just that he's not used to—" He stopped talking and looked

at Ramona, and then at the man. "I'm not sure what's going on here," he said in Cantonese, and then repeated himself in Mandarin.

The man smiled. "I congratulate you on your accent. Perfect in both languages. Remarkable. Perhaps you grew up on the mainland. Certainly you did. Or here. It's very unusual for a Westerner to speak one fluently, let alone both."

"Look at you," Ramona said, leaning back in her seat. "You had me going, mister I-don't-speak-a-word-of-it. I'm totally impressed. That's actually pretty hot."

"Trust me, I—"

"Will you introduce me to your lovely wife?" the old man said.

"We're not a couple," Faron said.

"My apologies again. Different flowers catch different eyes."

It was a Mandarin saying, prettier to Faron's ear than *Beauty's in the eye of the beholder*—and now, as a series of idioms and proverbs began to roll off his tongue at surprising angles, he felt the same unusual presence that had come over him in his hotel suite a few hours ago. But here there was no bed to look under. The presence seemed to be coming from within, like a sort of psychic déjà vu. It was as confusing as it was remarkable.

"*With love, water is enough; without love, food doesn't satisfy*," Faron said.

"Very good," the old man said.

"*The best time to plant a tree was twenty years ago*," Faron said.

"*And the second best time is now*," the old man responded.

"Oh yes, I love these. *A bird does not sing because it has an answer.* Do you know that one?"

"*It sings because it has a song*," Faron answered.

"Perfect. Impressive. In any case," he said, switching back to Cantonese, "I won't keep you any longer. Enjoy your meal. Just wait till you try the dumplings here."

And with that, the old man returned to his table and picked up his playing cards. His grandchildren, tyrannosaurus versus pterodactyl still in hand, played on at his feet without a care in the world.

"Pinch me," Faron told Ramona, offering his arm.

"You're funny," she said. "That was so cool. I'm impressed. You've definitely got my attention here."

"Please."

She pinched his arm.

He backtracked in pursuit of a feasible explanation. The delicate tickle-pinch that Ramona had just then favoured him with was simply another layer of the dream, he decided. He needed a shock to the system. Time was wasting in this sleepless city, and here he was, already in bed, like a toddler down for naptime when the party was just getting started. He had only one night ahead of him before his meeting tomorrow, and he intended to take advantage of it rather than dreaming some trippy dream.

He stood, heart pounding in his chest considerably faster than it ever had, and walked over to the old man's table. He offered his other arm. "Would you mind?" he said.

"You're an unusual fellow. But in a most entertaining way," the old man said.

The pinch that sent a sharp pain signal up the length of Faron's arm to the insula and anterior cingulate cortex did nothing but make him flinch. "Again, please," he said.

"*The miracle, my friend, is not to fly in the air, or to walk on the water . . .*"

"*. . . the miracle is to walk on the earth,*" Faron said.

The man nodded and smiled and pinched Faron's arm even harder, which caused Faron to bark out a series of insulting curses as he pulled his arm back. He apologized immediately.

The little people playing on the floor laughed.

"My grandchildren seem to appreciate your colourful Cantonese," the old man said.

MAYBE THE JOKE was on him. At the bar they visited after their meal, Faron tried to temper his galloping excitement. An evening of madness had taken hold and he saw no choice but to dwell graciously among the inmates of the asylum until the fit passed. The night would find its balance once again soon enough, he thought, and so he didn't resist the fantasy as he walked through the brightly lit patches of language that popped up all around him, Ramona at his side, on their way to the back of a loud, colourful bar where they sat at a table set with a single plastic flower.

He ordered their drinks from a waitress who seemed less impressed with his command of her language than the people at the restaurant had been.

In this altered view of the world, his heart required answers, but no answers were forthcoming. Knowledge felt effortless and effortlessness felt threatening. Ramona placed her hand on his forearm. The game she'd engineered was beyond him. This illusion of language was part of the game. He should not be surprised to wake up and find himself in a back-alley clinic with tubes in his nose and a hole in his side where a kidney had been removed. The drinks came. He turned the olive in his martini and wondered if perhaps this delusion wasn't the result of some alchemy of exhaustion, alcohol, and excessive travel. He looked at his hand. It was steady as a rock. Perhaps he'd become so manically perceptive and supercharged with the ghostwriter's gift to recreate the lives of others that it wasn't language he'd mastered at all but the ability to enter the very thoughts of those he engaged with. He ran the edge of his thumbnail against the bottle of Advil in his pocket. When he shifted in his seat, the thing rattled like a child's toy. *Too many of these, as well—this with the booze. No wonder,* he thought.

"I don't even know what language I'm speaking anymore," he said over the music.

"This one's English, I'm pretty sure," Ramona said.

He removed his arm from under her warm hand and ate his olive, confused in his state of perfect comprehension.

She lifted her Negroni. "To the mysteries of language and the deep blue sea."

Faron admired her dogged shamelessness. She was adept at indulging the fantasy, game again for the sport she'd introduced at their meeting at the hotel steps, the make-believe she'd spun about their time together in Paris. They sipped and watched the Hong Kong expat crowd. It was a place Ramona came often for this simple reason. Half the clientele were white and shared among themselves the language Faron wrote in. The Germans and the Scandinavians flirted creatively with the Brits and the Americans in the idiomatic chit-chat and wet pickup lines learned from the movies and TV shows of their adolescence. Faron counted in his head. He'd watched maybe three Chinese language films in his life. Jackie Chan did more fighting than speaking in two of them. It was a hopeful explanation until it wasn't an explanation at all.

Nearing three in the morning, when they stepped into a cab parked at curbside, the driver reached his hand back to Faron, expecting the passenger to give him a card with the name of their hotel, as was always the case with tourists. Instead, the man looked up, surprised, and smiled into his rear-view when Faron told him his destination.

"You got it," he said.

Through dark streets lit like petals on a wet black bough, Faron silently recited the Pound couplet in his head, and with it came the perfect Mandarin translation, brightly articulated without any effort at all. He closed his eyes and wondered when this would stop.

"I'm back in the reef tank as of eight tomorrow morning," Ramona said.

He didn't tell his new friend what he had on for tomorrow, not even in the vaguest terms. As they coasted down a wide boulevard lined with office towers, silent revellers to left and right, he doubted he was capable of taking on the task of writing the Iranian's story now. In an instant, at this vulnerable hour, it all seemed too much for him. She'd doused herself in gasoline, for god's sake. He would never be able to understand that, let alone commit to something with such absolute determination. And if he could not understand someone, he could not write about them. She was a woman so fearless that with a single lit matchstick she'd made tremble the regime that had ruled her country for decades. He was not equal to the task. He'd never be able to capture the spirit of such a person. Tomorrow he would meet Ms. Khajenouri and explain his concerns as much as possible, and apologize for wasting her time.

Ramona kissed him good night when the cab pulled to the curb. It was a night to remember, she said, and thank you. "We'll always have Hong Kong." She didn't wink when she said this. She was good indeed, he thought, and in the game till the end. They waited until she was through the first set of glass doors of her building before Faron resumed his journey.

Now that the two were alone, the cabbie spoke ceaselessly as he drove. At a red light, he arched his body and looked over the back of his seat and glanced down at Faron's shoes, as if he was checking that his passenger wasn't a life-size puppet managed by some ventriloquist hidden down there.

"I've been driving in this city for twenty years and haven't heard a single foreigner who could speak the language right—until you came along!"

"It was high time, I guess."

"Ah, the mystery of language, the way babies learn is fascinating!" the driver said with unbottled enthusiasm. "Do you have children? Little shitting monsters one day, the next they're getting married and going on vacation!"

"None," he said. "I've got a niece in Guangzhou. She speaks Mandarin."

"Another impossible language for Westerners."

Faron, hopping over to Mandarin, shared his praise with the cabbie for that city's morning tea ritual.

"You're more Chinese than my grandmother! You sound like Radio Beijing. Unbelievable! I can barely speak my own language. And look at you. I sound like a mule when I speak. A mouthful of marbles. My wife tells me with no smile on her face that she married a donkey. You sound like a filigree, my friend, a champion racehorse!"

"*In this case, the donkey's lips certainly do not match the horse's mouth*," Faron said.

"Wonderful," the cabbie said.

"I grew up in Canada. I got here a week ago."

"It's true you look more like the blond Simon and Garfunkel

fellow than you do one of my people. But looks aren't everything! Some people have a gift, I suppose. I drive. My gift is driving a taxi. I know this city better than anyone. I know all the hotels. One night at the Metropole costs more than I earn in five months driving this old shitbox," he said, caressing the dashboard. "You're doing well, my friend. I have no resentment there. I say, Good for you! Money makes the world go round. A man of your talents deserves all he can get."

As he drove, the man lifted an admiring gaze again and again to the passenger in his rear-view mirror. Faron was not immune to the cabbie's delight—he smiled and chatted on with him—but he felt the same unusual sensation creeping up on him that had caused him to look under his bed earlier today. Now the otherness was *inside* him, though, not hiding somewhere in the cab, its presence as close and real as his own breathing. Maybe a turn for the worse in his mother's condition had thrown its complicating shadow over him from all the way back home. He checked himself for the silent chills of premonition that might crawl up his spine at such a moment, but he felt nothing odd in that regard. He resolved to call her the moment he stepped out of the cab. On the far side of the planet, yesterday's mid-afternoon sun still warmed the spring fields of her modest farm. He imagined her there, waiting on the front porch for the return of her loyal son, diminished now and frail. It was a heartbreaking thought that obliged him to choke back the wave of emotion he felt awakening inside him.

He turned his stare to the side window, his face now turned glum with the reality of his mother's condition.

The driver glanced up again at the rear-view with a look of concern. "I can pull over if you're going to be sick, my friend."

Faron shook his head, speechless in all languages. The man put his foot back on the accelerator and the cab sailed on long enough for Faron to regain himself.

In the car port at the Metropole, he palmed over a small stack of bills and thanked his driver.

"You are a rarity, my good sir. Delighted you're feeling better," the driver said when he counted the handsome tip.

Faron got out and tapped the roof of the car. "*A journey ninety percent finished is still only halfway done*, am I right?"

"A philosopher as well as a big tipper!"

Faron dialled his mother's number after the cab pulled away, and watched a pair of young lovers kissing on the promenade while he waited for her to pick up. The automated voice message she'd refused to personalize answered and told him the party he was calling could not be reached at this time. Deflated, he pocketed the phone and headed for the revolving doors.

FOURTEEN

MILDRED CROUCHED IN A STAND OF TALL GRASS ON THE SOUTH-western shore of the peninsula and watched the group of Kazakhs huddling below at the water's edge. The coastline was at its darkest at this hour, but she was close enough to hear their voices in the pre-dawn of that day of the Pure Brightness Festival. Conditions were perfect for the crossing. The bay was calm and the cloud cover choked all light from the sky. She'd slept rough here on the floodplain that was the bird habitat three kilometres west of Shenzhen, waiting for one of the smuggling rings that carried migrants from the mainland to Hong Kong. She was cold and hungry, and the sports coat she'd taken from the foreigner was thin and offered little protection or comfort. She hiked the collar and closed the coat up under her chin, but still she was cold as she sat watching the darkness for signs of one of the marine border patrols that hunted the illegal crossings on these muddy lowlands.

She wore a baseball cap she'd found yesterday on the side of the road, and now she pulled the red brim down low over her face and settled deeper in the grass, waiting like this for what felt like hours until a distant rumbling carried to shore over the black water and she saw three short flashes of light. The sound of the motor grew louder and the flashing signal was returned by one of the illegals on the shoreline, and then the skiff's motor fell to a murmuring neutral as the short vessel emerged slowly into view like a wyvern from a faerie mist.

The shadowy silhouette standing at midship called out to the group, and Mildred rose quietly and came down from the grassy rise toward the illegals at the water's edge and slipped into their numbers. It was still dark enough for her to appear as one of them without raising suspicion as they waded into the bracing water and climbed up over the rub rails. They had already paid the boatman's master for the crossing, and so the pilot was not occupied with the counting of heads or collecting his fee as he boarded his cargo. He hauled Mildred up like the rest of them and she righted herself on the bottom boards and claimed a spot on the forward thwart, head down, the hat brim still pulled low over her face.

In the whispered exchanges around her she heard a dialect spoken in the west, mostly incomprehensible to her. Under the foreigner's coat, she wore a strip of bubble packing she'd found in a heap of trash, fastened around her midsection and secured with twine, a poor facsimile of a lifejacket inspired by stories of drowned migrants. The pilot settled at his station and leaned into his controls, and the motor's propellors jumped to life again. His cargo, as one body, readjusted their centres of gravity and leaned forward into the cold dark. The vessel rose to speed and slapped hard against the surface as it cut the bay, the vibrating motor held now at a steady pitch. She pressed the cap to her head and watched the faint glow of the city on the far shore of the peninsula, wondering if her journey might soon be ended, and suddenly the girl beside her called out to the pilot and the skiff angled hard to the north and Mildred saw the Coast Guard gunboat looming in the black night.

The pilot dropped speed and the rumble of the motor fell to a soft growl as the cutting beam of a searchlight began sweeping over the water. Mildred closed her eyes and began to pray, though she had no god to pray to. She knew she would not be mistaken for a Kazakh if the vessel were boarded. Her identity would be found out and she'd be sent back into the clutches of her tormentors. She gripped the edge of the thwart and felt the swells carry the vessel in deep, rolling arcs that forced its passengers one by one to lean toward the sea and throw up what little they had in their bellies. Others emptied their stomachs for fear they'd be discovered and thrown overboard. Only a few seemed immune to the sudden plague of nausea that came over the group.

When the girl next to her leaned over the side too, Mildred placed her hand on her back and steadied her and held the child's hair from her face. After she sat back down again, she wiped the child's mouth and pulled her into her body and shared what little warmth she had to give.

On like this they crawled over the bay, the motor turned to a low rumble to minimize the noise that would carry so dangerously over the surface. The pilot kept to his detour while the towering ship was still in view, then slowly, as the gunboat receded into the dark, they began to pick up speed and the wave of nausea slowly fell away.

The searchlight became a dim pinprick in the night and finally the throttle was opened and they resumed their journey to the far shore.

FIFTEEN

THE METROPOLE LOBBY WAS EMPTY BUT FOR A TRIO OF SLOUCHing insomniacs when Faron crossed the echoing space in the direction of the elevators. Seated on couches between two stone pillars, they looked up from their phones, as if hopeful he might have come with the answers to the questions that were preventing the mercy of sleep, but Faron had precious few answers that night, only questions of his own. After trying his mother's number a second time, and getting the same message, he stepped into an elevator and felt the pressure in his middle ear slowly build as he was delivered again high above the clouds.

He stood, eyes forward, working his jaw, until the lift slowed and stopped and the doors rolled open and the pressure began to equalize. He exited the elevator and walked down a deserted corridor, searching for the room number he'd seen on the bar chit that Gideon had generously signed earlier that evening. When he stopped in front of what he hoped was the right door, he felt the pressure in his inner ear return to normal. He didn't have to knock twice. The door was opened quickly and there stood Gideon Kastner, cane in hand, wearing a wide grin.

"I'm glad to see you've come through your first night safe and sound. You look like shit. Come on in."

It sounded like there was a small party going on. There were voices and muted laughter.

"I'm interrupting," Faron said.

"Not at all, we're expecting you."

Gideon led his guest through to the main room of a large, finely appointed suite and introduced him to a group of individuals seated on armchairs and sofas. They all rose and shook Faron's hand and welcomed him with pats on the back and wide, admiring eyes. Gideon handed him an unopened bottle of Perrier.

"Go on, you look parched."

"I'm not sure I understand any of this," Faron said. "You were expecting me?"

"No one ever understands at first. We all have our own story. But you're the new guy with the twist. Welcome to the Lost Souls Club."

This was Gideon Kastner's group of fellow conventioneers, this mad collection of soul transporters, or whatever he'd called them.

"Really. It's super late."

"No, no, please have a seat," Gideon said.

The group settled back into their armchairs and sofas, attention turned to Faron. The circle of sympathetic faces leaned in.

Faron took a seat.

"Let me do the introductions," Gideon said, gesturing to the woman on Faron's left. "This is Advika."

Faron smiled politely.

Advika was carrying the soul of a man who'd died after emigrating from Hong Kong to the Vancouver area in 2011, Gideon said. She was a court stenographer, spoke in short, nervous sentences, and wore a burgundy sweater and green slacks. Next was Amir, a handsome young man and host to the unbound soul of a lovesick insurance agent from Shenzhen who'd succumbed to a heart attack while on a family vacation in Sharm el-Sheikh. Beside Amir sat a forty-year-old podiatrist from Boston called Mr. Voight. He was carrying the soul of a dental hygienist killed in a traffic accident on Route 1A on his way in from Logan International. Also present was a Malaysian lawyer named Sannan Megat, who hosted the immigrant soul of a theatre critic who'd fled China in the first year of the Cultural Revolution. Finally, of course, was Gideon Kastner, whom Advika had identified as the poet Wystan Hugh Auden when she'd called Faron's room twelve hours earlier.

"This is all great fun, really, but I need to get some sleep," Faron said.

"We can relate. Your resistance is natural. Ask anyone here. We all dug our heels in. That's why we're a community. We all helped each other. It takes time. Through our doubt we found the truth. I knew you were one of us as soon as I saw you. It comes with the territory. You'll see it too in people like us if your passenger stays with you long enough. There's a sort of glowing presence we can see around each other. I think you have some sense of where this is going."

Faron did indeed have a sense of where this was going, which was straight into the story bank he always added to whenever he travelled. It would be a good one he'd trot out over a bottle of wine with Setareh and Mikkel—about the night he'd met a bunch of crackpots and woke up the next day realizing he'd been so stoned on painkillers and booze that he'd dreamed all sorts of entertaining madness.

He rose from his seat. "I don't even know what day it is." He pulled out his phone and looked at the time.

"It's a bit much at first," Gideon said. "Don't feel you're unusual in that way. Eventually your passenger comes to the surface. He'll introduce himself one way or another. Mine expressed himself pretty fast. Not that I knew those poems were his. Have you seen any signs yet?"

Faron remained standing and said nothing.

"Alright," Gideon said. "That might be a good thing. Less trouble for you that way. We think the stronger the presence, the harder it is to shake them loose. Like I said at the bar. A pit bull on a chew toy, this Wystan Hugh Auden. With any luck, your guy will go gracefully. Or gal."

"Likely tomorrow will tell, with any luck," Mr. Voight said. "Technically today."

"What's today?" Faron said.

"The whole country pauses to remember their dead," said Gideon.

"The Pure Brightness Festival," Advika said.

"Tomb-Sweeping Day," said Sannan Megat.

"Conditions are optimal—it's the perfect day for a transmigration," Gideon said. "There's a channelling of spiritual energies that's favourable to the passenger's journey. A springboard into the next world. We're all hoping for the best."

"A springboard?" Faron said.

"Call it what you will."

Faron retrieved the bottle of Advil from his pocket.

"Far from guaranteed, of course," said Sannan Megat.

The last few pills bounced around inside the container when Faron gave it a shake. He popped it open and downed two more, then picked up the bottle of Perrier he'd set beside him and twisted the cap. He took a long drink.

"He's right," Gideon said. "But it's their best day to exit the middle world. The Tibetans call it the bardo. Purgatory for others. It's like a gap between realities where the soul gets trapped on the way to dying. They're stuck until they find the person or place or emotion out there in the real world, some connection, some link that sets them free."

"A gap between realities . . ." Faron said.

"Yes," said Gideon.

Faron took another swallow of Perrier and wished now for the comfort of the routine he'd felt so wonderfully free of as he'd watched the view of the harbour only hours before. The adventure he'd set out to find this evening had left him breathless and confused, and now he only wanted the safe grounding of the familiar. Or was this still just some fool's dream ignited by the hallucinogenic cocktail of booze and pills thrown back while nursing a possible concussion after a series of sleepless jet-lagged nights in the grips of an upside-down time zone? It was a wonder he didn't think he could fly. He'd almost believed his dinner partner when she'd turned to him with wide eyes and complimented him on his perfect Chinese. Who knew what the cab driver was up to with his enthusiastic fictions about his passenger's multilingualism.

"Those pills, what are they for? That bump on your head?" Gideon said.

Faron told them about the drone and the prisoner and the warder.

"I tripped over someone's foot."

"Who was flying the drone?" Gideon said.

"Some street vendor. An old woman."

The circle of faces closed in.

Gideon withdrew the bullet pendant from inside his shirt and let it rest in the palm of his hand, an *ah ha* expression impishly creeping across his face. "A mere bump on the head. Just consider yourself lucky you didn't have to get blown up or shot in the process."

FARON WAS PRACTICALLY vibrating with exhaustion when he got back to his suite sometime after five that morning. It was far too late to spend even another second puzzling over the unusual events of his day. He flicked on the bathroom light and removed the toothbrush from his toiletries bag. Relieved that he was moments from sleep, he looked up and saw a man seated above the vanity, half in and half out of the mirror, positioned as if caught in the act of entering through an open window. He jumped back and gripped his heart with a trembling hand, the other held out in defensive posture.

"What the—?" he said.

The intruder, an Asian man who looked to be somewhere in his mid-forties, raised his hands in an appeal for calm. "Sorry," he said. "Sorry. I know." His voice was not threatening at all. If anything, it was almost calming. "Take your time," he said.

"How did you get in here? What do you want?" Faron looked around for something to defend himself with.

The man, gesturing to the floor, said, "May I?"

The stranger stepped down from the mirror, like a cat burglar entering through a jimmied window, and took a deep breath when he felt his feet touch the real world for the first time in seventeen years. He pinched his cheek and slapped his legs with his hands. "Oh, this is lovely. Oh, how I've missed this. You have no idea!"

"You've been here before? This is my room now. I checked in yesterday afternoon." Faron closed and opened his eyes again, but the man was still there.

"You hit your head pretty hard today at the station," the stranger said. "You're a wreck. You haven't had a decent sleep since you landed."

Faron once again decided he was dreaming. What else *could* he believe? And so, in this dreamscape, he would declare his objections. Like an attorney in a courtroom, he challenged the absurdity of what he'd just witnessed—a man emerging from his bathroom mirror.

"I put it to you, members of the jury, that I'm already asleep in that big bed out there," he said, gesturing with a defiant finger. "I've been asleep for hours. And may I sleep for many more. I rest my case. Now disappear."

The intruder said nothing.

With an eye still on the stranger, Faron squeezed a blob of Crest onto his toothbrush. He opened the tap and began to clean his teeth.

The stranger stood to the side, waiting, pleased to see that his host was a fastidious man in his personal hygiene, actually counting his strokes, as he himself used to do.

"And you'll have me think I'm talking to you in Cantonese right now? Or is this Mandarin?" Faron said through a mouthful of minty froth.

"I know both," the stranger said. "And so now you do too."

"Because you're in my head? Not because this is a dream."

"Right."

"Marvellous," he said, still brushing. "Whatever you say."

"You remember the blindfolded woman at the station?"

Faron spat and rinsed and placed his toothbrush in the holder to the left of the mirror where the intruder had been sitting. "Why, you know her?"

"In a manner of speaking," the stranger said.

He rinsed his mouth again and then stood at the toilet and relieved himself. He washed and dried his hands, then went back out into the main room and stopped at the window. The cloud cover had moved off, revealing what looked like the greatest city in all the world, its pearls of luminescence aglimmer at this humbling hour. He exhaled audibly and glimpsed his reflection, this time in the dark glass of the window, and Jiang Ming stepped forward again.

"When you fell—"

"I was tripped," Faron said.

"Yes. And that's how I ended up here . . ."

"She was avoiding you, tripping me like that," Faron said. "And what do you want with her, anyway? She's afraid of you."

"She has no idea what I am or that I'm here. She's read my books. Of course, she knows who I was. She smuggles my books onto the mainland. But that's different. She's my bridge, the person I need to get where I'm supposed to be."

"Which is?"

He pointed vaguely to the view of the city beyond the windowpane. Far off, the first touch of dawn had begun to play over the soul menagerie that was Hong Kong. As the thin light rose on the horizon, Faron's image against the glass began to fade.

"Quickly, man, listen," Jiang Ming said. "I wouldn't even know how to begin to answer that question. But it's in your reflection that you can see and hear me. You'll remember nothing of this until I appear again. You don't even notice what language you're speaking. You won't know I'm here. Afterwards, you might feel lightheaded."

As the windowpane brightened, he listened to the stranger tell of how, since his death so many years ago, he'd tested those he felt might be able to deliver him from this transitional state that held him. He'd begun to fear that he'd never find the right person, that he'd remain trapped forever in this purgatorial otherworld. It was not a question of physical boundaries and borderlines, he said, but of that most profound release from the state that held him. He needed to find his perfect match. It was nothing he understood, but when his cue came, he said, facilitated by the old street vendor, he was summoned to Shenzhen, and there in the railway station, when he saw the prisoner, he knew his long wait had come to an end. She was the perfect expression of all he needed to be carried forward into his liberation from the bardo. His light had grown brighter, stronger. He'd approached her again while she was held captive in a house in the countryside; and finally, at the station a second time, as he was angling himself just so, his glowing blue hand on the bookseller's forehead, a foreigner—"you," he said—got in the middle of it with a thumping crash.

"And here I am," he said.

Faron felt an odd weightless shifting in his heart, like the invisible pressures that had grown in his middle ear as he'd ascended in the elevator, but this weightlessness now expanded in his chest and he felt that this nonsense before him, as biblically supercharged as Moses parting the waters of the Red Sea, was as real as the nose on his face. His centre began to slip in a direction that might welcome such madness as truth—that he was talking in a language he had no knowledge of to a man trapped inside him—and suddenly he felt the powerful cut of truth open him with a surprising blade.

"I won't remember a thing?" he said.

"I will appear as a mild form of déjà vu. A heart murmur. Vertigo. A body echo. Indigestion. Nothing you'll identify as me."

"I'll go about my business?"

"Yes."

"Oblivious?"

"Yes."

"What about those people upstairs? They all spoke about their passengers. They knew what was happening to them."

"It takes months for the guest to assert himself to the conscious mind of his host. Look at that war correspondent. That Kastner fellow. He wrote Auden's posthumous book thinking it was him doing the writing. You can hardly blame him for that. It took him years to see otherwise. I'm not blaming the poor man. Sometimes a second traumatic event needs to occur."

"You're not saying I need to get shot, I hope."

The question was not a serious one until he said it, at which point it became a new concern. Faron did not know this man. What he was capable of he had no idea. He wondered if he wouldn't be marched like a marionette into the middle of traffic to create the conditions necessary to maintain uninterrupted contact. Maybe that's what Auden had done to Kastner. Got him shot at West 45th and 7th in order to make himself plainly known to his host. Who knew how long the poet had been looking for such a disaster. Perhaps this was his visitor's next move.

"No, not at all, my friend. Nothing like that. We just need to find the bookseller. *You* need to find the bookseller. I'm trapped here until you do."

The half-light of dawn finally washed away the last of their shared reflection and Faron was alone again. He shook his head, abruptly returned from a prolonged daze, and felt an odd vertigo, and that familiar sense of otherness filled the room.

"Is anyone there?" he called out.

The query was met with silence. He staggered backwards into bed and touched the remote, and the blinds obediently descended over the world.

SIXTEEN

THE SKIFF LOADED WITH TWENTY-ONE KAZAKHS HUGGED THE shoreline at the northwest tip of the main island as the pink hue on the horizon pushed into the breaking day. The pilot idled the motor just south of Black Point, and urged his passengers overboard. There was no time to waste. With daylight coming, they would lose any small advantage and find themselves exposed and vulnerable to capture and detention by the authorities; they'd be forcibly returned to the mainland, where they'd face heavy fines or imprisonment. For Mildred, it would be much worse.

She rolled herself over the side into the shallow water and found bottom and walked up onto the sand flats. The cold night out on the bay had seeped into her bones. She was shivering now as she tore the bubble-wrapping from her chest and turned and saw the girl she'd helped on the boat walking slowly toward her. The girl looked much younger than she'd thought, a child of seven or eight, skinny and weak and too young to be alone.

When the child spoke in her incomprehensible language and reached for Mildred's arm, Mildred shook her head no and told her she was sorry, it wasn't possible. "You're safer with your people. Stay with them." And she pulled her arm away and started up the beach.

She pushed through a stand of marram grass and found Nim Wan Path, which looked like a bicycle lane cutting between green scrub and rock. It led north toward the highway that fed traffic off the Shenzhen Bay Bridge, where she would be challenged by the police at any one of the checkpoints or traffic stops; to the south, to the right, the path ran alongside Lung Kwu Tan Road, which followed the coastline toward the city, thirty or so kilometres distant.

She was thirsty and hungry, and the chill in her bones would let go only once she started moving. She'd walk until she found water and perhaps transportation, or maybe she'd go the whole way on foot, both options more achievable if she travelled alone. The girl was still waiting down there on the beach, split off from the others, watching her up in the tall grass.

The child waved, as if to say goodbye, and Mildred waved back, and she felt such a crushing sense of pity and remorse that she swore under her breath.

She called out, "Hurry up, then, come on," and the girl ran toward her over the sand and up the incline. She took Mildred's hand, and together they began along the path.

AT FIRST THE girl kept pace as they walked, the path's teasing camber a surprise of sudden palm and banyan trees and blue garbage bins and torn tarpaper and rusted corrugated-iron fencing. The early morning was silent but for the haunting bird calls that rose from somewhere deep in the forest and the soft tread of their footsteps and steady breathing. She slowed her pace to allow the girl to keep up. For a time she carried her on her back, and then, exhausted, put her down again, and they sat at the side of the road to rest. It was full light now, the day starting to warm. They walked on past a locked iron gate blocking the entrance to a narrow laneway that led down to a stone dwelling with a patch garden, where a man was digging roots. She called out to him through the fence, but he was either deaf or ignored her intentionally.

They continued on past a graveyard of junked cars and refrigerators piled in a cut in the forest, and where the road opened to a view of a wide expanse of water, she stopped again and waited for the girl. Up ahead a man stood at the side of the road, staring out over the bay. He did not move or turn to her. She took the child's hand and led her silently past the stranger, and on they walked under the gathering cloud cover.

Ten minutes on, a tuk-tuk trundled past.

At another bend, where the road entered the forest, they saw an old man wearing the reflective yellow vest of a municipal worker sitting on a rock outcrop, broom in hand, talking to a three-legged dog. When Mildred asked if he had any water, he reached into the bag at his feet and handed over a can of Sprite.

She gave it to the girl, who took down three long drinks and then shared the can with Mildred. The man patted the dog's rump and asked where they were headed, and when she told him, he said they still had four or five hours yet to go.

SOON THEY PASSED a scroll of corrugated fencing and shanties set far back in the trees. The road was winding and rarely straightened, but when it did, she turned and saw the girl trailing behind. Places of business began to appear. On the other side of a tall iron gate, a fish farm with green ponds and a young boy holding a carp by its gills came into view. A second tuk-tuk passed, and soon after that a small open-backed truck loaded with PVC pipe rumbled by, and then more shanties and fields of rice and white cabbage appeared.

After another hour of walking, the air began to smell of the canneries that dotted the coast on this side of the island, its fishermen now asleep on their front stoops as the two strangers walked hungrily past the blue and clear plastic sheeting that flapped languidly in the breeze. She didn't look at these men, or the women who worked in the fields on their left. The wide bay was always to the right, beach and rock and the calm surface muted by the clouds that troubled the sky with their nervous tones of uncertainty.

The road grew wider and trucks and cars and tuk-tuks began to pass with frequency. Children and dogs came chittering and barking down from the cinder-block dwellings that surveilled the road. The children asked Mildred where she was from and why her head was shaved like a man's and told her that just up the road she'd find a bus that would take her into the city on the Kong Sham Western Highway. They followed her for a short while longer, skipping and singing along, but they grew bored and splintered off back into the maze of shanties. The adults sitting on their front stoops did not take much notice as she passed. They looked up from their business only for a moment. Finally, after a long stretch of road, she looked behind her and saw that the girl was gone.

SEVENTEEN

WHEN FARON AWOKE STILL FULLY DRESSED FIVE HOURS LATER, HE lay without moving, staring into the shadows of a room he didn't recognize. The confusing vestiges of a fantastic dream hovered tantalizingly just beyond reach as it slowly dawned on him where he was. He knew the dream had something to with his late-night visit with Gideon Kastner, but nothing more. With the touch of a finger, the blinds rose and a new day's light flooded the room. He rolled out of bed and drank down a large glass of water. Below, the thick cloud cover over the city had returned.

He stripped off his clothes and stepped into the pattern-tiled walk-in shower and steamed up the bathroom so completely that a glance in the mirror afterwards revealed only the faintest hint of the truth that lay within his murky reflection. He dried off, wrapped a towel around his midsection, and found a message on his phone from Ms. Khajenouri asking if two o'clock was still fine with him. He was looking forward to it, he wrote, and was there anything he could pick up for her on the way? He'd already gotten her a package of specialty Persian tea and a gift box of the date and pistachio dessert called ranginak that Setareh had told him all Persians were mad for.

Within minutes he was dressed and riding the elevator down to one of the hotel cafeterias, where he'd grab something before setting off on his day.

He sent Setareh and Mikkel a short good-morning message and checked the news as he ate his breakfast. There were no updates about the standoff at the consulate. Ms. Khajenouri's short note had mentioned nothing out of the ordinary either. He enjoyed his coffee and toast and single poached egg and boarded the elevator again, pressed his floor number, and turned to his reflection in the mirrored wall panel to straighten his shirt.

"You slept in," the stranger said. "You needed it."

Faron remembered everything. "Oh, Christ," he said.

The man eased a foot down from the mirror and stepped carefully into the lift. "I can't explain it either," Jiang Ming said. "But trust me—"

Faron passed his arm cautiously through the man's chest. "I think the issue's my sanity, not my trust."

The lift came to a stop and the doors bounced open at the mezzanine level. Standing there was the Rubik's Cube girl from yesterday, accompanied now by a woman of about forty. She wore a green pantsuit and an extravagantly feathered hat, the sort of number the Queen of England wore to the Royal Ascot.

"You again," the girl said. "Good morning! Going up?"

Faron turned to Jiang Ming, who told him they couldn't see or hear him. "It's just you," he said.

"Yes, yes, going up," Faron said.

He pressed the button to close the doors.

"I was just telling my mom about you. This is my mother. I was telling her about the foreigner who spoke perfect Chinese."

The lift began its ascent.

"How do you do," the woman said.

"How do you do," Faron said.

"My mother doesn't believe a Westerner's capable of speaking our language. I told her she was being racist. Go on, say something else. She thinks I made you up."

The woman clicked a tut-tutting sound with her tongue and placed a hand on her daughter's shoulder and called her a silly melon.

"She may be a silly melon, but you must be very proud of her. She's quite accomplished in her chosen field," he said.

"Remarkable," the mother said.

"I breezed past round one yesterday," the girl said. "Round two and then the finals this afternoon. I'm feeling good. Nimble fingers, nimble brain." She held up her cube.

"I'll bet you win all the marbles today," he said.

"See what I mean?" the girl said to her mother. "Flawless. You two could get married. But no kids, you already have one!"

"Xiao Hui!" the woman said, blushing wildly. "Please excuse my daughter's impudence."

"*Gentle and graceful is the girl, a fit wife for the gentleman,*" Faron said, unwittingly quoting a classic Chinese poem. "Alas, I am tethered to another."

Jiang Ming watched with amusement.

"I guess you'll just have to keep searching, Mommy," the girl said.

The ornamentation in the woman's hat was an opal-blue and sea-green peacock feather that quivered like glowing ashes rising over the fire that was the poor woman's burning embarrassment. Faron watched the floors ticking away on the panel above the doors, trying to ignore the mischievous smile of the stranger standing next to him. Jiang Ming knew precisely everything about Faron, including the love triangle that had captured his heart. The awkward silence in the small space became a presence unto itself. *Life is indeed the ceaseless march toward the miraculous,* Faron thought.

"That it is," Jiang Ming said.

"My daughter's right, though," the woman said. "You certainly do sound like one of us."

"She doesn't know the half of it," Jiang Ming said.

"That makes two of us," Faron said.

"Who are you talking to? You keep looking at yourself," the girl said.

"My imaginary friend," Faron said.

"I have one of those."

She turned to her cube and spun the thing in her small hands and nailed it in sixteen ferocious spins. The lift slowed and came to a stop.

"This is you," the girl said.

"Good luck today," said Faron.

The doors rolled open.

"The kid's sharp, she'll do well," Jiang Ming said.

"It was nice to meet you. You've got quite the little firecracker there."

"It was a pleasure," the woman said.

The intruder vanished from Faron's memory as soon as he stepped off the lift, as did much of the conversation he'd shared with the girl and her mother. He walked unsteadily down the hallway, light-headed, struck by a powerful vertigo, and let himself into his room.

The same peculiar sensation he'd experienced yesterday had returned. It was the distinct awareness that he was being observed, though by whom or how he had no earthly idea. He looked around the room, resisting the urge to ask if anyone was there or to look under the bed again. The likelihood that hotel security turned hidden cameras on their guests was slight to zero. It *was* possible, though, that some degenerate had placed a spy cam in the room for some godawful reason. And the fact that he could not rule this out brought some small sense of relief—it would account for this creeping paranoia, unpleasant though the idea was of a reprobate voyeur watching his every move.

He took a seat and waited for the light-headedness to fade.

He checked the time. The car that had been arranged to deliver him to his meeting with Ms. Khajenouri would be coming soon. He got up to collect a notepad and pen from his suitcase and saw the book tucked into the mesh side pocket. It had slipped his mind since yesterday.

It really was something, that cover for *An Italian Affair*. The image of beautiful lovers locked in a passionate embrace was straight out of the Harlequin playbook, as shamelessly over-the-top and spicy as they could get away with here, he imagined. He flipped it open—he could not resist—and gave the first paragraph a quick read, curious to learn why books of this sort practically flew off the shelves. He read the opening paragraph a second time, then closed the book over his finger, confused. He read the name of the author, Dafne Hong-Collier. She was a hell of a writer, he thought. It took him a few more paragraphs before he understood that the book and the jacket were mismatched. He removed the cover and read the author's name and the title on the spine, and then he flipped back to where he'd left off and read until the alarm on his phone began to chime. He earmarked the page, placed the book in his satchel, and rode the elevator down to meet his car.

THE DRIVER WAS waiting for him in the porte cochère in front of the hotel's main entrance, and in a moment Faron was comfortably arranged in the back of the sedan. He watched the view from his window for a few blocks after they pulled out into traffic, and then his mind turned again to the novel he'd found in his suitcase. It was the book Beenhouwer had spoken of at the dinner party three days ago in Guangzhou—the greeting card chapter titles had given that away quickly enough—but how the novel had come into the hands of the warder at the train station, or if the blindfolded woman's crime had anything to do with it, he had no clue. The parallel was as distressing as it was intriguing. Here might be a second prisoner sending her call for help to the outside world through the story held within these pages. He'd seen her lips move, after all, and he'd thought for a moment that she was trying to send him a message before he'd discarded the idea as so much nonsense. He wondered now if he'd rejected the possibility too easily that she'd been trying to tell him something.

The city rolled by, his sense of unease growing. He read on, worried now but entranced by the story, until the driver pulled to the curb across from two cruisers and a tactical police van parked in front of One Exchange Square.

FARON WONDERED IF the building's security measures had anything to do with the Iranian dissident holed up in the consulate on the forty-seventh floor. Upon entering the grand atrium, he'd been asked to produce his identification and was then invited to pass through a body scanner before continuing on to the bank of elevators.

He wanted to check himself in the mirror once he boarded—

it occurred to him that every elevator in the world had been turned into a narcissistic box of self-reflection—but its walls were lined with a freight padding that looked shabbily out of place in an office tower that was otherwise so properly elegant and modern. He straightened his shirt as best he could, the lift rising, and when the doors rolled open, he saw the standing floor sign for the consular office pointing to the right. He proceeded down the hallway, full of cautious anticipation now, and pushed through a door that opened to a reception area smaller than he might have expected for the consulate of a country as important as Japan.

To one side of the room, a dozen or more people were seated. A lumpy security guard stood at attention beside a flag and a framed photograph of the Japanese prime minister. On the wall opposite the flag was a digital screen displaying the number 56.

He approached the woman seated at the reception desk and announced the nature of his visit. She seemed a pleasant and efficient gatekeeper, roughly Faron's age, and responded in excellent English. She was dressed in a grey suit and wore black-framed glasses that, together with her hair, which she wore in a bun, gave her the studious look of a librarian or academic. He presented his passport and watched her enter his details and time of arrival into a registry. When she was finished with this, she returned the passport and picked up the phone on her desk. He recognized only his name when she spoke in Japanese to a person on the other end. It sounded wonderfully musical in her language, the stresses on the consonants and vowels oddly inverted. She hung up the telephone and, thanking him for his patience, invited him to take a seat. Someone would be along soon, she said.

He was pleased that he'd not been issued a number. His business here would be expedited, he thought with some relief, but he was disappointed when he was not ushered through directly. Certainly his meeting with Ms. Khajenouri was far outside the routine concerns of work visas and passport renewals, and therefore merited no small degree of special attention.

Reluctantly, he settled into the nearest available seat and found himself staring at the prime minister's likeness, hung directly across from him. He was wondering if the prime minister himself might be involved in the negotiations concerning Ms. Khajenouri's stay here when suddenly his phone pinged. A message from Setareh had just come in. He clicked on it at the same instant the frosted-glass inner doors swung open and a man called out his name. He pocketed the phone, message unread, and followed the individual through the doors.

They passed into a large office space abuzz with functionaries tending to their consular duties, then proceeded to a second set of doors and down a hallway, at the end of which was an elevator, an open-faced Otis in the old cage style. They stepped onto the elevator and rode it to the forty-eighth floor, where Faron was passed off into the care of a second consular official. This man introduced himself as Mr. Saito, chief assistant to the consul general. He was very pleased to meet Mr. Jones, he said in fine English, shaking Faron's hand and bowing deeply.

"Ms. Khajenouri is eager to speak with you. Please follow me."

He placed his open palm lightly on Faron's elbow and guided him forward along a carpeted hallway.

"I have read two of your books," said Mr. Saito. "It was my responsibility to learn about you, you see, in order to permit this meeting. And then I became curious. I enjoyed your portrayal of Becks and lovely Posh. Being hounded so, the poor souls! Fame is not the natural state of man, certainly, but oh how we love to watch the famous squirm!"

"Your English is very expressive," Faron said.

Mr. Saito directed his guest through a series of hallways—speaking all the while of how exciting it must be to meet the famous people he wrote about—past conference rooms and small office spaces and finally to an antechamber distinguished by a large oak door.

"Welcome to the Imperial Room," Mr. Saito said, pulling the door open.

Faron stepped into an elegantly decorated chamber of dark wood and sofas and deep armchairs and large paintings hung on panelled walls. At the far end of the room was a green-granite-encased fireplace in which a pretty horizon of blue flame burned silently. Bookshelves and side table lamps and potted plants and Bakhtiari rugs suggested the richness of an Oxford don's smoking room, and though there were paintings where normally windows would be placed, the air smelled fresh and springlike.

"This is lovely, thank you. The interview will be conducted here?" Faron said.

Lamya Khajenouri rose from the deep armchair where she'd been reading, quite obscured from where Faron and the consular official stood at the door. "Oh sorry, yes, yes, we shall speak here, if that's alright, Mr. Jones," she said.

In nine silent steps she crossed the room and greeted Faron with a Western handshake and a Persian kiss on both cheeks.

"I'm very grateful you've come," she said.

"It's a pleasure to finally meet you," he said.

Mr. Saito did the formal introductions and quietly withdrew.

In person it was not difficult to see what the camera had found so captivating in Lamya Khajenouri. She was professionally attractive in the way many actors are, perfect features and so on, but this was secondary to the warmth and easy confidence he felt in her presence. They were still strangers to one another, despite their correspondence, and in her quiet formality and grace he observed also a shadow of caution, or perhaps exhaustion—there would be some sharp edges waiting beneath that poise and beauty after her years of exile and asylum.

She directed him to an armchair set in front of the fireplace and angled her own chair slightly toward his. Between them sat a wooden tabletop globe, its northern hemisphere opened and rolled back at the equator to reveal a chessboard within. A game was in progress.

"I see you play," he said.

She was currently engaged in a game with an Iranian friend exiled in Mérida, Spain.

"We are scattered all over the world, of course, you know that. Scattered souls, all of us. But here we are at last, you and I, face to face. I want to thank you for coming."

"I'm a great admirer of your films and your advocacy. You're an inspiration to many people."

She nodded and smiled. "And your sister, how is she? And your mother, more importantly. I'm very sorry to hear she's not well."

Faron had no desire to talk about himself or his situation, but he knew that to gloss over these concerns might suggest a petulance or impatience that might misrepresent the simple exhaustion he felt on these matters. His mother's health was failing, he said, and he was eager to get back home. Sadly, his sister had rejected his proposal, but he didn't regret the effort in coming, and seeing her and meeting his niece for the first time had been wonderful. For that alone, he could say the trip had been worth it.

"Well, then, you tried, and that's important," she said.

After letting the moment settle, he asked if she had any news yet about the diplomatic standoff. "You don't think they'd actually make good on their threat, do you? Come knocking down these doors? It's day ten of the ultimatum tomorrow, isn't it?"

The expression on Ms. Khajenouri's face showed no sign of optimism.

"It's a question of my host's resolve. They're negotiating, I'm told. But I've made some people in Tehran very unhappy. We see how they've crushed the protests that followed the murder of Mahsa Amini. That hope we saw in the streets has gone underground again. The young women in my country are the real inspiration, not me."

"Would you go back if you could? If things changed there?"

"Nothing will change in my lifetime. We have small advances, and then they kill more young people. We're fighting on behalf of the next generation. But Beijing risks the sovereignty of its own consulates around the world if they follow through with their threat."

She rose from her armchair and crossed the room to a small serving station and returned in a moment with a teapot and two glass cups on a tray. Also on the tray was a clear bowl containing a bouquet of wooden sticks coated with golden sugar crystals. She placed the tray on the mantel above the fireplace and poured out the tea.

"In Iran this is said to cure all maladies, of the body, of the heart, of the spirit—it's our miraculous cure for everything. As children we're told of its wondrous powers. If you skin your knee. If a girl breaks your heart. It has magical qualities, we like to believe this. We are an optimistic race, and perhaps a bit foolish too. We choose our mythologies with blind faith. Perhaps this is the nature of faith."

"Chai nabat," he said. "I have a friend who makes this."

The pause hung for a moment.

"I've waited too long to tell you. For that I apologize."

He put down his cup. "Apologize?"

"You wouldn't have agreed to come if I'd told you why I

wanted to meet you."

"I'm not sure I understand," he said.

"The charade was necessary."

His confusion deepened, and then it gave rise to the uncomfortable impatience of a man who learns he'd been lied to, but has no idea why. Maybe for some political or public relations gambit that would sink him in the middle of the diplomatic crisis that surrounded her. But he was no pamphleteer, she knew that, and certainly she understood that he was no partisan willing and able to swallow a burning match, as she'd done. The struggle was not his. He was only a writer who'd learned to throw his voice in the sort of trained ventriloquism that had earned his industry's respect but changed nothing in the world.

"Do you know the name Arman?"

"Of course," he said, curtly.

"Yes," she said. "My husband."

Faron had researched her life well enough to know about the journalist whose body parts began turning up in the Montevideo harbour two days after he checked into his hotel there in January 2016. It was her husband's death that had brought her to the fight. He'd read about the investigation that caused the Uruguayan government to recall their ambassador from Tehran, which was met by a corresponding move on the Iranian side. The Uruguayans had concluded beyond a doubt that Iran had sponsored the killing.

"May I have your phone, please?" she said.

Faron reached into his pocket and placed it on the board

without disturbing the chess pieces. She picked it up, and his satchel, which he'd placed at the foot of his chair, and walked silently to the other side of the room. She placed both items under the seat cushion of an armchair, then sat back down again across from him.

"You're going to tell me someone's listening," he said.

"Would that surprise you, here?"

He said nothing.

"You are not interested in politics. You write about celebrities."

The truth and the insult were indistinguishable.

"You avoid politics. That's fine. But politics does not avoid you. You are part of the story I'm going to tell you about my late husband."

"I never met the man. How can that be?"

"This happened years ago in Tehran," she said, "long before you heard his name. Arman was a handsome young man, a graduate student in journalism. He was known around campus as a charmer. He was very talented. He wrote beautiful poetry. Girls fell in love with him easily. We all competed for his attention.

"He noticed two young women who visited the same coffee house at the same time every day that he did. He began to sit with them, to tell them stories. He took them out, introduced them to his friends. They went to parties. Soon they fell in love with him. He was charming and polite and told funny stories. He paid them equal attention. It became clear that the women were destined to be enemies. They competed foolishly for his favour. Each began to believe that she was the woman whom he cared for and that his interest in the other was falling away. It will be no surprise that one of those women was me."

"You won the war of hearts."

"Yes. In a manner of speaking. I went to him in Qatar. He was already with Al Jazeera by then, graduated and moved away. We were married in Cyprus. My mother and father had died many years before. There were no relatives to attend the wedding. But it was a joyous occasion. I stayed with him there for a week before I went back home. I was happy. I had won Arman's heart completely. I took his name, for personal reasons. It is not traditional for Iranian women to take their husband's surname. But I did."

Her new husband returned to Tehran when he could, she said, every month or six weeks, and she visited him twice in Doha the following winter. They spoke often by telephone and planned that she would join him abroad in a matter of years, perhaps even in America. By then she was studying the work of the poet-filmmaker Forugh Farrokhzad and the reality-bending movies of Abbas Kiarostami at the University of Tehran's College of Fine Arts. He respected his young bride's decision to stay in Tehran until she finished her degree, she said. She was making short films that played close enough to the line that her academic supervisors found nothing to report to their overseers. She narrated these documentaries in a haunting voice-over in direct reference to Farrokhzad's *The House Is Black*. Casts were minimal. She used real people living their real lives. Her thesis project was a sixteen-minute documentary that followed a Tehran bus driver through his day. It was screened in Istanbul and Cairo and in the Persian communities of Paris, Berlin, and LA. It won no prizes, but it got her noticed. She began to travel and Arman still came home to Tehran, but less now because he was always working. He was the same man she'd always known, she said, loving and devoted, though he was consumed by his job and wearied by an unrelenting schedule.

After years with Al Jazeera, he filed a series of stories about the Iranian nuclear weapons program for the BBC. The reportage brought his name to the top of the list of journalists that the regime would attempt to silence. It was impossible now to return home.

"He knew what they were capable of," she said. "It was his business to know. He wrote about dissidents. He knew the threats and dangers they faced. And these would extend to him. It was an open secret, that Iranian agents were operating abroad, as they are to this day. But you cannot imagine your own assassination. If you truly understand, you do not continue."

"He was a courageous man," Faron said.

"He suspected his phone had been compromised. By 2013 he was sure of it. Mine as well. We changed our phones regularly—we believed this would help—and spoke in our own private shorthand. The secret language understood only by a wife and her husband. But we were growing distant. There was too much time apart. Three years they tracked him. They were waiting for their moment. And then it came in Uruguay. He was in Montevideo for a story. He was writing about the physicist named Ardeshir Abbasi who'd gone missing from his post at the Malek Ashtar University of Technology in Tehran."

"I remember the name," Faron said.

"It was understood that my husband led them to an even more valuable prize than himself. Months after Abbasi's disappearance, a video was posted online showing him, or someone claiming to be him. In the video, he said he'd been kidnapped and tortured by the Saudis and the Americans. Then a second video came. A month later. Six weeks, maybe. The same man, Abbasi or someone playing him, claimed he'd defected with secrets from the Iranian nuclear program, and he was living in the West now. Maybe the second video was made by the Israelis or the Americans to discredit him in the eyes of the regime back home. Maybe it was made to sabotage trust, so he could never go back, the Israelis sabotaging the Iranian nuclear weapons program without firing a shot. Either way. He lost trust on both sides."

"And Arman went to meet him," Faron said.

"After months of negotiations, yes. Abbasi agreed to meet with Arman. Through my husband, Abbasi would make his appeal to the British public. But the assassins were ready. Most of this you likely know. Most of this was reported."

"Yes," he said.

"What was not reported was how they knew where to find my husband and Abbasi. They suspected it was a cellphone breach. But Abbasi made no mistakes. He didn't use a cellphone.

He was not so careless. And Arman too. They knew how to communicate secretly. And my husband and I never spoke of his travel plans. We knew it was dangerous. It was a different phone that was used to track and target them. Not his. Not Mine. Not Abbasi's."

She sipped her tea and then continued.

"The Uruguayans checked the phones of his colleagues and associates and friends. The investigation was at a standstill until the NSO Group's Pegasus document was leaked."

"That's how the Saudis tracked that journalist in Istanbul," Faron said. "I read about that. They used the Pegasus spyware."

"Jamal Khashoggi, yes. They tapped the phones of his family members—his wife, I believe. There are over fifty thousand names on that list. Journalists and their spouses, politicians, human rights activists, academics, even President Macron of France. One of those compromised phones led the assassins to my husband's hotel room the night he was killed."

"I'm so sorry," Faron said.

"The authorities seized the phone as soon as the name associated with that number was recognized. The spyware was discovered on the phone. This is when I became convinced that my husband was having an affair."

In an instant the man she'd mourned for years was not the man she'd thought he was. The realization had been crushing, she said.

"We were not a perfect couple. By no means. But I still had love in my heart. He'd treated me like a fool. I suspected this woman was only one of many such women. He was a charming and idealistic man when we married. He turned into a coward and a liar. He was that all along, I see that now. But I didn't surrender to despair when I discovered my husband's true character. I was already committed to the fight, you see."

Here was a story of the wounded soul that struggled on in the face of crushing revelations, Faron thought. He could tell that story, if in the end she wanted him to—if that's why she was telling him this—from the human angle of the broken heart. In that moment she became so much more to him than the glamorous figurehead in her fight for human rights. She was a woman who refused to give up. Her struggle was personal and private as much as it was about politics. Wasn't that it? It was about living bravely in the shadow of betrayal. For years she'd fought for the cause she served, despite these anguishing reversals.

"And this leaked document," he said. "That name. Did they tell you who it was?"

When Lamya Khajenouri disappeared for a moment in thought, he regretted asking the question. What did it matter, the final name in a long history of deception? She smiled a rueful smile and reached forward and placed her glass among the pieces on the chessboard.

"Our tea," she said, "this chai nabat—you see how it doesn't cure all maladies. It doesn't cure the broken heart. It does not protect us from a lover's betrayal. What we are told as children . . . those silly tales."

Her trust and faith in love, her freedom, her country—so much had been taken from her. As he sat there imagining the depths of the solitude that held her, he felt once again the slow, creeping sensation of being observed come over him. He turned and looked at the door, expecting to see Mr. Saito. No one was there. He turned back to his host.

"And now it seems you've entered this story," she said. "This story that has pursued you in a most unusual way."

"Why am I here?"

"Patience is bitter, but to a good end," she said. "The woman who led the assassins to my husband was the woman I sat with at the coffee shop in Tehran thirty years ago. The woman against whom I won the war of hearts, as you called it. It was not such a definitive battle as I'd thought. In the end, it seems we finish at a draw, she and I."

She shifted slightly, turning her body, and with her right hand she closed the northern hemisphere of the globe between them and gently rotated the sphere so that Faron was looking at South America.

"Do you see Montevideo there?"

"Yes."

"Do you see the city across the river?"

"Buenos Aires. I've never been. I have friends who go there," he said.

"Montevideo is a short crossing from Buenos Aires. Yes, I know. Where your Iranian translator spends every January with her husband."

Faron looked up from the globe, the threads of the story now spinning dangerously together in his mind.

"Yes, Setareh Azad. She was the one. It was her phone that led the assassins to my husband and Abbasi."

"The woman in the coffee shop," he said.

"Yes. My sister."

EIGHTEEN

BEFORE SHE LEARNED THE TRUTH, SETAREH AZAD HAD BELIEVED she'd won the battle of hearts waged between sisters. The blissful first months of her engagement to Arman were clouded only by the pain she knew this union would cause Lamya when she was finally told. It was the worry that stayed with her in a time otherwise filled with happiness. Setareh and Arman were hopelessly in love and to be wed in the new year, once he returned from Qatar, where he was working with an Al Jazeera television documentary team. She would reveal the truth to her sister when Lamya got back from a trip to Ardabil province, where she'd gone with classmates from the university to scout locations for a new film project.

On the evening of Lamya's return, Setareh knocked softly on her bedroom door, practically sick with remorse, and told her that her heart was heavy; she knew Lamya had loved Arman, but she'd given herself to him and they were to be married. Perhaps one day she might feel happy for her, Setareh said, after enough time had passed.

Lamya was still unpacking from her trip, her suitcase open on the chair by the window. She looked down at the tangle of clothing, overwhelmed by grief, Setareh thought, and when tears rose in Lamya's eyes, Setareh believed the pain was so great that she would never be forgiven.

"I'm sorry," Lamya said. "I'm the one who must beg forgiveness," and she showed Setareh the ring on her finger and told her that she'd not been in Ardabil province but in Cyprus with Arman, where they'd been married in a civil ceremony on a joyous day shadowed only by the brooding prejudices of a troubled conscience.

THERE WAS NO apology or excuse or remedy for the wound that had been opened between the sisters, an act of treachery so vicious that Setareh felt she would die.

She would never forgive Lamya for stealing away the man she'd loved, to whom she'd given herself, heart, body, and soul. Nor would she forgive the man who'd whispered such convincing lies. The betrayal was impossible to ignore or to forget. Over the months that followed, every moment of every day seemed uniquely dedicated to the task of reminding her of this humiliation. Their mutual friends closed ranks against Lamya for a time, recognizing the unpardonable breach of faith, and offered Setareh consolation as best they could. They spoke with her in hushed tones and smiled bravely for her and told her she would find happiness one day, the man she'd promised herself to had proven unworthy of her love, better done with him now rather than later. They saw her as the good sister wronged by the one who'd learned to use her beauty as a spider uses its web.

Three months after the betrayal, Setareh sat waiting for one of these friends at a coffee shop near their childhood home when Arman took a seat across from her and said his heart was still hers. He'd committed a terrible mistake; he was in love with her, not Lamya. Could he ever right this wrong? This roused in Setareh such a fury that the owner of the shop rushed from the back room with a knife in his hand, believing a thief had entered his establishment. She rose from the table, apologized to the shop owner for the disturbance, and told her sister's husband that neither his nor her sister's name would ever cross her lips again. She no longer had a sister, she said. "You do not exist."

FOUR MONTHS LATER Setareh rented a flat in the 7th arrondissement in Paris and began her studies in the international languages program at the Sorbonne. The routine she found for herself helped calm the obsessive thinking about what had driven her from home. She immersed herself in the rhythms of life in the French capital, in her studies, in reading. After her classes were done for the day, she explored the city and took to visiting the bookshop on rue de Verneuil, directly across from the attic flat where Faron Jones sat at his window trying to write his novel—this fact known to neither of them until Setareh read his book many years later and understood with a lightning bolt of comprehension that it was her whom his protagonist had fallen in love with during that lonely year in Paris.

At first, before she recognized herself in the story, she'd enjoyed discovering the names of the streets and cafés that were familiar to her as they appeared on the page. She was reminded of the city she'd fled to following her romantic defeat, but now that difficult year was turned warmly nostalgic by the passing of time. When the young hero of the novel first entered the bookshop she remembered so well, she was filled with delight. It was called La Porte Rouge, on rue de Verneuil, and named only after a hundred-some pages, and upon reading the name of the shop, she pressed the book to her chest and closed her eyes in a dignified surrender to her youth and recalled the many silent evenings she'd spent browsing and reading in that enchanted place.

It was a haven for people like her who sought the comfort of books. The owner was a petite American woman named Sylvia who'd been in Paris for over forty years and didn't think at all about going home again. She was home, she said, among these books and the people who loved them. Setareh wondered what had become of the woman, and when she resumed reading, she was delighted again when, seated by the window at his silent typewriter, the narrator saw a young woman enter La Porte Rouge for the first time. He waited up there, watching the red door of the shop, and then he followed his curiosity down to the street and entered the store. He watched her take a book from a shelf and walk to the back of the room, where she sat on the cabriole sofa beside the little jade plant that Setareh herself had sometimes quietly dusted when the owner of the shop wasn't looking. She saw herself as she had been at the time, young and in retreat from love, sitting just as the woman in the novel was. She remembered the purple fabric of the sofa and the paintings and photographs on the walls and the slow creaking of the wooden floors as customers browsed from one shelf to the next. And then the convergence of art and life revealed itself to Setareh when the narrator watched the young woman remove a handkerchief from her shoulder bag and begin to wipe dust from the jade's leaves.

Within pages she knew beyond a doubt that it was her whom the hero of the novel waited for every evening at his window, though it was impossible to believe the world might contain such a marvellous occurrence as this. But the details were too perfect, too often: the blue paisley shawl tied with a rosette twist on the left side of the young woman's head; the handwoven galesh slides she wore; the leather shoulder bag with dragonfly embroidery. She recognized herself in the routine of her evening visits too, always arriving at the bookshop just after seven, and always pausing to study the display window before entering; and the way, regardless of the weather, she wiped her feet three times on the doormat before she pushed open the red door. Her browsing habits were observed and described with great care, and how she slipped off her shoes and tucked her feet up under her when she sat on the couch beside the potted jade at the back of the room. When she made a purchase of a book, which was often—but always in deference to her monthly budget—she did so on a Saturday, depending on what was left over after doing her food shopping for the week.

She read the novel in one sitting and knew as she landed on the last paragraph that she would bring this book to life in her language, both for the fact that it had moved her so deeply, and for the fact that its author had captured her in her youth in such a surprising way.

The final pages recounted her last visit to the bookshop before she left Paris as she herself remembered it. She'd bought the French translation of Turgenev's *Spring Torrents*, which told of a man in his later years so relentlessly tortured by the nostalgia of lost love that his life no longer meant anything to him. The bookseller named Sylvia wrapped it in brown parcel paper and cupped Setareh's hand in hers for a long moment, speaking to her as Setareh nodded, listening. The narrator observed this moment from his position next to a bookshelf, knowing it was his last opportunity to speak with the mysterious young woman. And yet he did not act, not for fear or nerves, but for the sharp desire to capture this moment and cling to it forever. She was the perfect embodiment of all that he would ever aspire to and yet never hold. It was a naive and idealistic fantasy, but as she read the ending of the novel, she loved and admired the undamaged heart of the young man who'd observed her with such care and gentle patience.

She'd sat in the glow of the book afterwards and wondered how long the author had been able to safeguard the purity of that moment before his life steered him inevitably into the harder realities of adulthood. But already at that young age, he'd known too well what she herself would only learn much later: that some lives were too fragile to risk the sorrows of love. The hero never saw Setareh's face clearly—he'd said so in the novel—always partially hidden as it was by the shawls she wore, not in religious observance but as a symbol of her solemn retreat from the world. She wondered what direction the story would have gone if he'd stepped bravely out from the shadows and offered a salve against the betrayals she'd suffered. What a different turn her life might have taken. She wondered who he was, if she'd ever noticed him, consciously, watching her from across the room. She'd smiled at more than one handsome young man at La Porte Rouge, of course, but she'd never spoken to anyone except the bookseller herself. The author's photograph on the back of the book showed the face of a young man staring into the camera with an intent gaze, still more boyish than handsome, an attractive and trusting face, but not a face she recognized.

She didn't tell Faron who she was a month later when they met for the first time after he'd signed over the translation rights. Her silence was an act of deception, yes, but to tell the writer who she was would threaten to alter the novel. It would change the ending of the story, and so she held her silence as she sat across from him at the various Toronto restaurants they took to meeting in, and slowly she fell in love with the man who'd written so beautifully of his tender obsession with the young woman she once was.

SHE TRANSFERRED HER studies from the Sorbonne in Paris to the Université de Montréal after that lonely year and in the spring she met a young man who'd spent eighteen months in Haiti with Médecins Sans Frontières and was now in Montreal to speak at a university recruitment drive on behalf of the association. His name was Mikkel Austerlitz. They traded idle comments about the cafeteria food while standing in line at a lunch counter, and when he asked if he could join her—they were both alone—they set their trays across from one another at a table by the windows with a view to Mount Royal and spent the rest of the afternoon talking about Haiti and Paris and Tehran. Later in the evening, after a walk in the old town, she felt a playfulness that was entirely new to her when he let down her hair in his hotel room and told her with a smile that he had a feeling that, as of this moment, they were both happily doomed. She was not a virgin on what they would later refer to as their wedding night, but she discovered that what she'd hurriedly learned from Arman about the act of love had been nothing but its simple mechanics. Here, a world was unlocked for the young lovers. And in the thrilling curiosities of its new pleasures, Mikkel and Setareh found their perfect match. They met every night that week, and when the recruiting drive ended, he stayed another ten days, until he was obliged to return to Haiti and she to her regular life as a student at the university.

They saw each other when they could in the years that followed. He came to Montreal three or four times a year and she joined him for weeks at a time in Port-au-Prince and Kigali and

La Paz. Finally, after twelve years, she came to Toronto, where he'd accepted a post at a downtown hospital. They did not marry. Neither had any use for the idea. They were already wed, besides, according to the private mythology they held between them.

Setareh followed her sister's career with the wintery emotions of one who knew too much time had passed and circumstances were too altered for them to re-enter each other's life. She struggled with this truth, but knew enough to let their lives continue on their separate paths. She never told Mikkel of the sister who'd betrayed her, or even of the betrayal in any general sense. Her life was filled otherwise with the love of a good and interesting man and a career that challenged and sustained her. She worked steadily as a medical translator in the hospitals and clinics around the city, once presiding over the surgery performed on a Parkinson's patient who was kept awake during the operation so that a series of questions could be directed at him while the surgeon probed for damaged pathways. As she interpreted these questions, masked and standing at the foot of the operating table, the upper fifth of the patient's skull removed like a bone-white bottle top, and then interpreted the answers, she feared that any word wrongly translated, however slightly, might lead to some neurological catastrophe. Her work as a literary translator introduced no such drama into her life. It was a quiet and cerebral passion that she pursued not for remuneration but for her love of the languages she worked in and the novels and poetry she admired.

In their home on the island, a short ferry ride from the city, they lived happily, peacefully, and took pleasure in the small routines and patterns of everyday life. They travelled together, not often to begin with once they settled in Toronto, but in the years that followed, they grew weary of the northern winters and began spending time in Buenos Aires, where Mikkel owned a one-bedroom flat that looked east over the great Rio de la Plata estuary.

ON THE MORNING of her forty-second birthday, Setareh Azad received a message from the man who'd betrayed her many years before in Tehran. It was a simple happy birthday message, like any of the dozens she received that day on social media, and said nothing to suggest the history they shared. She ignored it, resisting the urge to open his LinkedIn profile. Instead, she read some recent stories he'd filed on the BBC Persian website. Three months later, at Nowruz, another message appeared, similarly pleasant, similarly anodyne. This too she ignored. That evening, as she celebrated the Persian New Year with Mikkel, she tried not to think about her sister and the years that separated them now. The past was the past, she reminded herself. She was happy with her life and felt no need to look back. She would do nothing foolish. The past would stay where it belonged, in distant memory.

The messages continued to arrive with greeting-card regularity on various significant dates of the Persian and Western calendars. At last, when the telephone call came, she was so unnerved to hear his voice that she said nothing, only held the phone to her ear, as if frozen in time. He said he wanted to see her. She held her silence and hung up, but an hour later she pressed redial, disturbed by her rude behaviour. It rang six times before a man picked up and told her she'd reached the editorial office at BBC Persian. She said a man named Arman Khajenouri had called her from this line. The voice asked her to wait, and then she heard her first love say her name.

After a stuttering pause, she apologized for hanging up. It was a shock to hear from him after so many years, she said.

He understood completely, and was sorry for bothering her, but he was doing some research on a story in a certain country in South America, he said, and wondered if she'd like to meet. He'd seen her posted photographs of Buenos Aires. He knew she was there now. He was flying in a few days. For security reasons, if she agreed, he would call from a pay phone when he landed, and they could arrange a meeting, but he had absolutely no expectations, he said.

What harm can it do? she thought.

The following morning she found a text on her phone inviting her to click on a link to a gallery of pictures from the London Book Fair that she'd attended last March. She deleted the text—she had no idea who the sender was—but the no-click Pegasus spyware had already installed itself on her phone. Five days later, when Arman texted from Montevideo, their exchange was not the private matter they thought it was.

ON THE AFTERNOON he saw Setareh Azad disembark from the ferry in Montevideo, Arman Khajenouri immediately regretted the nostalgia that had compelled him to arrange this meeting. It was not for his safety or hers that he felt this regret, but for the fact that in seeing her again after so long he realized he was a sentimental old fool. He waved to catch her attention, and as she approached, he saw in her eyes that he was much diminished from who he'd been when she knew him. He'd not aged well. He looked like an old man already, no longer young nor handsome nor self-assured. And now, placed beside this woman whose self-confidence and beauty had grown just as his had fallen away, she would only see the man he no longer was. Time had not treated them equally. She still walked with a sway in her hip in a manner that was unconscious to her but aroused in him the unachievable desires of a younger man. His marriage was ending, he would tell her, and it was true; it had been ending for a long time. In the way of these things, cast adrift from his wife's attentions, he'd turned to the past, and in the past he'd found the memory of Setareh Azad. Would she take back this regretful old fool? In the compliant mythology he'd created about them while lost in the desert of his dying marriage, he'd assembled this fantasy and lived within it for so long that it became a plan he was willing to test.

Now, in the bright morning at the pier in Montevideo, he regretted all this and felt clownish and inept with his loose belly and mop-grey hair and ten-cent smile. She was kind. She didn't mock him as he deserved, but he would feel aged and at a disadvantage to walk with her through the city; he might even be mistaken for her father or uncle, the difference was so acute between them now, his murderers already watching, and she permitted him to link his arm in hers as in the old style when men courted women, and she was pleased despite herself to see the man as a harmless collector of memories, his betrayal of her deep in the past and reduced in the filtering light of history.

They walked together up from the port past the Point Terminal, where passengers and mariners and members of the Iranian intelligence agency lingered, and on into the city that would see his death before midnight the following day.

They sat on a terrace at the edge of a green park of swing sets and a carousel and watched the pigeons peck at fallen crusts and puddles splashed from a fountain. He talked about his life and his journalism, and finally about Setareh's sister and her work in the film industries in France and America that had brought her such renown, and how with each new project and her growing fame he'd felt her moving further away from him. He was not guiltless, of course, he said. He'd made far too many mistakes in his life to pretend otherwise. They lived as strangers now and had done so for years. She was remote and glamorous and cold to him, and he was helplessly drawn to the past, stuck there at the moment of his life's greatest regret until he understood that he might be released from the shame of his heartless betrayal of Setareh if only he came to her in a spirit of humility and regret. She was more beautiful than he remembered, he told her.

"You are an old fool," she said, "but a sweet old fool."

He smiled, nodding, and told her he had no right to contact her. He apologized and thanked her again for crossing from Buenos Aires. He knew she was married to a handsome man, a surgeon, no less. It looked like they were happy together—he'd seen their pictures—and he knew enough not to presume anything; he was simply a wounded soul looking for comfort in his past.

She did not bother to correct his misconception that they were married. It didn't matter. They were happy, she said. She'd told Mikkel about the purpose of her visit to Montevideo, that it was to meet an old flame long extinguished. He was not a jealous or unreasonable man, she said.

"Yes, I hated you both," she said. "Love at that age makes us all equally blind and selfish. I hated myself as much as I hated you and my sister. It was a heartless betrayal, what you did. But it's too long ago now to hate anyone. Now there is only emptiness. I feel nothing at all. I'm sorry about you and Lamya. Hers is a different world from mine. I no longer know my sister. Not at all. And look at us. It seems we're the little people she lived among once upon a time."

He didn't speak about the story that had brought him to the Uruguayan capital, and she didn't ask after he told her it had something to do with back home. They talked about the old days and about the mutual friends neither of them had seen in years. She didn't want to speak of the difficult politics in their country. It was like speaking of the air or the darkness at night, always the same. They dined early at a small restaurant on a wide street busy with pedestrians. They ate cuttlefish and Galician-style octopus on potatoes and shared a bottle of wine and found a few pleasant memories to linger over before it was time for her to leave.

He walked her back to the port, where she caught the eight p.m. ferry, and watched the lights of the boat sail out into the estuary and knew this was the last time he would see Setareh Azad, though he did not know how close he was to the end of his life, the assassins already there, waiting. He walked slowly back to his hotel and looked over his notes in preparation for his meeting the following day with Ardeshir Abbasi, the physicist who'd disappeared from his post at the Malek Ashtar University of Technology. He calmly smoked a cigarette on his balcony and watched the night sky and felt the great regret of the aging lothario who'd betrayed the only chance at love he'd ever had.

ON THE FERRY back to Buenos Aires that evening, after she messaged Mikkel that she'd boarded safely, Setareh took the stairs to the upper deck to feel the sea air on her face. It was a warm January night, so pleasant here compared to the hard winters in the north. There were only a few passengers on board up top, backpackers and business commuters. Most gravitated to the railing on the port side to see the big water below, and out beyond, the dizzying breadth of the Atlantic Ocean. She was grateful for the brief return to her past that was this visit with

Arman Khajenouri, for in it she'd been reminded of the life she'd narrowly escaped. He was selfish and cowardly, and now, worse, a pitiable man frightened by the reality of his vanished youth, drawn to a distant memory of love to escape the emptiness he'd created in his life.

As the ferry neared the port of Buenos Aires, she stepped away from the railing, serene in these thoughts, and saw a paperback book abandoned or forgotten on a seat, its cover lifting and falling in the breeze. The upper deck had cleared now; she was the last one up there in the open air. She picked up the book and saw the title—*Strangers at the Red Door*—and read the jacket copy, which told of a young man's vividly rendered year in Paris and the unrequited love affair that consumes his life. She turned to page one and read the first paragraph, and then the second, and liked it enough to slip it into her shoulder bag.

The wind came up in a surprising gust and she descended to the exit, where she found Mikkel waiting for her at the bottom of the gangway. He greeted her with a kiss and together they walked arm in arm through the melancholy streets in the direction of home.

NINETEEN

LAMYA KHAJENOURI WAITED FOR FARON TO SAY SOMETHING. THE Imperial Room was quiet, the blue flame in the gas fireplace a soft, wavering glow.

She'd known nothing of her sister's short visit to Montevideo, only that the Uruguayan authorities carrying out the investigation suspected that a phone had been used to track her husband. Whom it belonged to they had no idea. They tested the devices of those in Arman Khajenouri's circle, and then, four years after the murders, the family relation between the sisters was discovered in the leaked document that was found to contain the surname Azad, which the famous film director and actress had abandoned years earlier when she married Arman Khajenouri in Cyprus, an act intended to set her identity apart from the sister she knew she'd wronged.

After she was informed of the discovery of her family name on the leaked document, and it was then confirmed that the Pegasus spyware had been found on her sister's phone, Lamya wondered for only a moment if this was a story about the wronged woman exacting revenge on the sister who'd betrayed her many years ago. Had she waited decades to finally and triumphantly lay this retribution at her sister's feet? It was an impossible theory of vengeance for the woman Lamya knew her sister to be. Even from this far remove of half a lifetime, she knew that Setareh was incapable of the sort of betrayal she herself had committed. But why Setareh had spoken to Arman she could not begin to imagine.

"But an affair, no, never," she said.

Faron stared at the blue flame in the fireplace, trying to make sense of all this, and then he turned a hard look on her. "This is between sisters, if there's any truth in what you say. I don't know why you're telling me this. Or why she wouldn't have told me."

He'd been annoyed at first when he understood that a lie had been used to lure him here, but Setareh's silence on the matter of Montevideo was of far greater consequence. He'd been told nothing of this until now, if it was true—that a story of murder had woven itself into Setareh's life. It was a cold statement of how little he might know her. She rarely spoke of her years back in Iran. For so long he'd believed this was due to the trauma left by the war and the venomous morality police who plucked women from the street with casual brutality. It seemed equally apparent now that she spoke little about her life at all. Desperately, he looked for a charitable explanation. Perhaps it was a feeling of remorse for her role in Arman's and Abbasi's deaths that had kept her silent. Didn't that make sense? Her phone had been used without her knowledge to lead the assassins to their prize; she could not be blamed for that. But the holes in what he knew about her life were suddenly filled with suspicion.

"As a writer of other people's stories, you're bound by confidentiality with respect to your potential clients. Their vanity demands your discretion. I understand that. But it was not my vanity that required your silence. It was my shame. Yes, it was a lie that brought you here. But you wouldn't have come otherwise."

"You've wasted my time," he said. "I don't even know why you're telling me any of this."

He was ready to leave now. There'd been too many games, too much subterfuge.

"Your novel."

"What about it?" he said impatiently.

"That's why I asked you to come. I read all the books my sister translates. First in the original, then her translation. This is my only contact with her. I hear her voice in her translations. It comforts me to hear the voice of the sister I no longer have. The book that interests me is the one Setareh is translating for you. She posts about the books she translates."

Silence hung for a moment.

"So what?" he said.

"I'm trapped here, the hopeful shut-in, as you were, seated at your window as you waited for Setareh every evening to enter La Porte Rouge."

He stared at her, confusion on his face.

"In your novel, she's the young woman your hero falls in love with the year after I betrayed her. The one who you loved. The one you waited for and created stories about. The one you perhaps love now. And the one who loves you."

The expression on his face told her he'd had no idea who Setareh was.

"I'm sorry," she said slowly. "I thought you knew."

"And what, she just magically steps out of the past like that?"

"Magically, no. She read your book and found you."

"You couldn't know this. Neither of you could. Sometimes we imagine ourselves and the people we know in the books we read. There's nothing unusual in that."

"But this is more than imagining," she said.

She told him she'd been intrigued by certain details that his hero noticed about the young woman he was infatuated with in his novel. And then she began to see the parallels to what she knew about her sister's life in Paris from the letters Setareh had sent to their friends, who after closing ranks against Lamya began to speak to her again. The letters told of evenings at a bookshop called La Porte Rouge on rue de Verneuil, where she sometimes spoke with the woman named Sylvia who owned the shop and invited the young people who came there to sit and read for as long as they liked. These letters had been shared with Lamya not as gossip but out of concern for the sisters torn asunder in a battle of the heart.

But this was still only the suggestion of the truth, Lamya said, the threads of conjecture not so completely tied off as to be declared fact, until she found Setareh's Farsi Twitter posts where she commented on the books she translated. In a series of posts, she described finding the novel that someone had left behind somewhere, and then herself forgetting about it for years, until she saw it again, tucked away on one of her bookshelves. In a later tweet, she wondered if the world had ever seen the publication of a novel translated by one of its very own characters.

"*In the chaos around us there lie invisible bridges between life and art.* These are my sister's words," Lamya said. "Your novel was widely published. Where she found it I have no idea. From then on, she pursued you. This isn't magic. This isn't coincidence. Coincidence reunites characters at the end of a story, not at the beginning, when it brings people together for the first time. Why she kept this from you is a question I can only guess at."

Faron stared at her in dismay and confusion. Setareh wouldn't have kept this from him, he thought; he could see no reason to. For their fates to be as determined to bring them together as Lamya Khajenouri's claims suggested could be no less than a victory to be celebrated, not a failing to be secreted away. Years ago, he'd become so inexorably and lovingly obsessed with a beautiful stranger that he'd written her into his novel, and now, impossibly, they'd met and fallen in love.

"There's no good reason for her not to tell me if it were true," he said.

"Perhaps to preserve the integrity of the ending of the story.

Perfect lovers destined never to meet. The eternal longing of unrequited love must be preserved—isn't that what your hero decides when he watches her buy the Turgenev novel on her last day at the shop?"

"I was a boy in love with a fantasy."

"You were a great artist."

The comment shocked him. How far he'd wandered from his first lofty ambitions he could barely understand. He was neither young nor a great artist anymore. The courage of youth had left him long ago. Wisdom perhaps had installed itself where courage had once burned, but wisdom was tired and cautious and grey.

She got up and walked to the cabinet where she'd prepared their tea. She pulled open a drawer, removed a folder, and returned to her seat.

"I made films before I became a prisoner here. You know this. I intend to make them again. The impasse will not last forever."

She handed him the folder.

"You see, I've brought you here as a petition for my sister's forgiveness."

"What is this?"

"Through you, through your novel, and through this"—she gestured to the folder—"through this, two sisters can end their long silence."

He broke the seal and removed the unbound screenplay.

"You see, the young woman narrates the film I want to make,"

Lamya said. "She must tell the story. It's her turn to speak. Her voice is the voice I hear in her letters home. This is how I step back into my sister's life. This is my plea for redemption. I'm asking for your help."

He'd been played in a game he didn't know existed—not even a player, but a pawn moved between opponents who'd expertly held their secrets. And as he thought this, he felt the strange otherness come over him again, as if to warn him that the game was not yet finished, that he was still being played, a note of caution being sounded. He rose abruptly, startled by the sensation, and the unbound script spilled onto the floor. The pages were wildly out of order now as he took a knee and piled them back together and stuffed them into the folder.

"I think you'll have to do this without me," he said, standing again.

"Without your novel, this story goes no further. There can be no film. The future dies here."

"I'm sorry," he said.

He became aware of a muffled ringing, like an infant's muted cry, and remembered his phone. He crossed the room and reached under the seat cushion, but it had fallen silent again. He waited for the caller to leave their message, and then he listened to the voice of his mother's caregiver. She was staying on with her long into the night, she said; her condition had taken a violent turn. He should come immediately if he wanted to be there at the end.

"I have to go," he said, slipping the folder into his satchel.

"Can I do anything? Can I help?" Lamya said.

She walked with him down the hall, to where a young woman informed him that Mr. Saito had been pulled away on urgent business and that she would escort him out. She led him and Ms. Khajenouri to the cage-style lift and down to the lower floor, through the administrative offices to the reception area, and stood silently with them while they waited for the elevator. He nodded absently when Ms. Khajenouri wished him luck. "And please let me know," she said.

He boarded and pressed Lobby.

As the lift began its descent, he knew his mother might be gone before he got back, but he would try; there was no way he would not try.

His thoughts were crowded now with what he'd just been told about his mother's sudden sharp decline. He tried to clear his mind of these and to think positively. He'd make it back in time, yes, and maybe the charmed fate he'd longed for only a few minutes ago might also afford such miracles as the one he was hoping for now. But the fantasy that his mother might rally long enough to provide him the closure he needed was a naive and selfish idea.

The elevator slowed and came to a stop, and the doors opened to a view of Mr. Saito and three uniformed police officers speaking with building security. As he walked through the lobby past Mr. Saito, he hit the number that had just called his phone. The same voice that had left the message answered. Yes, she said, she was at his mother's bedside now. It was not possible to tell how long she had left, but her pain was being managed, and she was resting.

He hung up as he met the revolving door sideways, pushing through with his right shoulder, and the momentum of the door clipped his heel and galloped him forward, causing him to stumble into the arms of a woman who was just then attempting to enter the building. He didn't have time to notice the sports coat she was wearing or the raw skin of her chaffed wrists as they fell together. He didn't notice her general state of dishevelment after a night of sleeping rough in Shenzhen and the crossing from the mainland and the hard walk on the coastal road. He didn't notice any of these physical things—the beautiful eyes and tonsured scalp and ragged clothing—as they stumbled together on that spring afternoon of the Pure Brightness Festival.

What he did notice at that instant, as Mildred Chen herself did, was that every detail, every thought, every first and last emotion they'd lived and known as their own private experience was now shared, each perfectly in sync with the other in that lightning flash when the spirit of Jiang Ming appeared and placed his glowing hands on their heads and apologized for all the trouble he'd caused; it certainly wasn't meant to be as complicated as this, he said. The moment rolled forward at a leisurely pace as they fell, unaffected by the pedestrian logic of time, and in that instant they each knew the joys and sorrows of the others, and together the three travelled back to the beginning of their lives, when the world was so fresh and unknown that language was not yet theirs and they could only point to the shapes that fascinated them; and so too was the world naive beyond reckoning, a pure burning innocence, and here they lived on in perfect balance in this unusual trinity of souls, glowing and uproariously free. Soon they would untangle and dust themselves off and face one another as strangers at the entrance of One Exchange Square, and the spirit of the dead novelist would finally be released into the sweet hereafter. But for now, held in this long moment of the mighty everlasting, they were finally and for an eternal instant united as their purest selves.

AFTER FARON HELPED her to her feet, they stared at each other for a moment, bashful as old friends following a reckless indiscretion. The air between them crackled with energy, and in languages unknown to the other, they began apologizing for their clumsiness. The blindfold had obscured much of her face, but yes, it was her; he could see it in the shaved head and his sports coat and the mouth and lips he'd watched so closely when she'd tried to communicate her unspoken message.

He told her it was him, the man from the train station, he'd seen her not once but twice, actually falling over her the second time, but the gift of language had vanished and so he pantomimed a blindfold being tied over his eyes and pointed to his wrists, and then to hers, and a shiver of sympathy rose up his spine when he saw the abrasions there. She nodded—yes, she remembered his face, she'd whispered her apologies into his ear, and taken his jacket—but she was unsure of his intentions now, and she picked up the ball cap that had fallen from her head and started for the revolving doors. He called to her and retrieved the copy of the novel from his satchel and raised it in the air.

"I think this is yours. Please, take it," he said.

When she saw the book in the stranger's hand, she felt such a powerful release of emotion that she let out an audible gasp, nearly reduced to tears. The terror she'd felt over these unbearable days lifted and she was filled with gratitude that fate had chosen not to abandon her completely, that she should be reunited with the book that had shaped her life, that now, in these difficult and marvellous parallels, *was* her life. She nodded and thanked him, attempting to regain herself, and he passed it to her and she held it close to her chest, and then she turned and Faron watched her disappear through the revolving doors.

THE METROPOLE LOBBY was busy with young people spinning their cubes when Faron got back to the hotel just after five that afternoon. The urgency of his situation had returned to him now, since his encounter with the woman in front of One Exchange Square. While in the cab on his way back to the hotel he'd left a message for his sister and called his agent, asking to get him on the next flight home. He considered calling Setareh, but it was still too early in Toronto. He typed out a quick message to say what was happening and hit send as the cab pulled into the car port.

Now, the girl named Xiao Hui from the elevator bounded

up to him and spoke in a language he could make no sense of. Her face was agleam. She showed him her ribbon and the small trophy shaped as a Rubik's Cube. It was a first prize in her age category.

"Fantastic," he said.

She drew a strange face for him and waited, then spoke again in long, bewildering rhythms.

"I'm sorry," he said. "I don't—"

She answered his stubbornness with an even more perplexing barrage of Chinese. When he raised his hands in surrender, she scrunched up her face in exasperation, then romped triumphantly back to her circle of friends.

At the elevators, he checked his cell for messages. There was still nothing from his sister, just an email confirmation for the flight his agent had booked him on. He pocketed his phone.

The elevator doors opened and out stepped Gideon Kastner. "You're looking frazzled. You okay?" he said.

Perhaps Faron could summon a courteous minute for the man who'd told his fantastic story about the transmigration of souls.

"I'm flying out tonight," he said. "There's a family situation back home."

"Sorry to hear it."

"Thank you," Faron said, holding the door.

"I see you're travelling alone now. That glow you had . . ."

Faron regarded the man with a confused look.

"Nothing, nothing. That was fast—good for you," he said. "You don't have time for a drink, I don't suppose."

"I'm afraid not," Faron said.

"Well, then, it was a pleasure."

They shook hands.

"*You owe it to us all to get on with what you're good at,*" Gideon said. "That's Auden's best advice, as well as mine."

"I'll remember that," Faron said.

He stepped into the elevator and nodded goodbye, and the doors closed between them.

TWENTY

MILDRED SLIPPED INTO A BLUE SMOCK SHE TOOK FROM AN UNtended housekeeping cart in the lobby at One Exchange Square and rolled the cart past the police and officials conferring at the reception desk. The hat brim pulled low over her eyes, she waited for the elevator to arrive, and then ascended to the Japanese consulate, where a sense of urgency quickly spread when she revealed her copy of the banned novel and stated her request for political asylum.

She was a bookseller and the publisher of New Light Editions, she told the officials who gathered around, forcibly carried over the border to the mainland and drugged and kept against her will and made to sign a document waiving her right to speak with a lawyer or a family member. After a brief round of questioning, they escorted her into a back office and gave her a glass of water and waited for her to speak again. She was a piteous sight, her nerves so jagged that her hands trembled visibly when she spoke about the forced medical examination and the sham video confession and the handcuffs and blindfold. She described the warder and her escape, and soon her identity and the alert and arrest warrant issued by the mainland authorities were verified by the consulate. Into the second hour of her interrogation, as she was escorted down a hallway, she noticed a woman in an adjacent office sitting quietly at a computer console. She'd seen a photograph of the Iranian dissident only once, moments before she herself was detained at the crossing, but it was enough for her to know who this was. Ms. Khajenouri's dark hair had taken on a dusting of silver since that UN address, and she was thinner—the stress of living under a death sentence, Mildred thought—but she was a poised and beautiful woman who could not be mistaken for anyone else. She looked up from the computer screen and smiled and emerged from the office like a butterfly from a cocoon and introduced herself as Lamya Khajenouri.

AFTER THE LAST round of interviews that day, she showed Mildred to the kitchenette lounge one floor above the main consular offices and prepared for her a sandwich and bowl of instant noodles while the new arrival washed her face and hands at the sink. It was likely she hadn't eaten in days. From the officials she'd spoken with, Lamya had learned something of Mildred's situation—that she was a Hong Kong publisher and bookseller and had been illegally detained—and now, as she set the cafeteria-style tray of food on the kitchenette table, Lamya removed the phone from her pocket and pushed it across to Mildred.

"Call your people," she said in English. "They need to know you're safe."

The bookseller, to Lamya's mind, had the appearance of a roadside traveller, her clothing too well-worn, the exhaustion and stress clearly written on her face. The shaved head and badly chaffed wrists suggested a cruelty she could only begin to imagine. The hunger could wait, it seemed. The poor woman picked up the phone and dialled.

After three years in the consulate, Lamya had some Cantonese—she mostly spoke English and French with the staff here—but she would have understood the emotion in Mildred's voice in any language. The bookseller was speaking with an aunt, she knew that word, and *sorry* and *worried* and *police,* but not the word for *handcuffs* or *blindfold.* She stood at the window, listening, and when Mr. Saito entered the room, called away from the negotiations in the lobby, he joined Lamya and waited patiently until Mildred ended her phone call and set the phone on the table.

They shook hands and he welcomed her on behalf of the government of Japan. He regretted the makeshift living quarters, he said, indicating the cot that had been hastily set up in the corner of the room. They were doing everything possible to arrange something more agreeable, and private, and one of the female staff would come around soon to see to the clothing and personal care items that were required for her stay. He provided whatever additional details he could about the official process that was now being set in motion to support her case. She thanked him, and now she sat at the table and ate the meal Lamya had prepared for her.

THE MYSTERIES OF the two languages that stood between them invited a child's unguarded creativity—there was much hand-gesturing—and the slow settled patience of the wise. That first evening in the Imperial Room, before Mr. Saito appeared with the news about the ultimatum, the distant memory of the high school English that Mildred believed had completely abandoned her began slowly to return. They shared a pot of the chai nabat that was said to be the magic cure for all and found that Lamya's phone, too, was useful in breaking down those mysteries. It sat on the chessboard between them, like some charmed talking stone, and with Mildred's rudimentary English and Lamya's phone, they asked and offered more than the simple outlines of their lives. And then the door opened and Mr. Saito crossed the room with a smile and shared the news that Beijing had agreed to quietly issue a face-saving statement regarding the suspension of its deadline. Lamya rose and embraced him. What powerful negotiating tools he and others had employed she would never know, but she felt such a deep relief on that night, and in the following days, that she would pause in the middle of some domestic task, brushing her teeth or putting on a pair of shoes, and consciously give thanks that she was still alive.

The day after the ultimatum was suspended, Mildred's aunt

came to the consulate and saw her niece for the first time since her disappearance. They sat together talking quietly, settled now after a reunion that had seemed on the surface one of pure relief and joy but carried with it the unspoken truth that the sinister forces that had disturbed her life so profoundly had not been defeated, but only temporarily stalled. Mildred told the story of her abduction and then listened as her aunt spoke of how the authorities had come to the shop every day since her disappearance to confiscate boxes of books they wouldn't have cared about only weeks ago. It was retribution and a warning to any bookseller foolish enough to stick their neck out as they had. Her aunt had barely enough time to inform their associates at New Light Editions that a raid was coming, she said, but at last they'd been able to clear out the small office near the City University of anything incriminating. All of them were frightened but unbowed. They would find a way to continue.

"BUT WE MIGHT lose everything," Mildred said when she told her aunt about the plan she'd been turning over in her mind. She believed it was the right thing to do, she said, but she would do nothing without her agreement.

Her aunt had built up the bookshop over decades. In it was held her every first and last dream; it was her livelihood and her lifeblood, and out of it had grown the fearless small press that published the books her niece carried over the frontier. She was sixty-nine years old now and tired easily. Sometimes she toyed with the idea of stepping back. The body was one concern, yes, but fear did not enter the equation.

"The hornet's nest has already been stirred," she said. "Do not hold your tongue any longer."

THE PRESS CONFERENCE was held in the consulate's media room the following day. Members of the local and international news services crowded the small space and raised their hands like a classroom of eager freshmen after Mildred Chen spoke about her illegal detention and forced removal from Hong Kong to the mainland. With her aunt at her side, she named the booksellers who'd been disappeared before her, one of whom was still missing to this very day, and spoke of the psychological torture she'd been subjected to and of her escape and the crossing back to Hong Kong. The AP and Reuters were there, as were *The Economist* and the *Hong Kong Free Press* and the *Oriental Daily News*. The senior correspondent from BBC *Newsnight* out of Hong Kong asked for the name of the novel she'd attempted to carry over the border. She lifted it from the lectern and held it high above her head. It was from that day on that Jiang Ming's *Beijing Soul Asylum* became widely known as the most dangerous book in China.

THAT EVENING, AFTER the press conference, Lamya and Mildred sat again in the Imperial Room and spoke into the talking stone, speculating how this new pressure on Beijing might affect their lives in this consular prison. They nervously watched the Twitter feeds reporting on the story rack up their frenzied shares and breathless comments. The city was outraged that yet another of its citizens had been subjected to the extraordinary rendition that was in direct violation of the Basic Law of the Hong Kong Special Administrative Region. *Never back down. Never surrender,* they said.

Lamya tried to describe to Mildred what life in Iran had been like in her youth and the outrage and resentment that now burned there against the political class. Their countries were perhaps not so unlike, she said. The causes they were fighting for spoke to basic human freedoms, and maybe one day they might celebrate a shared victory. When she asked her companion if she had a young man waiting for her with whom she'd planned a future, Mildred said she was not interested in men or marriage and that in her language and culture—she typed the word into the phone—an unwed woman after the age of thirty was called "the orange at the bottom of the barrel." She was far too deep in the barrel to care, she said, and didn't mind it one bit down here with all the other oranges. The irreverence of the comment endeared her to Lamya, who typed out the equivalent phrase in Farsi.

She herself was "a pickled sour vegetable," said the talking stone, and Lamya smiled and told her there were so many old fruits and vegetables locked up in this consulate, they should start their own market garden.

It was a quip that sparked an idea.

TWENTY-ONE

FARON PARKED THE RENTAL BESIDE THE BLUE SEDAN WITH THE Victorian Order of Nurses emblem stickered on the driver's side door and got out and stood for a moment in the warming sunshine of the cool afternoon. He could see nothing had changed about the house at the end of the gravel lane; it was as it always had been, a tough, modest home, though inside it now crept the most profound change of all. The rolling fields beyond still lay unclaimed by spring growth, and the line of poplars that marked the gravel drive held steady in the light breeze. On the rural road, up through the trees, a car sailed past, and then the quiet of the day returned.

The silvered outbuildings behind the house, humbled and bruised by another long Ontario winter, sat in stalled expectation, gates and doors hanging open, the industry of a previous season cruelly interrupted by his mother's abrupt change in circumstances. Beside the compost heap the wheelbarrow he'd used on many occasions was positioned tray down where he'd left it in the fall, a single spade reclined loyally against its fat wheel. The pond he'd dug years ago in front of the house was thick with the skeletal remains of last year's cattails. Soon it would be alive again with the music of frogs and blackbirds. In the strips of grass off the gravel lane and at the edges of the path leading to the house, bashful welts of crocus and bluebells were emerging. These were new here since Hong Kong—eight, nine days. The cold earth was pushing new colours into the world.

He walked up the path and visored his eyes close to the window and saw the hospital home-care bed and the dim flicker of the television. A dark form crossed the room and stopped and turned in his direction. His mother was there, sleeping on the bed, a sheet pulled to her shoulders.

The nurse opened the door and greeted him and he stood beside the bed and touched his mother's warm hand and waited for her to stir. She was even thinner now, her cheekbones rising through the taut skin, the death mask already hinting at its final sad measure. The infusion pump at her bedside controlled the drip rate of morphine sulphate and electrolytes into her blood—this her one last connection to the outside world, he thought—and when he lifted her hand into his own, careful not to disturb the catheter secured there by a transparent dressing, the hand felt so feather-like as to be hardly there at all.

The nurse spoke with the heavy Caribbean accent he recognized from the message he'd listened to at the consulate, and in the telephone call soon after. She seemed efficient and kind, a large woman enviably prepared for the wide spectrum of human frailty. It was odd to hear his mother's name spoken by a stranger, and he wondered if this caregiver had come to know her in ways he didn't and never would in these last few days. The end of life was the greatest confession of all.

A second bag of intravenous drip was stored in the refrigerator, but this one should be good until tomorrow, she said. She showed him how to change the bag in any case and told him she could be here in under an hour if necessary. Otherwise, she'd be back in the morning. There was nothing to do now but to wait.

HE SAT AT his mother's bedside and messaged his sister again after the woman left. The message went unanswered. It was obvious now that she was dodging his calls and ignoring his messages. In the end it would be him alone, as he'd feared, and the rift between the two women would live beyond their mother's death. In time he would forgive Jana the bitter pride that had dug itself so deeply into her heart, but not tonight, as he sat here, aggrieved and angry for the selfishness that would turn a blind eye to their mother's death.

He didn't tell his sleeping mother that he'd gone all the way to China to persuade Jana into one last kindness. Instead, he spoke that night of the weather and the heavy traffic out from the city and the bluebells coming up and the things around the property that needed tending to. He spoke of the inconsequential so that they might rest for a time from the hard truth that was coming. She slept on, cast deep in her narcotic sleep, and when somewhere out there in the dark the coyotes began their sorrowful yowling, he finally lay on the couch and waited for dawn.

IN THE MORNING, she woke up when the nurse rolled back the infusion pump to change the IV bag. She looked around the room, confused and disoriented. Faron picked up her hand and told her she was home. He was here with her, he said, and then she fell back to sleep.

HE DETOURED ON his way home after picking up supplies that afternoon and rolled up in front of the church his mother had attended since moving here almost twenty years ago. He'd come here twice, at his mother's request, to consult with the pastor on the matter of her funeral service, this shortly before his trip to see his sister. The man was a high-strung and convivial fellow who spoke well of Faron's mother and the good work she'd done with the charity he ran through the church. Now, when he saw the prayer box planted conspicuously in the lawn beside the walkway leading to the church's front entrance, he felt a hurry of anger rising in him. He slowed the car and pulled over.

It was little more than a white birdhouse propped up on a four-by-four post with a miniature A-frame roof and a fist-sized blue swing door fastened on a small silver hinge. He silenced the engine and watched the prayer box, as if daring it to spin upward into the air like the fairy drone had done. But no miracle would propel it forward into the supernatural today, no more than prayer could cure the body or cleanse the world of murderous theocracies. Lamya Khajenouri might already be under escort to Iran, for all he knew—he'd avoided looking at the news since getting back, and she'd sent no messages since their meeting. His own life had become a taunting question mark. He hadn't forgotten the alarming revelations Lamya had shared with him, and again he considered why Setareh had kept silent about her connection to the bookstore in Paris.

He'd sensed no duplicity in her when she'd wrapped her arms around him at the airport after he'd come through customs, though he was looking for it—some slightly bitter taste when she kissed him at the arrivals gate. The reason she'd told him nothing about Montevideo was clearer to him now; it was no more complicated or less profound than remorse at knowing she'd been used to lead the assassins to Arman Khajenouri and Ardeshir Abbasi. It was not about secrets, but the shame in knowing she'd been used in such a way. No, recourse to prayer and a belief in the everlasting was absurd, insulting even. After the wasting illness that had reduced his mother to near nothing, the false hope of prayer seemed only a cynical ploy designed to feed on the dying. He was not prone to anger in the least, nor contemptuous of the faith people leaned into, but he suddenly felt the need to expose the fraud for what it was.

He threw open the car door and marched up the holy lawn. Nobody was around, the street empty. He thrust his hand into the box and pulled out a fistful of ringed and lined papers, sealed envelopes, quartered foolscap, and the blue airmail onion skin from the old letter-writing days. What he would do with these he had no plan. None of this was thought through or clear in his mind. He imagined gasoline, and a match, and remembered the courage of Lamya Khajenouri. But this was foolishness, he knew, and in an instant he was overcome with shame when he looked down at the crumpled prayers in his hand and recognized this disgraceful act of vandalism.

He returned the prayers to the box and closed it, and then he saw a small blue sheet that had fallen to the grass.

It was folded in half and now creased by his outburst. When he picked it up, he saw his mother's name written on the outside fold. This caused him to hesitate. He turned and looked left and right. The church doors stood open, but no one was there.

He opened the fold and read the prayer and felt a surprising emotion take him.

It was gratitude for the fact that someone in his mother's life, a perfect stranger to him, had been moved to offer this simple, beautiful devotion. It was not the prayer so much as the strength it was meant to impart. He closed his eyes and felt shame again for invading this small house of prayer with his selfish doubt. He mumbled an apology to the box, as the woman at the station had mumbled hers into his ear, and then he slipped the prayer into his wallet and drove back to his mother's small troubled home.

SHE WAS AWAKE and holding the hand of her caregiver when he got back. He put down the bag of groceries and came to her, and the woman passed his mother's hand to him and he sat beside the bed and asked if she knew who he was.

"Oh my son, my son," she said, and her voice trailed off.

He placed his other hand on hers. "Yes, I'm here."

Later that night, when they were alone again, her breathing became hard and gasping, and then suddenly a great emptiness filled the room. He touched her cheek and whispered her name. He placed his fingers on her wrist, held them there for a minute, and then two minutes, and finally sat back in the chair, defeated and alone, and knew she was gone. She'd wanted an end to the solitude that had ruled the last months of her life. He knew the way people lived had little to do with how they wanted to die. She'd spent the last thirty years insisting on the fierce independence that had frozen his sister's heart against her. And here was the price, to die in a home that she'd filled deliberately with absence. He forgave his mother her stubborn pride and her rigid sense of personal justice, as he would forgive Jana one day, for they were equally afflicted, as he himself was, pinned as they were like butterflies in a collector's book of old, dusty grievances.

He kissed her forehead and removed the catheter from the

back of her hand, covered her face, and then he stepped into the kitchen and called his sister.

FOR THE THREE days between her passing and the afternoon of the funeral, Faron sat at his mother's kitchen table, drinking coffee and looking at photographs. He had no idea where to begin. He searched for pleasant childhood memories, but they all seemed to come back to him half formed or grey. There was no point to be made of them, no story he could tell. Once again he was faced with the challenge of writing someone else's life. This time he was stumped. He could speak of his mother's hobbies, find some parable buried within those interests. But he was not looking for parables. He would not wring pretty lies from the metaphors and symbols he saw if he squinted just so. Straight biography was likewise of little use. Her life had offered few choices, a mother at seventeen and again at twenty-one, and a headful of dreams exploded like crystal on a concrete floor. It was remarkable that she'd even had dreams, a luxury not often available to women of his mother's generation. She'd carried hers daringly on the surface in her teenage years and spoke of them with a deadly serious expression on her face. Glamorous women would vie for the privilege of wearing her designer gowns. Her name would be spoken in the fashion capitals of the world. Her classmates resented the snooty ambition. It deflated their own modest goals, she'd told her son, which ranged between secretarial college and an engagement ring. Miss Aren't-I-Wonderful would learn one day, they'd said, she'd be put in her rightful place.

And then in grade eleven the humbling prediction came true when she woke up one morning with a bout of the flu. She lay in a fever bed, sweating and sick to her stomach, and five weeks later the doctor at the clinic where she'd had her arm splinted one day when she was six told her and her mother that she was pregnant. Her mother slapped her face that night, while her father mourned quietly in the front room, contemplating the end of times. With all the shame and fear that followed, there was scarce room for the dreams in her heart to survive, and less so in the quiet of night after she married the boy three months later. The first baby came, and then the second, and with them came the death of hope. What young mother in her time had it any way other than grindingly hard? It was so long ago it barely mattered. Their father hung around for close to a decade before he split for the other side of the country at the ripe old age of twenty-seven. The deadened dreams gave way to exhaustion and resentment, first for the man she ended up calling That Selfish Prick, and then for the two kids he'd left behind.

For years neither Faron nor his sister had any idea what they'd done to etch that scowl on their mother's face. Finally it began to dawn on them. They were the embodiment of her loss, and the easiest, closest targets at hand. At first the anger was dispersed equally. But Jana was her mother's prettiest thing, and the one who reminded her of herself and her foolish dreams; she'd better get it through her head just what sort of trouble you can get yourself into if you think your dreams are worth more than a puff of smoke. It was her mission to remind her daughter of this fact as often as possible.

Faron was in high school by the time the icefields between his sister and mother had been permanently valleyed with treacherous chasms. He tried to insulate his little sister against their mother's moods. By then he'd learned his role as emissary between the two. But when university called him away, Jana was left to meet their mother's selfishness one on one. After she finished grade twelve, she came to Toronto and stayed with her brother for a week, and then she rode a Greyhound to California to put as much distance between herself and her old life as she could afford. That was all it took for their mother to bolt the doors to her forever, and there began what became the eternal freeze-out.

HE TORE UP his notes and tossed them into the basket an hour before the service. The pastor suggested he speak from the heart. Dozens of people came, including Setareh and Mikkel, who embraced him and offered their condolences, and settled respectfully into their seats. They'd called him twice in the days since his mother's passing. Both times he'd messaged them back to say he was managing, just busy with arrangements, and not to worry. It was true, but he was stalling as well, unsure what to do with the grey mists of doubt that had taken up in his heart since that surprising meeting with his lover's sister.

Most of the guests were in their seventies and eighties, though there were several younger men and women too—some of them young enough to have children in tow. He guessed they were all fellow parishioners come to pay respects to a member of their congregation. In the adjacent room, where the service was to be held, most of the seats were already occupied. He walked slowly through the crowd, shaking hands and accepting condolences, and finally, when the pastor called the service to order, he took his seat beside Setareh and Mikkel and looked at his mother's coffin for the first time, a plain model with no ornamentation, as she'd requested. The pastor welcomed the assembled guests, offered a short homily, and then invited Faron to say a few words.

He rose and approached the lectern and, after pausing a moment, he introduced himself and said his mother would be pleased to see so many kind faces; it was a comfort to know she'd been a valued member of this community.

Speak from the heart, the pastor had said. And so, if not from the heart, he spoke from recent memory about the young woman he'd seen at the Shenzhen train station.

He didn't share why he was in that city, or even when this was, but he said that we might choose to believe that the young woman in handcuffs and blindfold had been on her way home, granted a pass to see a relative before they died, and we can only hope she made it in time to say her goodbyes. He did not mention that he saw her at the same station six days later, or that, as if by some miracle, he'd practically fallen into her arms outside the Japanese consulate.

He didn't mention the odd particulars of their meeting, for he recalled nothing of how, in that moment outside the revolving doors, a spirit had slipped from one to the other and vanished, but not before the three of them had lived and felt in that instant an entire life together.

Nor did he mention the miracle of language that had assailed him—all memory of that was gone now—or the diver from San Diego with her odd games or the grandfather at the restaurant or the man who had transcribed Auden's posthumous masterpiece, *Songs of the Blood Moon*; it had all become a faraway whisper in his mind, like the memory of a dream from long ago. Perhaps he would have time later to remember and understand these things, but that time was not now.

What he spoke about instead was the curious tradition called Pure Brightness Day, when a small paper replica of something that was dear to the departed is burned and in the rising smoke is carried the essence of this thing to the spirit world. It was a beautiful thought, he said, to trust that those we've lost might still be among us somehow in some form. And no, he did not know if the woman at the train station had made it home to say goodbye to her family member. But he had, and he was grateful for it.

Here he paused and looked at the casket, and his thoughts turned to the box from which he'd stolen a prayer. He retrieved the paper from his wallet and spread it flat against the face of the lectern. The prayer did not quote the writer his brother-in-law was so fond of, but it did happen that it was signed with the name Charles. The hand in which the note was authored suggested that he too was old, a man of his mother's generation.

He'd placed it in his wallet with the intention of reading it to her when he got home that afternoon four days earlier, hoping she might take some comfort in hearing some kind words from this Charles fellow. But the thought had abandoned him that evening as her condition worsened. He read the note again now, silently, standing before the crowd of mourners. The man was likely here now, silently grieving the loss of a relationship that for Faron would remain a mystery.

Without reciting the prayer, he sat down again beside Setareh and folded his hands in his lap. The pastor rose and thanked him and spoke about Ida Jones not with the dutiful charity that Faron half expected but with a genuine admiration and respect for a woman who'd been widely loved in her community. She was, at heart, a truly genuine soul, the pastor said, and she would be dearly missed. Setareh placed her hand on Faron's now, and he watched the coffin and wondered how it was possible we could be such different things to different people, and whether it was even right to question who the real person was—the mother that his sister could not forgive, or the generous friend who'd been so deeply admired by the people in this room.

AFTERWARDS, HE FOLLOWED the hearse to the cemetery and waited under a chestnut tree for Setareh and Mikkel to pull in.

The day was cool and the sky dappled with clouds. They walked up the treeless hill where his mother's grave had been dug, and soon the casket was brought up and cradled on a heavy webbing of rope and lowered into the ground.

He removed the paper from his wallet and silently read the prayer again.

The webbing came up and the casket remained. He tipped a shovelful of earth into the hole and stood to the side with Mikkel and Setareh and watched the sextons begin filling the grave. He struck a flame and set it to the corner of the paper, and the smoke carried the prayer up and away, and then they walked back down the hill together to the cars.

Setareh asked if they could come back to his mother's house with him. It might be a good idea, she said, for him not to be alone. He thanked her and said he'd be fine, really, but being alone was probably what he needed right now.

THE SMELLS IN the darkened living room of his mother's house startled him when he got back from the cemetery. They were not the smells of her last month of decline but of her lived life and habits and routines. Her clothing and the old magazines and bathroom soaps and the red rubber boots by the side door—all these smells he felt with startling clarity in the back of his throat. It was unnerving how completely she still seemed to occupy the house. He almost expected her to round the corner and slip into those old boots and invite him out for a walk to admire the peace and quiet she'd found here and the hummingbirds that coloured her feeder with their dazzling blur and the beautiful deer that invaded her garden. He spoke her name quietly, almost believing she'd respond, and then he moved through the rooms without touching anything, as if this were some personal museum or shrine that must not be disturbed. Later, he went back through the house a second time, room by room, and selected the items he would take back to the city.

He didn't see many things in the end that he wanted. Most of his possessions, and Jana's, had been given away or discarded long ago when their mother left the family home where they'd grown up. He chose a few framed photographs, a palm-sized wooden carving of an elephant, which, for no reason he knew, was his mother's favourite animal. He found the copy of his novel, which he'd dedicated to her, signed in his youthful handwriting, and, because he saw little else, he claimed a ceramic salad bowl that he'd given her years earlier. There was nothing else. He went through the house a third time. Saddened that he could find so few things he could carry forward from her life into his own, he pulled open the night table drawer in his mother's bedroom and found the letters he'd sent to her from Paris, tied together with string.

He leafed quickly through the envelopes, but didn't open them; instead, he pulled open his mother's closet and immersed himself in its crowded tapestry of smells and colours and textures. It was years of living that hung before him, empty shells still vaguely claiming their owner's shape. He stood here, allowing for memory to rise in him, and then he closed the closet and went downstairs and read the letters.

He was moved by the voice of a son who'd loved his mother much more deeply than time had allowed him to remember. He'd bowed to the passing of years, which should not have been surprising, but it was. Time's arrow had wounded his heart and now, on the other side of his mother's death, the heart was toughened and cautious, and he wondered if his efforts to reconcile his mother and sister had come of a sense of duty and not of love. Was it even useful or fair, he wondered, to compare the youthful heart, such as his had been, to the adult's at midlife and beyond? He would not survive the test. Could any adult manage the passage to fifty and beyond and still hold the purity of heart and soul they'd begun with? The question bothered him. It was not to be answered. Too much time had passed, and yet not enough to allow the wisdom required to know one way or the other.

In one of the envelopes he found a pressed flower with a faded ribbon tied around it, as if in a surprising gesture of sentimentality.

He got up from the kitchen table and stood at the window over the sink and looked out into the dark as the wind came at the window at sharp, whistling angles. The old refrigerator clicked on. The dead house was alive with sounds. Outside, a coyote howled.

The idealism he'd carried with him into middle age was just so much rote thinking by now, a sort of mental sloganeering that masked the heart's failure to feel as it once had. It was a terrifying thought. He'd lost something of himself in this hungry march through time. In these letters from Paris he heard an unguarded and caring voice full of love for his mother and a deep wonder for the new world around him. In the intervening years he'd allowed only half an effort in understanding her, and now, with little more than the memory of the man he no longer was, he sat again and read on and heard the voice of a second coyote rise and fall and the wind whistling at the window. He'd moved so far and so inexorably in the opposite direction of youth—and so he'd lived on—yet here on the night of his mother's funeral, this lonely fact filled the room like the private howling of a third animal lost in the dark. Here in these letters, as if trapped in amber, was his innocent soul before time had dug in its claws.

He wondered what she'd sought in keeping these at her bedside. Did she read them late into the night, hoping to summon a voice from the past, as he himself was doing now? The thought of her stranded in the loss and nostalgia of days long ended saddened him. It would have been easier to know that the letters were there for no particular reason, that she'd not reached for them at a lonely hour. He didn't want to think that, in her sleepless nights, she'd attempted to recapture something she no longer had, which was the abiding love of her children. Had she struggled so, yet found it impossible to simply pick up the phone? She'd not spoken of this fading love or of the letters or of her rift with Jana or her insistent retreat from him and his sister. She'd not spoken of it and neither had he. In the winnowing tumble of days the subject of *feeling* had been carried off by an indifferent wind. She'd not let on that tenderness was anything she was interested in, the sport of her righteous independence so strictly observed. But it had always been there, that crushing need never spoken of. In her last years, while she was still healthy, she'd guarded her solitude with clumsy precision, on her own terms, and said nothing of the absences in the heart. The pressing routines of solitude were too deeply entrenched. There had been too many sacrifices made to give ground now, and by the time she came out here to this lonely plot of land, she spoke openly of the virtues of selfishness.

ON THE MORNING after the funeral, Faron closed down the house and stood on the front porch and watched the old man coming up the lane. He walked slowly, a cane at his left side, and nodded as he approached, his stride slightly broken when he lifted the cane and signalled hello. Faron walked down the lane to meet him.

"Good morning," the man called out.

"Good morning. I'm guessing you're Charles."

"I am Charles. Old Charles."

"I saw you at the service," Faron said.

"Yes."

"Thank you for your prayers."

The man nodded. "Your mother asked me to give you this."

He pressed an envelope into Faron's hand, offered his condolences, and walked back down the lane.

TWENTY-TWO

WITHIN WEEKS THE ROOFTOP THAT LAMYA HAD REFERRED TO AS a sanctuary in her correspondence with the ghostwriter would become the lush garden that would occupy them into that anxious summer of waiting. They ordered soil and planters, and Mildred's aunt, whom Lamya thought a kind old soul, brought flats of seedlings and the small hand tools they needed to begin transforming the space into a cultivated field of green.

The bookstore had been shuttered the day after the press conference and now stood in escrow, held by an unnamed party that in a lightning move purchased the building and declared the business closed. They'd taken mercy on the old bookseller, however, and did not eject her from her small flat above the store; but now, downstairs, those portraits of the great writers Mildred had learned to admire as a child watched mutely as the abandoned bookshelves quietly gathered dust.

For three days in a row following the press conference the three women climbed the stairs to the bulkhead doorway on the rooftop of One Exchange Square and stepped into the liberating sunlight and wide views of the city and the bay. Up here they did not feel their confinement so deeply, or the political and bureaucratic chaos that swirled around them. The world seemed briefly theirs on those fine April days, peaceful in a way that surprised them. The worry was always there, yes, and the reality that their lives had been so narrowly confined, but in the canyons of busy streets below, Hong Kong was a toy city over which they donned their gardening gloves and bamboo sedge hats and filled pails and planters with soil. They introduced the tender roots of watercress and napa cabbage and eggplant and soybean sprouts to the black earth they arranged in their waiting buckets, and Mildred's aunt, mourning the loss of the bookshop, began to feel a renewed purpose and hope that she might be able to open it again one day, or that when her niece was permitted to finally leave the consulate, they would take their savings to Singapore, where she had a brother, and there rebuild the bookstore.

More bags of soil were emptied into the pails and planters they secured, and the greenery spread, and soon they saw the beginnings of a small functioning garden. Building management turned a blind eye. Their sole condition stipulated that these activities steer clear of the HVAC systems, sky windows, and maintenance sheds. The rooftop was theirs otherwise. Consular officials, including Mr. Saito, emerged from the bulkhead stairwell and inspected the patchwork garden with curious looks of amazement and wonder. They sectioned off the agreed-upon allotment and began planting directly into the smooth river stones that mottled the rooftop. In time they would see what sort of harvest they'd produce, but more important was the shared purpose they felt while they waited out their confinement.

On most nights, after the evening meal, the two women met in the Imperial Room, where Lamya read and wrote notes on her screenplay while Mildred reviewed the manuscripts she received from around the country and abroad. The future was on hold for both of them. Lamya knew nothing of what the ghostwriter had made of her request. He'd not messaged her since their meeting. She would give it more time, though the waiting was terrible. For Mildred, the future of the small press was uncertain, but the voices calling out to be heard were many. Queries and manuscripts came to her via the unpublished email address she'd shared years ago in the secret network of activists and academics for whom New Light Editions had become a solemnly defiant island of free voices.

Seated in the glow of the fireplace one evening, Mildred was alerted to an odd presence somewhere in the room. She looked around but saw nothing unusual. Lamya was reading on her laptop, a cup of tea at her side. The fireplace, the table lamp, the chessboard in the centre of the open globe—there was nothing here out of the ordinary. But she felt it, some strong presence, like the sudden memory of a departed loved one or the shy touch of a mysteriously parallel life.

And then it was gone.

TWENTY-THREE

FARON GOT THE 8:30 FERRY OVER TO THE ISLAND THAT EVENING, two days after his mother's funeral. It was dark and cool by the water now, and he watched the city lights as the boat pulled away from the quay. They glowed east and west on the shoreline as far as he could see, and when the colder wind came up in the middle of the crossing he went below deck and from there he watched the black silhouette of the island come into view as the ferry cut its way forward.

Setareh and Mikkel were waiting for him when he came down the ramp once the ferry put in. She kissed him and held him close and asked how he was, and he breathed deeply, his face in her hair as they embraced. He loved the smell of her skin, its warmth, how it tasted when he kissed her. He did not want to let go, but finally he did, and Mikkel shook his hand and they hugged like old friends, and he said they had a good bottle of wine and a hot meal waiting back at the house.

The low roar of the ferry's engines fell off in the distance as they followed the narrow path and passed the cottages that usually delighted Faron for the whimsy of their architecture. They were of the miniature sort unique to the island, like little hobbit homes, but tonight he didn't think much about them or the pleasant domestic images they often conjured in his mind. His mother's house would soon be cleared out and listed, and before long one family's dreams would be replaced by another's. It was a hard thought, how objects seemed so casually to outlive their owners. His account with the funeral parlour had been closed, and he'd seen to the last of the municipality's taxes, and the overdue heating and water bills. All of that was wrapped up now, his mother's legacy tied in a sad tight bow. He'd finally spoken to his sister, who'd said the proper things about loss and memory and the unforgiving passage of time, but she'd seemed eager to turn the discussion to the practical matters of the estate.

They opened the wine when they got to the house and Setareh took the tahdig rice dish off the stovetop and turned it over with an expert flourish to reveal its perfect golden-brown crispness. Mikkel placed the wine and glasses on the table while Faron stood at the bookshelf, watching them, wondering how this night should end. He'd left his satchel containing the screenplay on the bench by the front door.

They got caught up on the lighter day-to-day matters they could recall from the past two weeks, those smaller asides invited into the conversation to help divert Faron from the heaviness he wanted to leave behind. He could not be sure he wasn't telegraphing his uncertainty—he was useless when it came to hiding behind a smile—but in Setareh he only saw and felt the woman he'd fallen in love with and could not help but love still. He was as powerless without her as she was incapable of hurting him, he decided, and why she'd held the secret of La Porte Rouge in Paris and the tragedy in Montevideo he might never know for certain. Truths such as these, locked away in a lover's heart, could not be held as a sign of dishonesty or lack of trust, but rather as a nod to the careful devotions required in loving someone in an imperfect world.

"Tell us about Hong Kong," Mikkel said. "How was it?"

He told them about the American poet and his wild claims, and the reef tank diver who now, in his clarifying mind, seemed more a sort of dream meant to prepare him for the shadow reality out of which people emerged from his past, as Setareh had done. Perhaps she'd even recognized him as the author of *Strangers at the Red Door* and devised that odd tribute in its honour. Whatever the case, hers was merely an inventive game played by a flirtatious stranger who spent nights submerged in a fantasy as colourful as the shimmering otherworld of that reef tank. He told them about the Chinese girl at the Rubik's Cube convention who yammered on at him as if he knew what she was going on about, and about the hotel that rose so high over the city that his suite looked down over the clouds; he spoke of the splendid view of the harbour and wandering through the chaotic and thrilling backstreets of Hong Kong and the dinner party at his brother-in-law's university where he'd met the American translator. He saved the story about the blindfolded woman for last.

"And then she was there again at the train station when I came back through six days later, sitting exactly where I'd seen her the first time."

"Synchronicity," Mikkel said.

"And then a third time, outside the consulate."

"Imagine, in a city of eight million," Mikkel said.

Setareh had been circling the rim of her wineglass with a ringed finger when he said this. Her finger stopped. He did not name the country of the consulate.

"And your new client," she asked. "How did that go?"

"It depends," he said. "I'm not sure."

"Depends on what?" she said.

"I don't think I know enough yet."

After their meal, they settled in the living room, seated across from the fireplace. It was a warm and welcoming space Setareh and Mikkel had created over the years, a cabin-like two-bedroom bungalow with plank floors and colonial-style interiors. There were windows everywhere, black now but for the dim lights of the marina sparkling through the trees.

"You promised you'd read to us," Mikkel said to Setareh. He was opening a second bottle. "'The whole marvellous thing,' you said."

"'Heartbreaking,' you said," Faron added. "I haven't even congratulated you yet. Not in person. With everything going on. I'm sorry. Congratulations."

"Thank you," she said.

Mikkel poured out the wine and Setareh left the room and

returned with the manuscript. She sat between them and turned to the first page and seemed about to begin when she suddenly stopped. She was hesitant, Faron could see, nervous perhaps, and he wondered if she'd caught the remark about the unnamed consulate. She would know where her sister had been for the last three years, of course. Her case was widely reported on.

"There will be tweaks here and there," she said, returned now from her pause. "There always are. I've already sent it off to the editor in LA."

"I'm sure it's perfect," Mikkel said. "But hold on."

He took down a copy of *Strangers at the Red Door* from the bookshelf, then returned to the couch and opened the book to the first chapter.

Setareh softly cleared her throat and began.

Faron understood not a single word as she read, of course, but in the ancient rhythms of her language he heard the echoes of his youth and felt again the hopeless rush of love that had stirred him on those cold evenings when he followed Setareh into the bookshop and watched as she selected a book and carried it to the back room, where customers could sit and read for hours. It was his moment to decide now, as it had been his hero's moment so long ago, on that last evening at the bookshop, and he wondered if he'd make the same mistake again and say nothing.

She'd stepped out from his novel and into his life but had held that secret close, and in doing so she'd respected the hero's decision to choose the innocence of unrequited love. To declare herself now would introduce the Persian flaw that would become the imperfection in a novel she herself considered perfect. He did not place such overwhelming responsibility on a story he'd written so long ago, yet the prospect of altering the novel had troubled Setareh, he could see that now, and for this reason she'd kept the truth from him. Yes, her silence had been an act of devotion, an unspoken gift to his hero's eternal youth, held forever at the tantalizing edge of possibility.

We only have what's before us in the dying of our days, his mother had said in that note given to him by Old Charlie, *this and the cooling embers of the past*. He'd read her words and wept on the open deck of the ferry on his way over, before his retreat below deck, and felt such a seizure of remorse that his hands trembled and the note fell from his grasp and was taken up and carried off on the wind that rose up in the middle of the crossing. She'd known of his journey to visit his sister after all, and she thanked him for the love and the hope that held yet in his heart. *You are my son, even now when I'm gone. And I am your mother, who did what she could and sometimes succeeded and often failed, but love was always there, too quietly, perhaps, or distracted or selfish, but my love was always there with you, and still is from wherever I am now.*

And here, for a brief moment summoned from some distant shore, the spirit who'd wandered for so long returned to Faron Jones and marvelled at the rich and complicated layers of love and longing and loss that resided in this man's wounded soul. He embraced Faron and told him that his mother was where she was supposed to be—*Grieve now, but know she's at rest*, he said—

but the ghostwriter heard only an unusual humming in his head and the echoes of the wind coming across from the bay.

Setareh lowered the page and touched his hand. "Are you alright?"

"Thank you, yes," he said, trying to smile.

"What's wrong?" She touched his face and gripped his hand. "Tell me."

"The novel is yours now as much as it is mine. You can make the changes you need to."

She kissed him then, not quite understanding yet, and he got up and walked silently to the front door.

"You're not leaving?" she said.

He took up his satchel and came back into the living room. "No, no," he said. "I'd like to stay, if that's alright."

"Of course," she said.

He sat down again, reached into the satchel, and removed the screenplay. It was a hazard of pages, bound by a single elastic. He looked at it briefly, as if reconsidering, and then he offered it to her.

She took it and set it atop the translation resting on her lap. "What is this?"

"It's from someone who used to be important to you. Some of the pages will be out of order. Go on, have a look," he said.

As she turned to the first page, he knew he'd found the breakthrough he needed to tell this story the only way it could be told. There was just one way, and here it was. The golden key was his. *You owe it to us all to get on with what you're good at,*

Gideon Kastner had said as they stood at the elevators that last afternoon at the Metropole. He'd lost nothing of himself since writing those letters to his mother back when the world was still new and lit with the dreams of the young. He understood this now. There was time yet for courageous advances and humbling retreats and the forward march into the unknown. There was room yet for hope.

He watched Setareh begin to read her story, as it was told by the sister whom one day she might learn to forgive, and he felt the past and the future hold in perfect balance, the moment theirs, and he knew that it was here where he belonged, exactly.

Acknowledgements

The first seeds of this novel were planted during two separate visits to China in 2015, the same year five Hong Kong booksellers disappeared and were found later to be in the custody of Chinese authorities. Alex W. Palmer's feature story "The Case of Hong Kong's Missing Booksellers," published in *The New York Times Magazine* in 2018, provided valuable context and detail. Also valuable was *The Guardian*'s December 28, 2019, report on forced labour in Chinese prisons and the Chinese Christmas card scandal at Qingpu Prison in Shanghai province.

I am grateful to Robert Ward for his careful attention; and to James Bi for his advice on certain practical matters regarding Mandarin and Cantonese; and to Maryam Z for inviting me into the beautiful world of Persian culture and tradition.

The author wishes to acknowledge the support of the Ontario Arts Council.